I0714137

BRUCE R. GUERIN
RECOMMENDED
WORKBOOK PRESS
THE MISSING
CHILD

Copyright @2021 by Bruce R. Guerin

This publication contains the opinions and ideas of its author. It is intended to provide helpful and informative material on the subjects addressed in the publication. The author and publisher specifically disclaim all responsibility for any liability, loss or risk, personal or otherwise, which is incurred as a consequence, directly or indirectly, of the use and application of any of the contents of this book.

WORKBOOK PRESS LLC
187 E Warm Springs Rd,
Suite B285, Las Vegas, NV 89119, USA

Website: https://workbookpress.com/
Hotline: 1-888-818-4856
Email: admin@workbookpress.com

Ordering Information:
Quantity sales. Special discounts are available on quantity purchases by corporations, associations, and others.
For details, contact the publisher at the address above.

Library of Congress Control Number:
ISBN-13:   978-1-956017-13-7 (Paperback Version)
              978-1-956017-14-4 (Digital Version)

REV. DATE: 20/07/2021

The Missing Child

Bruce R. Guerin

This book is dedicated to all our Missing Children throughout the world: The United States Marine Corps, and the hope we will all share in a better life tomorrow. To serve as a Marine has been the highest honor of my life.

Today, the Corps is still a place where young boys can learn to become men. They can learn honor and fidelity in our ancient code of brotherhood and to all my brothers in arms, Oorah and Semper Fi.

For my son, Kristen, who lived not long enough to create his own epitaph, except that which is inscribed on my heart and restless spirit. Your life and death have made me a better human being. I dedicate this book to you and to my wife, Rhealyn, who is my lifetime companion.

BR Guerin

CHAPTER ONE
THE CALL

The unsettling ring of the damn phone awoke me from a profound slumber. My first thought was, *who in the hell could be calling me at this ungodly hour?* It was still dark as I glanced at my watch and saw it was barely 6:00 a.m. With an extreme sense of irritation, I left the comfort of my bunk to pick up that damn shrieking phone.

It was frigid on my boat, and although I have heat and air-conditioning, I'm too damn, cheap, and pigheaded to use them even on the coldest of days.

I yelled into the phone, "Hello, this is Jake. Who in the hell is calling me at this ungodly hour?"

I heard an eager, determined female on the other side of the line. Her voice was whiskey deep and expressed a sense of annoyance at my tone. I'm familiar with that tone of voice from women; I've met lately in my chosen profession. Her speech divulged all her fears and an extreme sense of loss.

She spoke loudly. "Mr. Reynard, my name is Jeanette Alexander, and we share a common acquaintance in Maryanne Phillips. Maryanne gave me your number. She told me you had a gift for finding missing or kidnapped people. Maryanne said, 'Jake's the person; you turn to when the police are stuck or have given up on finding someone who is missing. She told me to reach out to you, specifically. I'm sorry for the hour, but my family is completely distraught about my sister. You worked as a New York City cop with the missing person's unit in Manhattan for six years. Now, you work as a private investigator on one case at a time. You work when you want and only on your own terms. Could you, by any chance, meet with my father and me to discuss our situation tomorrow? We are desperate about my sister's disappearance!"

That was when my inner alarm bell went off. Julia Alexander—was all this about her disappearance?

I asked, "Is this by any chance about Julia Alexander's

disappearance?"

"Yes, Julia's my younger sister, and if all you know about her kidnapping is from the newspapers, that would be a very misleading perception as to who my sister was and how she led her life."

I said, "I understand; I knew your sister at one time. I'm aware that if you heard about me from Maryanne, she told you, I just take a limited amount of cases. It's when or if I feel I can affect a change in their statuses. I would have a few questions before I can decide on this case. I can see from your phone's ID that you're calling me from Palm Beach. I would say that from where I live in Sarasota, that's a four-hour drive. Allow me to drink my morning coffee, and I'll call you back in about an hour. Ms. Alexander, we can arrange a time to meet at that time."

"Mr. Reynard, I'll stay at home to await your call."

I asked, "There is one other thing, Ms. Alexander. Will your father be attending this meeting? I would require his presence. Is he aware that you called me?"

"Yes, he knows all about this call. He'll be here tomorrow morning, specifically to attend this meeting with you in person. He's flying in from New York this afternoon."

I said. "Alright, I'll call you back later, Ms. Alexander, goodbye."

This was about Julia, after all. How many Julia Alexander's could there be? I had been expecting this call for six months.

I still recall that evening clearly. It was at that event three years ago that Julia revealed her remarkably unspoiled demeanor to me. I was struck blind by her astonishing beauty and kindness. That impression has always remained with me.

She walked over and spoke to each one of us standing security that night. She asked if we were hungry or thirsty. She wanted to know if we had been offered anything to eat or drink by the catering staff. Julia knew we were all off-duty cops, working part-time at her charity affair. She returned later to each one of us in turn with soft drinks and sandwiches that had somehow magically appeared from the hotel kitchen as if by wizardry. It struck me at the time because all those other people at that event showed little regard for us. I thought she had a lot of class to respect us as people. Cops are usually only appreciated by people with money when they are in distress.

Most of all, I remembered her eyes. They were incredible. She had the darkest blue eyes; I've ever seen on a woman. She possessed this self-assured smile. It was not one not easily forgotten by me or anyone else; who'd been exposed to it? She spoke to me last that night, "I don't know if we have enough food for a huge guy like you." I stand six-four and a half.

I spotted a massive mustard-stain on her dress that she must have acquired from making the sandwiches herself. I swept her up like a toy. Then I set her on top of the bar while she frantically attempted to maintain her composure.

I called the bartender for a glass of club soda and a clean bar towel. Then I went about cleaning her gown without a word spoken by her. I said, "You may want to warn me if your boyfriend shows up, as I have my hand halfway up, your dress. He might get the wrong impression. I don't want to be bludgeoned from behind for undertaking a good deed."

She said, "There's no boyfriend here or anywhere else for that matter."

Then she gazed down at me from her perch and showered me with her great laugh, "You really do know how to sweep a girl off her feet. I had to find a cop to save my dress and, in the process, give me an original line. You have possibilities, as a flirt anyway. You should come down to our shelter and entertain our residents. We can always use some muscle with a sense of humor. It's the Twenty-Third Street Shelter if you ever find yourself in need of a cold beer or a hell of a lot better sandwich than this one. I'll make you; the ultimate New York corned beef sandwich with my own two hands."

This was all whispered with her own playful, mischievous smile. Then it occurred to me that I was being flirted with by this stunning girl.

I replied. "I might just do that. Even if it's only to catch an eyeful of you in a pair of jeans. I bet you're as alluring as you are in this mesmerizing gown."

She said, "Any more of this blarney, and you will seriously turn my head." Then she held forth, "Please come down, and I'll make you an exceptional feast after I have put you to work repairing a few things that require a man's touch. That's all

I can commit to for now. I guarantee you that it will be like me, Mom, prepared to grab my Da's interest." That offer was whispered to me with her world-altering grin.

Before I could get another word out, she leaped from her perch on the bar and swept across the ballroom. She bestowed a beguiling gaze in my direction from across the room. I didn't intend to go down to that shelter, but she had surprised me. That's something most women can never accomplish.

Her standing socially was too far above my own for indulging in anything but this cute flirt. I didn't pursue the matter until I found myself on a rainy day off duty with nothing else to do. I lived downtown in the West Village at the time. So, I walked across town and stopped in at the Twenty-Third Street Shelter. True to her word, she put me to work all day with an endless list of handyman chores.

We teased and flirted with each other all day as I worked on her seemingly endless list of small tasks. She acted as my assistant, carrying my tools everywhere as we went along. Then, we shared a first-rate lunch that she'd prepared for us herself.

In the last few moments we spent together before I left, we were standing near each other quietly in a hallway alcove. My hand grazed against hers. Rather than rapidly withdrawing it, Julia laid her hand on mine and peered up at my face. I stood frozen at that moment, and then as if by some unspoken command, she lifted her face to mine. I kissed her gently with an increasing and dominant passion. Softly at first, but as our kiss grew, we became entwined as my hands found her face, and an overwhelming desire began to course throughout our bodies. I broke from the kiss first and labored to pass it off with a smile.

Before the next moment passed, she'd invited me to Sunday dinner at her family's home on Park Avenue. I told her I had the watch that Sunday, which was a total fabrication. In my heart, I knew we had nothing in stock but this great day and that utterly implausible kiss.

That memory of our day together remained with me a long time after the day ended. She called me at the station house twice, but I never returned her communications.

I mulled over all the stories written about Julia's

disappearance. I'd read all about it in the New York paper's months ago, and I recalled the newspaper's version went, something like the following:

(BILLIONAIRE'S DAUGHTER GONE MISSING)

Miss Julia Alexander of Palm Beach and Park Ave New York, the youngest daughter of Wall Street tycoon Charles T Alexander, was declared missing while traveling to Burlington, Vermont. She was last seen visiting friends at the University of Vermont; Ms. Alexander may have been the victim of foul play or is simply off on an adventure.

The newspapers went on to paint her as some kind of typical debutante. It was hot news for a while, then the story slowly receded off the front pages. It eventually vanished entirely after her father posted a five-million-dollar reward for any knowledge of her whereabouts. This had to drive the cop's nuts as that always brought out all the crazies.

Of all the women I ever held any illusions about, Julia stood alone. We'd shared-nothing, but that single kiss. We had only those moments spent in idle chatter and flirting, but I was left with such a promise of so much more in those; bottomless indigo-colored eyes. Consequently, I tucked her aside in that secret place we all possess within ourselves. Though I knew of her abduction, I stayed away from it all until receiving this phone call.

Her father finally summoned me. I knew immediately I would go see him. I would search for these people who abducted her with everything at my disposal.

I tie my 1989 Bristol 48.8-foot ketch *Switchel* up at one of the moorings located between the City Marina and the Sarasota Yacht Club. I've always loathed tying up at the public docks. I refuse to deal with all the boozing live boards. Who wants to live on a boat and not be able to sleep at night because your next-door neighbor is having a drunken argument with his spouse or lover?

I'd found my peace among the great purple and gold sunsets. The comings and goings of the other boats from the yacht club only enhanced the beautiful colors in my view.

As my thoughts drifted along with the outbound current, I began to shiver and finally gave in to those unrelenting northerly winds. I retreated below to my main saloon and acknowledged the biting winds by turning on my generator and with it the heat. What the hell? These cold temperatures didn't occur that frequently in Florida. In New York, if it were fifty-two degrees, I'd be sunbathing.

I lived aboard the *Switchel* and would never live in a house or condo again. This was, by far, the most unique aspect of my life. I had no attachments, no mortgages, and a complete unrestrained sense of freedom from all responsibility.

I would generally be in Sir Francis Drake's channel sailing the upper Caribbean now. However, when I was ready to get underway in November, my most recent shipmate, Ann, decided to reconcile with her philandering husband, Bradley. You simply can't handle an ocean crossing alone on a boat as large as mine.

I couldn't blame her. After all, I live an odd existence for a woman who wants a home and children. At least, I offered her refuge while she figured out what it was that she wished to, and of course, there were compensations of a more personal nature for us both.

I required solitude, and the women I've shared time with

usually coped with that for a while. Invariably, they wanted more than I was willing to give them.

My father and mother possessed an awe-inspiring sense of love for each other. For forty-four years, my father watched over her. When he lost her in the end to cancer, he retreated to seclusion and his books. Perhaps, it is in the genes. They loved each other but rarely said or showed it with any overt acts of affection in front of me. I was possibly never having seen or felt that closeness as a child created the perspective I possess. I wanted no attachments, no losses, and, most of all, no grief.

I'd worked at the missing person division of the New York Police Department for nine years after leaving the Marine Corps. In all that time, I'd made detective second grade and a respected name for myself within the department. In the end, it was like every other quasi-military outfit. You end up working under some ass-hole whose ambitions run more to power and politics. The victims and the urgency of getting them back alive seemed to take a backseat to everyone else's personal agenda. That yearning for influence and promotion becomes more important than the job at hand.

That situation arose in the kidnapping of Madeline Kintner, a four-year-old girl from Queens. Billy Miltanosky and I caught the case and interviewed the person working from the inside, whom we believed assisted in the child's abduction. As we were interrogating him, our new lieutenant, an idiot by the name of Wainright, stopped us in our tracks. This mutt was about to give up the location of his confederates for a deal when Wainright told us we had to release him from custody.

When you interrogate witnesses, you acquire a second sense about them. Billy and I knew he was on the brink of giving up his partners. However, Wainright demanded we let him walk for insufficient evidence. I insisted we hold him on a federal ticket under the Patriot Act. This lieutenant told us he wouldn't tolerate the FBI becoming involved in any of his cases.

We had this guy in the box for twelve hours. Billy and I knew he was ready to roll over when Wainright blocked us. We argued with him. This guy came from an administrative position in the city hall. This was only a temporary assignment until the new captains' list came out next month.

A street patrolman discovered the little girl's body ten days after that suspect's release in a dumpster on Forty-Third Street. The medical examiner put her time of death two days after we'd released that inside guy from our custody. Little Madeline had been sexually abused, then she was choked to death by her abductors.

I knew then; the life of a cop was over for me. Being a detective was too political for my personality. Plus, I'd formed no genuine relationships all the time; I'd worked at being a policeman other than my partner, Billy. My only friends were other cops and their wives and the occasional fix-up until Julia, and I had destroyed that opportunity.

I'd become abrasive and irritated all the time. If I really wanted this kind of life, I would have to learn to accept all the bullshit better than I'd been capable of in the past.

My drinking became a problem again. I'd beaten that demon once before and regularly drank only beer. Lately, the hard stuff had made its presence known to me once again. After that, the little girl was discovered. I spent an entire evening with Mr. Daniels and paid a heavy price the following day. That was a standard Marine Corps drink: Jack Daniels with a few chips of ice.

I experience that people in high-stress jobs use some form of synthetic outlet to relieve the pressure. Mine was alcohol, and I'd already battled that addiction once before. I knew it was time to take my anxiety level down. I had to clean up my act if I wanted to keep my commitment to myself. I must consider myself first and screw this pointless job.

The day after that little girl's body was autopsied, I resigned and turned in my badge and gun. I had no plans, but an account with over six hundred grand from my dad's estate and some stocks I'd purchased in my 401(k) account along the way. I got in my old Volvo and started driving south with no plan or place in mind. I only wanted the sun and peace.

When I drove into St. Augustine, Florida, I exited for a meal. It was two days before Christmas and was as rainy and cold as in New York. I kept on driving until I saw those first rays of sunshine. It was off, in the distance, off route, I-75 in Sarasota. I took that first exit ramp with no plan in mind and began to seek out a bed for the night.

I stayed at the Mango Inn on Route 41 for two days and made my way about town. The beauty of this little paradise overwhelmed me. On Friday at noon, I found a furnished one-bedroom condominium overlooking the public marina downtown. I learned that the unit owner was a guy named Duke McGarrity, who happened to be a retired Marine Corps Major and a mustang. I'd served on a Force Recon team, and that earned me his approval from the beginning of our relationship.

I not only received an inordinate deal on the apartment but found my first new friend in Florida. Duke and I'd shared the combat experience. Duke served in Vietnam and I in Africa, Kuwait, and Afghanistan. Duke displayed a Silver Star and two Purple Hearts in a case on the wall outside his office. My two Bronze Stars and three Purple Hearts were tucked away in my duffel bag.

In those first few months, Duke and I fished off his boat and drank a few beers twice a week. Beer or wine is tolerable for me, but the hard stuff meant I was trying to escape to some degree. It was the built-in barometer for my state of mind. I was learning to relax and live at peace within myself.

One day, a new topic of conversation came up. It seemed that Duke had a friend with a daughter in California. She'd fought a complex drug problem and then went missing this month from her father's home. It was peculiar, as his daughter was recently released from her second rehab program and was sticking close to home. Unexpectedly, she disappeared from his house. The local cops dismissed it because of her priors for drugs. They tend not to take those types of disappearances too seriously.

I understood why they thought this way, but Duke made a strong case for helping this guy. It seemed one of Duke's Purple Hearts would have been awarded posthumously had it not been for this friend of his. I know about those types of roots, and they run deep.

I made no promises but decided to consider it for him. The client sent us a file that Duke obtained from the L.A.P.D. Through some connection or another of his. I combed through it, seeing nothing at first glance. Then I came upon it. She got a second shot at rehab by turning the state's evidence against her former dealer/boyfriend/pimp and brother.

The father's name was Jonathon Cutler, and Samantha was his only child. After a quick computer check, I told Duke if Cutler wanted to pay expenses and put me up while I was out there; I thought I had an idea that might help me locate his daughter.

The following day, I received a notice of a first-class ticket to Los Angeles awaiting me at the Sarasota airport, and five thousand dollars had been wired into my account for expenses. Duke thanked me profusely and said anything I could do would be appreciated. Duke once was the Provost Marshal or head cop at Camp Pendleton. He was on excellent terms with many of L.A.P.D.'s finest, and that's how he'd obtained that restricted file.

I knew; I had resources out there if I required them. Culter told me to call if I needed his assistance, and he'd put me in touch with the right people to help me. I arrived in Los Angeles and found Samantha in two days by tailing her former boyfriend's brother, Raff. She had aided the cops by testifying against his brother, but he hadn't pulled any time on his drug charges.

He'd restrained her against her will and hooked her on heroin again. Then he put her out on the street for rent. When I found her, she was a complete mess. I confronted this Raff. I told him any further contact with her would result in his long and painful death. He made the mistake of attempting to prove he was a tough guy.

Most of them try to prove how dangerous they are. However, but Raff wasn't totally committed or highly trained.—meaning he'd kill because he knows to know the danger of leaving an opponent alive—these petty crooks always fail. They don't have the training or temperament to do the job of killing spot-on.

I always carry a razor-sharp three-inch buck knife in my left front pocket. I left Raff with a clean, deep six-inch wound down the right side of his face. It would serve as a reminder and instruct him, what would lie in store for him in the future should he ever decide to seek her out again? He knew he could lose more than a whore from his stable. He understood from the intensity in my eyes; that I'd kill him the minute, he tried next time. He pissed his pants when I cut him and gazed at his own blood.

In my experience, people who make a living off of women are cowards. Their aggression disappears when confronted by someone willing to take that final radical step.

In this world, we need people willing to lay down their lives for the greater good. We live in a time of repeating history. We exist with fanatical zealots and power-hungry despots, which are in the business of wholesale terrorism. People who seek and gain power by exploiting other people's fears with violence and bombings must be eliminated with deadly force.

I believe in a moral world, a society where predators aren't allowed to exist with impunity, and where we all possess an innate sense of right and wrong. The problem is that real evil does exist. With the training, understanding, and determination, people like me must balance the scales, or it all turns to crap.

I took Samantha to a cheap hotel off Sunset Strip, where no one would ask any questions. There we set upon a bit of rehab program of my own devising. There was little or no sleep with her constant begging for a fix during those first days, and it was infuriating. After all, I wasn't a damn drug counselor.

If I ever had to do this again, I would have taken her to a professional. I went about that filthy business of cleaning her up with no letup in the process. I did this for a snitch once before, and it was a gruesome piece of business.

We emerged from that cockroach-infested room five days later with Samantha physically intact. She was basically untouched by her withdrawal experience. We spent the next two days in a suite at the Regent's Beverly Wilshire Hotel and Spa, taking care of the balance of her drug aftereffects. Most of all, it allowed us each time to catch up on some lost sleep.

Two days after her recovery, I returned her to her father's intact. I asked that we all sit down and talk together. I began by explaining how I'd suffered from post-traumatic stress disorder and how the Veterans Administration at the time was of no real help to me. I had just returned from Africa and a particularly ruthless mission. A good friend led me by the hand to a doctor located right here in Los Angeles.

Dr. Bradley Milton experienced his own post-traumatic stress after Vietnam. He'd established a nasty drug habit during his second tour there. Now, Brad devoted his life to helping others by tutoring them via his own design rehab program. He told everyone who came to him, "All you have is yourself and those who've shared these same experiences. You must relive them together to let it go and be free of it forever.

He believed it's not the negative emotional state of our experiences that shapes our destinies. It's the feelings and emotions we experience during those incidents that tend to rule us. Those feelings can only be shared with someone who has experienced those identical emotions and lived through the same events. Once they are transferred to a safe environment, they cease to control us, and that's when true healing begins.

I told them that it had worked for me. During my treatment, I began to learn about my drinking problems as an outlet for my stress. We became great friends, having shared the same experiences as soldiers; we kept in touch throughout the intervening years.

Samantha was aware her father had broken down when he thought he lost her forever. This old tough, hard-bitten Marine loved her in a way; she couldn't begin to fathom. There was a lot of crying that night, but I sensed they shared a massive breakthrough. They decided on a plan that night that would entail treatment with Brad and more communication between them as a family.

In the morning, before anyone else awoke, I slipped out and grabbed the first flight home to Sarasota via Atlanta. I slept all day that initial day back. I was awakened with Duke pounding on my door in the late afternoon.

Duke said. "I heard from our mutual friend Jonathon Cutler. He told me you retrieved his daughter from a very nasty character. He said you helped them come to a new understanding as a family. In fact, they are off to Hawaii tomorrow for a long holiday. When they return, they're both going to that doctor friend you recommended. Oh, and by the way, it seems you left without your fee."

I looked at him and said, "We never discussed a fee, only expense money. This was purely a Marine helping another

Marine."

Duke replied, "I told him you would say that, but he asked me for your bank account numbers again. When you go to your bank, you'll notice a wire deposit for a hundred and fifty grand. Before you say anything, you should know that Cutler has a net worth of over fifteen million. He created a security company when he left the Corps and sold it last year after his wife Emily's death for an enormous gain. This is an insignificant amount of money for him. He said if it wasn't sufficient, just say the word because there could be no price too high for what you did for him. He knows about the cold turkey detox, the spa, and all those new clothes.

You cared enough not to bring home a street whore to him. He told me, 'I could never be able to repay Jake for his simple act of compassion. He gave me my little girl back with some dignity.' You brought her home with a bit of self-respect. The score stands that if you're ever in Los Angeles or need to take refuge in Hawaii, his home is yours, or anything else he can do for you. As for me, you've earned my sincere gratitude and respect. Few can say that in this lifetime. So tonight, it's lobster at Marina Jacks, and dinner is on me."

That night over dinner, Duke held forth his new idea, "You know, Jake, you should get your Florida State private investigator's license and a license for concealed carry. You should do this missing-person thing. It all seems worthwhile doing."

I said. "I don't know, Duke. What do I know about running a business?"

He responded. "That's the best part of this idea. I can supply the support, set up the books, do all the legal stuff, and take on only those cases you want. We would have no politics and, above all else, no one can tell us what to do about any of our investigations.

When we want to go out fishing, we go. I don't know about you, but I'm going crazy with this retirement crap. You will, too, believe me. It's only a matter of time. We're people who are meant to be in action, and you seem to have a special knack for locating these missing people. Nobody else would have thought beyond bringing that girl home. You thought about what her father was feeling, and you brought her back with a bit of self-respect. No, very few people would have thought of that. By the way, why did you?"

I thought about that for a moment, looked at Duke, and said. "If you'd seen as many of those faces of the parents who have lost children as I have, you'd know that answer. You'd do anything to make that look on their faces disappear."

Duke said, "You see; that's what I mean; you empathize with these people. I went to school at Stetson and acquired my law degree a few years back. I've been a member of the Florida Bar for three years. Every year, I pay my dues, and I wonder why I'm writing that check. Now I know why. So, what do you say, Jake? Let's do this together."

I looked at Duke, stuck out my hand, and said, "You've sold me, partner."

That night twenty-five months ago, marked the beginning of the Missing Child Group Inc.

I subsequently bought my 1989 Bristol 48.8 ketch, specifically for her ample headroom and superb sailing characteristics. She has a centerboard keel, which is excellent for Florida's shallow waters. I spent six months part-time and eighty thousand bucks customizing and refitting her. She was brand new, down to her keel.

The condominium I'd occupied became our office. I had all the computers and electronics on my boat matched to those we employed there. Once every three months or so, I'd motor up to the fuel dock and fill my boat with diesel fuel. I sat on my mooring with a million-dollar view of the adjoining keys. It gave me a sense of peace I've longed for all my life.

I paid for dinghy docking privileges at Marina Jacks, one of our first-class bars and restaurants located in Sarasota on the bay. Duke and I were regulars for their Friday-night happy hour. I drank my orange juice and ice tea mixture while Duke ingested his daily dose or two of single-malt scotch. A glass of wine or a beer on occasion was my only other vice.

I made the return phone call to Jeanette Alexander. We set up our appointment for the next day. I told her I would arrive at around noon or thereabouts.

She asked if she should send their corporate jet for me. I thought about that for a moment and told her, "No, I'd rather drive over." I didn't want to be at the mercy of someone else's conveyance. I detest wealthy people with their private jets in general. They live in a world where they presume they can buy anything or anyone.

We said goodbye, and I called my office.

A sweet, cheery voice answered, and I thought not for the first time what an astute choice Duke had made in hiring Brett Atwood. She was a Boston University graduate that had majored in computer engineering. That made her an invaluable asset to us. I asked her to get on the Internet and dig up everything she can on Ms. Julia Alexander of New York and Palm Beach. Then I asked to speak with Duke.

A moment later, Duke came on the line and said. "I thought you were taking the week off to work on that antique of yours?"

I told him something new had come up that required our attention. We talked about the phone call I received and my appointment for tomorrow.

"Duke, is that friend of yours from the FBI still at his

Washington posting?"

Duke replied, "Is it important enough to use that resource? He was still there when I last had contact with him, which was about four weeks ago. What information do we need from him?"

I replied, "Please give him a shout and see what the status is on Julia Alexander's abduction. It also might be a good idea to give them a heads-up if we decide to accept the client, her father. We don't want to piss those guys off or get into a turf war."

"You're right. I'll check it and make my guy aware that the client called us. Are you coming in today, or should I run any stuff I get out to you at Marina Jacks?"

"No, I'm picking up my new car today, remember?"

Duke replied. "Oh, I forgot all about that, and what time will you be done with that little task?"

I went on. "About twelve o'clock, or so the dealer said. It should be ready for pick up by then."

Duke said, "Good, we can meet at Hemmingway's for lunch. I'll give you all the information; I can get by then. Let's say about one, or do you require more time?"

I answered, "Okay, and by the way, please have Brett's check out the father? I recall his name is Charles Terhune Alexander. If I remember correctly, he owns a large Wall Street investment firm."

That accomplished, I started in on my boat chores. I'd planned to do some complicated boat maintenance today. I took apart the Genoa tracks and re-bedded them with stainless screws and fresh caulking. Once that was completed, I set off for the Volvo dealership to pick up my new Volvo S80 sedan. My old 850 had 150,000 miles on her and still ran like a watch. Nevertheless, as Duke said, "There's no use in making all this money and continuing to live like derelicts."

I broke down and spent the forty-plus grand for my newest toy. It took longer at the dealership than I thought it would, but it is what happens when the dealer has your money. Then there's fresh meat in front of the salesman. I loved it when automobile salespeople imbued their own language in your ear. My sales guy was out on a demo. I needed to wait. In life today, every job has its secret language. I would bet that if there were still shoeshine persons, they would have their own personal acronym, like SHOE—shoe shiners and honored operators and entrepreneurs.

I turned into Hemmingway's off St. Armand's Circle at one-thirty. I spied Duke sipping a glass of single malt with a large legal-size file folder sitting on the table.

He said, "Jake, I thought you got lost. I've already had my other tipple of the day."

I replied, "I'm sorry about the time. My salesman had another customer, and the new prospective buyer always comes first."

Duke asked, "Anyway, do you like the way your new car drives?"

"You know, I like old things. It's not quite the same as my other Volvo."

Duke said, "Yeah, I know what you mean. I love old cars, boats, jeans, and even a few gray-haired broads on occasion.

Anyway, before we get into this case, let's get you something to drink."

Duke waived the server over. She was a perky little blond thing that smiled with too many teeth. He ordered one of the same for himself and a glass of white wine for me.

When she left our table, he began to fill me in on Mr. Charles Terhune Alexander. "It seems that your potential client is the chairman of the board of the second wealthiest private investment firm on Wall Street. Besides that, he is the only son of some ancient money. His family's wealth goes back to the China silk trade. He's a graduate of Harvard, Summa Cum Laude, with a master's in economics and another in business from the Wharton School at the University of Pennsylvania. The word on him is he has an uncanny sense for discovering talent. He and his partners built this business from scratch with all the capabilities he found. His almost-eerie ability to forecast future economic markets is without equal, per our resources. His integrity is impeccable among his peers throughout the world of finance. On top of that, he is very close friends with our P. It seems they attended Harvard together and at one point pursued the same girl, which he won over as his wife.

He's a widower and has zero tolerance for people who don't share his grueling work ethic. He may try to quarterback you if you take this case on. So, get the rules straight upfront with him. He won't like them, but at this point in his circumstance, I think he's desperate as hell."

I said, "The thing that bothers me most is you, and I know likely; she's already dead. It's been too long, and I'm going to tell the old guy upfront. Even so, if he wants us to continue this search, we'll charge him expenses and hours only. That is, if it's okay with you, Duke, I don't want any bonus money on this one."

Duke said. "I'd better explain something to you. His net worth is about three billion nine, and that's with a capital *B* ... He can afford whatever it takes to accomplish this task. I'm only curious as to why it took him so long to go private in the first place."

I said, "I knew this girl, Duke. I met her in a very unique way, a long time ago. I can't even think about taking any money to find her. We'll charge him the legal hourly fee we posted with Florida. If he decides to take us on, that will be our fee. Otherwise, he'll think he can buy us and order me about."

Duke said. "However, you want to do this is all right with me, Jake. I didn't know it was so personal."

I said, "You'll laugh, but it's all about a corned beef sandwich. I collected on it years ago, and I never followed up on it. I've always regretted that stupid decision. What happened with your friend in the F.B.I? Have you been able to get any information from him as to where they are on the case?"

Duke replied, "He said it wasn't his area of expertise, but then he faxed me the entire file. He said he would scout around and find us more information. He also told me with all the terrorist threats, the bureau could hardly keep its head above water. Various people who were working on interstate crimes and disappearances have been busy doing this terrorist thing. Thus, too many things are being neglected. I know there has been no ransom request. The FBI and the local cops ran out of fresh clues months ago. It's probably not being worked actively at all now."

The server came back for our order at that point during our

conversation. Then, Duke ordered grouper, while I had the blackened redfish with a Caesar salad.

I'm afraid to eat fish more than twice a month. It's because I spend so much time out on the Gulf, and I see firsthand the mess we've made of our waters. Possibly, it's my French/Irish upbringing, as I love variety in food and eat accordingly. Cooking has been my diversion aside from working chores on the *Switchel*.

I'd invited Duke and, on a few occasions, Brett to eat dinner on my boat. I've always gone all out. They seemed to rave about my grandmother's bouillabaisse or my quail with a pecan raspberry sauce that I stole from a Chef in Savannah, Georgia. I made my own homemade pasta sauce with fresh tomato, basil, garlic, and other secret spices. They all loved my culinary expertise.

Duke had always accused me of being penurious with my money unless it came to good wine or food. I spare nothing to obtain the best of both. Before we finished the meal, he withdrew a large envelope and said, "This is the latest photo of her. I got it from my bureau friend by telefax."

I withdrew the eight-by-ten color photo from its envelope and recalled what I thought was one of the most notable faces I'd ever seen in my life. I remember her honey-brown hair and those beautiful, smiling, cerulean-blue eyes. These were self-confident eyes that pled quarter from no one.

Sometimes, you get a feeling, a reaction within a sense of purpose, and an obscure awareness of incompleteness. With that comes a total dedication to finding someone in my occupation. I had only had it happen once before, but I felt it now. I knew there and then that I would find Julia. I owed it to her. I would return her to her family no matter where it took me or whether she was dead or alive when I found her. I'd find the ones responsible for her abduction and deal with them in my own method.

Chapter Two
The Meeting

On Sunday morning, I took the scenic route across Florida, picking up Route 70 in Fort Myers. Then it was over to Okeechobee, and a cut down to SR98 and, after that, SR441. All the time, I was driving; that image of Julia was moving about in my mind. There was something else far more baffling. I couldn't quite get a grip on the circumstances surrounding her disappearance.

After perusing her file yesterday evening, it seemed noteworthy that no one noticed her absence in those first critical hours after her capture. At least, that was the timeline, as stated by the last person to see her, Ms. Patty O'Conner. It took too much time to contact her father on the phone. Then he had to explain to the locals who Julia was in terms of her significance.

It took almost twelve hours for the Missing Persons Bureau in New York to send anyone over to see Alexander in his office downtown. What was her friend Patty thinking? What did the cops think, or was everyone busy covering their own asses? Alexander was too important, also high up on the VIP list. The mayor must have crapped his pants. This was not NYPD jurisdiction, but Alexander was a resident of the state of New York. I wouldn't be surprised if some of my former colleagues had already gone up there. I'd have to give Billy a phone call later.

I left Sarasota at seven-thirty on Sunday morning. At nine, Duke called my cell phone with a lot more information from his source at the bureau. No, they were not actively working on her file. The lead agent for the Boston office, who was responsible for this effort, was pulled off for another case. We had his name and number in the file. Duke's friend at the bureau retrieved the entire record and FedExed it to Duke. The agent in command would sit down with us. Should it become necessary? He only required a letter of engagement from Charles Alexander.

Duke never ceased to amaze me with all his contacts. His time spent as a liaison officer with Naval Intelligence in DC had helped us on two prior occasions. Everyone loved the big Irishman. It was great to have a partner who could cover your ass, pick up a phone, and get things done that no one else could. That was at the very heart of our successful partnership.

In another case we worked on, Duke, at six feet four and two sixty, proved that time hadn't slowed him down a step even at his advanced age, somewhere between fifty-five and sixty. He was a good man to have on your side when things get dicey. I stood six-four-plus and weigh in at two twenty-five. I 'm no small guy myself, but Duke displayed a somewhat more significant presence when we stood next to each other. When we worked out in the gym together, he always managed to keep up with me no matter our difference in our age. That was in everything except running. That was where his single-malt scotch always presented itself.

That was where all our similarities ended. Duke was organized and process-oriented. Whereas I am the field operative personified. I improvised, depending on what the situation calls for in any instance. I had light dirty-blond hair, hazel eyes, and a smile I inherited from my mother. It created a sense of ease with people, and they opened up to my inquiries rapidly. I also inherited a piercing look from my father that could freeze a person dead where they stand. He'd been a union man during the Depression, a teamster, and one tough son of a bitch.

With his thirty-plus years in the Corps, Duke was far more traditional in his methods than I was. He undertook a certain appeal to the fair sex with his red hair and a ruddy complexion like his current flame, a widowed woman named Margaret O'Hara Ryan.

Major, I. Mc Garrity's s face had the map of Ireland pasted all over it. What that *I* stood for, he would never share. It was an annoying puzzle to me, as was his constant desire to be called Major or Duke, including all the women of his acquaintance.

This was hovering in my mind when I pulled over and turned onto the bridge of old Palm Beach. It was twelve on the dot when I turned into the gated property of Mr. Charles Terhune Alexander.

I parked in front of Charles Alexander's huge turn-of-the-century mansion. I noticed it was set back on what looked like approximately two-plus acres. The front of the house had Atlantic views on all three floors as it faced eastward towards the sea. We from up north call a Gatsby house, with an incredibly ornate facade from the Rococo era. It was impressive, and I knew that I was looking at thirty to forty million dollars' worth of real estate by today's standards, perhaps more. The other thought that passed through my mind was an invitation for any evil bastard to kidnap or hurt the people who lived within a house like this. Wealthy people who advertise their own wealth, well, it isn't the most intelligent thing.

I walked up to the front door, and before I could even strike on the ornate door knocker, it opened. I assumed right away that it was the eldest daughter, Jeanette. She stood five feet eight or nine and was no slouch in the beauty department herself except for the lack of her sister's beautiful smile.

She bore the same blue eyes that I'd seen in Julia's photo, but that was where the resemblance ended. Jeanette Alexander lacked that sense of the softness of feature and profundity of sweetness, I recalled in Julia's face. There was something about her thin lips and the hardness in her eyes. Perhaps it was only that she lacked warmth in her smile and light in her eyes.

She held forth, "You must be Mr. Reynard. Please come in."

I walked into an entrance hall that could have staged an NFL playoff game.

"Fathers in the conservatory, if you, please follow me."

I thought, *if he's in a purple smoking jacket holding a candlestick, I'm leaving at once.*

One left, and a right led us to an air-conditioned glassed-in greenhouse room where a short, stout man in his sixties was moving what looked to be pots of orchards around on a large table. He stood about five feet six inches tall, with silver hair, deep-set blue eyes, and a businessperson's smile as he came forward to shake my hand. He had on shorts that exposed a set of spindly white legs, which surprised me in this excessively formal setting. I expected to see him in a black pinstripe suit.

He said, "Mr. Reynard, I assume. Please come in, and we

can sit at that corner table if you don't mind all these flowers. Oh, where are my manners? You've driven a very long way? Jeanette, please show our guest to the lavatory. He can remove the dust from the road off of his hands."

I muttered, "Thank you, Mr. Alexander. I could stand a decent wash-up."

The eldest daughter led me out the same door we'd entered. We made a short left turn, and she pointed me toward a small door under the elegant central staircase.

She asked, "Mr. Reynard, while you wash up, may I get you something to drink—an iced tea or perhaps a soft drink or beer?"

I said, "Yes, I'd love a real non-diet Coke if you have any?"

I made my way into the ground-floor guest bathroom, and it was pretty much what I'd expected. There were gold fixtures with rose linen wallpaper and a large gilt mirror. It befitted the house. As I made my way back to the conservatory, I couldn't help but reflect on the question of how long the Alexander family had owned this enormous house. What in the hell were the taxes on a home like this? They were both at the table, so I went over and sat down in front of the Coke.

Mr. Alexander began, "Mr. Reynard; Perhaps, I should fill you in on this investigation so far."

I quickly replied. "Sir, there's no need for any of that because of my personal acquaintance with your daughter. My partner and I have already contacted people we know at the FBI. We are in the custody of everything they currently have, plus all the crime scene photos from the kidnapping scene. I might mention, they are no longer actively working on your case now. The FBI's attention was diverted by this current terrorist situation. They believed; they ran into a blind alley on your daughter's disappearance. As to the rest of this conversation, I would rather we conduct it in private, sir. Please, Ms. Alexander, don't be offended. I only wish to spare you any of the coarser aspects of this open conversation."

She snapped, "Mr. Reynard, I'm not used to being dismissed by the hired help. I needn't be spared any details of my sister's disappearance. I was told you were a man who enjoys candor. Well, let me be candid with you. There is no fucking way you will be employed by my father or this family without my approval. Are we totally clear on that?"

I said, "Yes, I understand completely. I'll find the door out by myself." I stood up to leave.

The elderly Alexander said, "Please wait for a moment, Mr. Reynard, please, another moment." The older man spoke clearly, and as I turned back to glance at him, I saw that look, the one only a father who has lost his child possesses. It gets me every damn time.

Mr. Alexander turned toward his daughter and spoke in a harsh tone, "Jeannette, Mr. Reynard, and his colleague; I believe his name is Duke, are not used to being spoken to in that manner. From everything I have learned about Mr. Reynard, were you a man who had spoken to him in this way, you would find yourself on your ass looking up at the ceiling. As we need Mr. Reynard a lot more than he requires us now, I want you to apologize and leave us alone for a while."

She replied, "But Daddy, do you realize who he is and how he knew Julia. He's that cop; she invited him to dinner, and he blew her off. He also requires a huge amount of money for his services. I didn't realize that until I spoke to Patty last night. He was that same guy who never answered any of Julia's phone calls."

He cut her off, "I don't believe that incident nor that any amount of money is going to be a determining factor as to whether Mr. Reynard decides to help us or not. I know of a case where he returned a three-year-old girl to her father, and per my sources, it cost Mr. Reynard and his colleague over twenty thousand dollars in expenses out of their own funds with no possibility of repayment. They were aware of that fact before taking on that case. Did I misstate my facts, or is my information correct, Mr. Reynard?"

I said, "Yes, it was something like that." Feeling no need to deceive him, I repeated, "Each set of circumstances merits a different solution. They all have their own individual problems and solutions."

Alexander looked once again at his daughter and said, "Jeanette, Jake—may I address you as Jake?

Then I positively nodded my head.

He went on, "Jake, isn't one of those ass-kissers; you meet and even date on occasion from my firm's offices. In fact, I'll bet I can tell you his terms of engagement for this entire matter, and that's if he decides to help us at all. Maybe, Jake won't help after the way you've insulted him. He will require expenses, support, and no interference whatsoever. His firm will report to me and only me when they feel the need. He will brook no interference by me or anyone else in his investigation. You see, dear, Jake is an independent man. He has already endured enough nonsense from people with half his abilities, and he won't tolerate it anymore. Have I summed up my facts correctly, Jake?"

I said. "Yes, sir, you unquestionably did your homework."

And I thought I wouldn't like this wealthy guy.

Jeannette turned at that point and spoke in a lower tone, "I'm sorry if I offended you, Mr. Reynard. It's only out of concern for my sister and the distress that makes me act in such an insensitive manner. It seems Julia was quite enamored of you. You're the only man; she ever invited to our home for Sunday dinner."

I said. "I understand, and believe me, if I thought it would have made any difference at the time, I would have done things quite differently. I'll keep you in the loop on any developments as they come up if we take the investigation further."

Mr. Alexander stood up at that moment and told his daughter that he and I would eat lunch on the terrace since it was such a beautiful day. The weather had turned somewhat warmer overnight.

I turned again to his daughter and said. "I will still want to speak with you before I leave, so if you can be available later, say, after lunch?"

She glanced at me, and I saw the tears rolling down from the corners of her eyes. "Of course," she said. "I remain at your disposal."

Mr. Alexander and I went out the double French doors leading to the pool area. He turned and said. "That was extremely difficult for her. You see, their mother died from a malignant carcinoma when she was ten, and she's had to look out for Julia, who's four years younger throughout their formative years.

He went on, "I guess if I had it to do over, I would have done things differently. However, that's all bullshit, as you probably know. We do what we do for a multitude of reasons. I have never been able to figure out how to be both a father and a mother. Thank God I had Levi to lean on.

"You know, it's rather odd. I'm so adept at seeing other people's dilemmas and problems. I can tell from the way a person walks into a room what he is and, most times, how to beat him at whatever his game is. I'm seldom fooled by people." I nodded as he attempted to impress me with his people skills.

You quit school, joined the Marines, and became one of their Special Operations people. Very elite, from what I understand, though not much is spoken about your unit's operations. I am aware of your many decorations for bravery. Even so, you walked away when they offered you a college education and a commission. It seems like you had a brilliant career lined up by military standards. You know, I had all that and a lot more research done on you and your partner. No one, and I mean, not one person, had a negative thing to say about either one of you. I think the term they used for both of you was *stand-up guys*, always finishing what they begin. Only don't try to quarterback them on what to do or how to do it. That could be the reason you left the Marine Corps and the New York City Police Department, or am I off the mark in my suppositions.

I replied quickly, "It was something like that. Mr. Alexander, the reason I wanted to speak to you in private is, there's a very high probability that your daughter is dead. You need to face up to this, upfront."

He replied, "I know that Jake, and please, I would really like it if you called me Charles, as all my closest friends address me. If you take on this chore for me, we'll be very close friends before this is over. You see, Jake, I need to know. I need to bury my little girl." As he spoke those words, the tears began to fall down his face, and his breathing became labored. "I'm sorry. It never seems to get any easier. I should have done something on my own from the very beginning, as Levi had advised me.

Jake, you need to understand that Julia is her mother over again. She is gentle and kind beyond understanding. Most of all, Julia is caring for others and a genuinely compassionate person. She shows tenderness in everything she does and thinks. She has a heart that other people only wished they could possess. God knows she loved all humanity with her entire being."

I was observing an entirely new aspect of Charles Alexander. It was one that I believed few people had ever viewed before, and a side of him I'd seen far too often, a father who has lost a child. You really must go through this experience to comprehend the depth of their pain.

I held forth. "It's because of that part of Julia's nature. I mean, after I made the connection as to who she was, I decided that my partner and I would do everything in our power to end this pain for you. I will return your girl to you and, in the process, find the people responsible and hold them accountable for this barbaric act."

That response simply poured out of me. I was entirely committed to finding Julia. I've had this highly acute sense of empathy since I was a kid. I don't know why, but it seemed I could always walk in the other person's shoes.

I've always felt this, and it got me into more than a few problems. Once, I walked into a gang-rape in our high school boy's bathroom, and I dived into three of my fellow football players. I went crazy for a minute, but I tore aside three huge guys apart. The kid who was the object of that assault followed me around like a puppy for my entire last year of high school. As for the fellows who did the assault, they stayed clear of me.

The tears began to stream down Charles Alexander's face. He raised up his head, considered my eyes, and said. "I knew you would help me, Jake. Somehow, I knew you would do this for Julia and my family."

At that point, a small Spanish-looking woman in an apron came through the French doors on the other side of the dining room we passed, carrying a large tray. As she approached, Charles wiped his face and said without a sham smile, "Jake, this is Ms. Lena Perrot. Lena has been taking care of the girls, Levi, and me for eighteen years in Palm Beach. She, along with Levi, who is sadly away attending his own mother's funeral, has been our family. Lena, this is Mr. Jake Reynard, and he is going to help us find the whereabouts of Ms. Julia."

I stood, extended my hand, and held forth softly, "Hola, Señora, Qué Tal?"

She smiled, looked up at me, and said, "Gracias, Señor. It is so lovely to hear your greeting in my native language. Señorita Julia, Siempre decía Español Conmigo."

With that, she began to place what looked like three exquisite'' fresh seafood salads before us. Charles said, "Jake, can we allow Jeanette to join us now for lunch? You see, she takes after me, and feeling left out of her sister's search will utterly frazzle her to no resolution."

I said. "Of course, I believe that Jeanette and I have reached an understanding."

He motioned to Lena and said. "Lena, would you please ask Ms. Jeannette to join us now?"

A moment later, the person in question came out, holding her head down like a rebuked child. So, I stood up and grabbed a chair for her at the table.

She looked at me. "I know we are in the South, but I'm not used to such manners, especially from someone I have just insulted."

I said. "Well, these are only basic Marine manners that my father and grandfather pounded into me quite a long time ago. There's also a little New Jersey etiquette thrown in for good measure."

She smiled and said in a low tone, "Had I known that I would have crossed that bridge to Jersey eons ago."

With that said, we all began to laugh in our own guarded manner, but it was sufficient to break the tension.

Charles Alexander looked at us both and said, "Jake has agreed to help us. I must say, I'm more than a little annoyed about what he told me regarding the FBI not currently searching for Julia. Jake, I believe you know of my personal wealth. However, what you can't say is the extreme affluence of my client base. They have had their wealth greatly enhanced because of my firm's efforts to manage their money. Perhaps you know that politicians must place their funds in what are referred to be as blind trusts. That means they can have no dialogue with the managers or input as to how their money is managed or invested for reasons of undue influence.

I'm sure you understand the premise. Most of these people's money, along with whatever pensions they are entitled to receive, is what they will look forward to when their government service is completed. I have personally overseen three standing presidents, twenty-two cabinet members, and thirty-four United States, Senators.

We still manage two former presidential accounts to this day and the current President's blind trust. I'm supposed to have some influence on these bastards. Now, I hear that these fools at the FBI have been doing nothing about Julia's disappearance."

I looked over and saw that he appeared to be turning beet red. I interjected my own observation. I said, "I know you want to call someone up the chain of command, and I understand you and the Presidents are close personal friends. Naturally, you want to raise holy hell. However, if you do that, you'll not only jeopardize any cooperation we can obtain, but you'll put my partner Duke's allies in jeopardy for releasing information to us as civilian investigators.

The feeling Duke and I got is that they would be more than

willing to help us on this matter. That's because they came up against a blank wall. If fresh eyes can find anything new, they would only benefit. Everything Duke and I do works because we're not hampered by jurisdiction or politics. It comes down to interagency cooperation. There was one time. I really wanted the feds in on a case. The person I worked for believed his own self-importance was more important than a little girl's life. Thus, her parents paid the ultimate price, and I couldn't live with that. So here we are today. Believe me, Duke and I have been able to help quite a few people because I decided to leave the official environment. I know it's difficult to allow anyone to handle something as sacrosanct as this is to you. Even so, Charles, you must trust Duke and me to use our contacts to resolve this tragedy for you."

"All right, Jake, I see your point. Your partner, Duke, he's the one with all those inside connections?

I replied, "Yes, Duke's the guy with all the political influence in our group. That was all acquired from his stint with Naval Intelligence."

I observed a small smile began to creep over his face. "I

think if my first name was Ignatius, I'd be fairly politically savvy myself."

With that declaration, I doubled over and began to laugh harder than I had in years.

I asked. "Are you quite sure about the name, Ignatius, sir?"

 He replied, "I'm completely confident. It's really his correct first name."

I entreated him, "Please never tell him that you know about this. He'd die if he knew I was aware of his secret. He's one the toughest old Marines you'll ever meet, and with that handle, now I know how he got so tough. He must have been fighting for his life since kindergarten."

Charles said. "But I still want to call the President and make certain that all doors are unlocked for you. Hell, I helped Jimmy Nickerson get nominated, and Julia's a goddaughter. My resentment could cost him between twenty and thirty million dollars within my own intimate circle of friends and clients. I've never called in a chip from him, and besides, he's a father and an ancient and dear friend from our college days.

We both chased the same girl for two years. I won that contest for her, and he and his wife got the White House. I think I got the better of him in that regard."

I said, "Okay, but don't allude to any idea that we already know it's a dead file; let him find that out on his own. When he proposes reopening the case, you can decline because too many people walking around on one another's feet only creates more difficulties than it solves. If we need more people, and we may, I have people I trust to work with us."

"Jake, when can you start? For that matter, what will you do first, and what about your fees for this search?"

I replied, "First, I'll begin by going to Vermont. I want to get a sense of where she was abducted. I'll attempt to interview some on-site people. Occasionally, time can work in your favor. When people get distance from an event, they begin to recall small recollections.

I need to investigate this from the beginning before I study what Duke will get from the Feds. Then I can compare what they should have to what I discover on my own. Expenses, we bill monthly. Our fees are an average Florida lawyer's fee schedule and not as high as most. Let's see where my efforts lead us. If this is an acceptable plan for finding out what happened to Julia. Charles, I can't accept any fee myself. I only need you to pay my staff."

He replied, "Yes; I already had my people wire a twenty-five-thousand-dollar advance for expenses, which I believe is your standard retainer. The rest will be wired to your corporate account."

I said, "I will need a letter of engagement signed by you so that the people we meet will know you have engaged us in this disappearance of Julia. They will be mostly other cops and people that can hinder us in the process of our investigations. I brought one with me, and it's in my car."

He said. "Jake, I get the sense you knew beforehand that you would help me?"

I said. "Yes, as Jeanette told you, I met your daughter three years ago at one of the charity benefits for her foundation in New York. When I saw the recent photo of her, it all came flooding back. Juliet stood out for two reasons that evening. First, her choice of dress that night set her entirely apart from the other guests. Most significant of all, she walked around to every one of us off-duty cops standing security with a tray of soft drinks and sandwiches she'd made herself in the hotel kitchen. She didn't have to do that, but she was thanking us for being there. She had obtained a mustard-stain preparing those snacks for us, which would have ruined that beautiful gown. She was utterly oblivious to it, and I helped remove it while we spoke to each other. I think to any spectator, it was funny when I lifted her on the top of the bar to remove those stains with soda water. She laughed and made a comment about how I'd swept her off her feet.

I donated my wages from the night to her charity work for the homeless. As you know, on a policeman's salary, I was captivated by her. We'd kidded and teased a bit. She invited me to come down and volunteer my fix-it skills at her shelter. I went over there on a rainy day the following week. We spent the entire day laughing and bantering with each other. Then, as if by fate, we brushed hands at the end of the day, which led to a kiss. That's when she invited me to your home for Sunday dinner. I've always regretted not seeing her again. Now, more than I ever did at the time. She's never left my thoughts.

I knew then; she was destined to spend her life with someone other than a detective third grade. She and I walked different paths in totally different worlds. She is an exceptional woman, and that has always had a substantial impact on me. I've never met her match.

Ever since Duke gave me that photo of her, I can't seem to get her face out of my head. I can't understand why, but I would help you with this no matter the circumstances. Sometimes you get a feeling. It's not a tangible thing, but you know that somehow you can affect change in searching for someone. Despite our different worlds, we are still connected."

Charles said, "Now, I think I understand this entire matter better."

"What Patty told me was the truth," Jeanette exclaimed. "You were that cop, and Julia really wanted to see you again. She called your precinct more than a few times, but you never answered her messages. Julia has always had that effect of being unobtainable to most people. She thought you were all tied up with your duty at first. It was assumed you were different until finally, Julia gave up when you never called back. She was extremely depressed about that. You must kiss terrific."

Her statement made me feel like a complete weasel.

Her father looked at me differently and said. "You don't know how much better your story makes me feel, Jake. I mean, I understand your commitment to our search. By the way, if you had come to our home for Sunday dinner, it would have been so Levi and I could look you over. Julia never believed in separate worlds. She believed in the power of love, and she cared deeply about people. That's the real tragedy. You would have been the first man; she'd ever asked home for Sunday dinner. She must have been totally captivated by you."

I said, "Now, you understand why I can't accept money or reward from you for doing this search. I have a moral obligation to myself where Julia is concerned."

Charles asked, "If I may suggest? I have my own plane at the local airport, and I plan to leave for New York in the morning. Why don't you fly up with my pilot and me? Mike will fly you on to Vermont. In fact, I want you to use our corporate plane to go wherever you need to in this investigation. I'm making it exclusively yours until this entire matter is resolved, one way or the other. As to the money part of this, let your partner Duke give me a call. We'll make a more significant deposit with him."

I replied, "That comment brings up a small but important point: Some of your money will go to paying snitches and other cretins that may possess information we need. There won't be any receipts for that money."

Charles replied, "I don't care about any of that, son. You have carte blanche to do whatever you feel is necessary. You have my complete trust. Listen, son, I've heard good things about you before we met, a lot more than I mentioned. Now that I've met you, I can see you're a man of honor. I don't get the opportunity to meet men like you these days. I think Julia chose you for a particular reason, and I've always trusted her judgment.

"Jeanette, Levi, and I share a huge apartment on Park Avenue in New York. I would like you to use that as your New York headquarters. I know you'll desire to speak to some of Julia's friends. The dining at our house beats the hell out of any hotel in the city, isn't that correct, Jeanette?"

"Yes, Daddy, and I see you're going to treat Jake like a part of the family. So, I'll tidy up my language and adjust my manners.

With all of us in agreement, I finished my lunch and moved my gear to what I thought was a guest bedroom on the second floor. I called Duke and filled him in on all the details of our conversation. Then, I realized I was lying on Julia's bed as I could still remember her smell. It was filled with the warmth and the sweetness of wildflowers.

Duke began to scold me for not discussing fees and didn't realize Charles had wired a twenty-five-thousand-dollar payment to our account yesterday for this meeting.

I snarled at him, "How can I discuss money with a father who is in tears over the loss of his youngest daughter? Especially when you know in all probabilities, she's dead. Duke, please just segregate that money from our normal expense money and return it. I have my own reasons for doing it this way. I screwed something up, which could have been truly great in my life some time ago. It was all because of my old stupid cop thinking."

Duke said, "Okay, I get the point. We'll do it your way. However, I will call him in New York over the next few days. Jake, not that it matters, but you seem to have taken an extreme fondness for this wealthy guy."

I said, "I wouldn't want to sit on the opposite side of a table with him in a business deal, but yes, I respect him. I only wish he'd gotten in touch with us sooner. There is something about this situation that doesn't make sense. Either Julia's dead, or someone is clueless as to who they have in their possession. There's been no ransom note. That bothers the hell out of me, and from what I know of her behavior, she wasn't the type to invoke thoughts of murder in anyone's mind. Unless we're talking about a serial killer, some Bundy type, I just don't get the point of her kidnapping. Anyway, hold on to what you got from your friend. I want to investigate this in the blind and compare it to what the FBI collected.

I'll be leaving tomorrow morning with him for New York. The *Switchel* needs a little tending for a while. Please tell Tim at the boatyard to adjust the stuffing box as I didn't get to it before leaving. Please ask him to check the bilges and batteries every two or three days. Duke, I don't want to come home to a sunken boat."

He replied, "It would serve you right. You should be living in a condo or a house like a normal person."

"Yeah, I know. I hear that from everyone. Good night, Duke."

Our dinner that night was served alfresco by the pool, and the evening brought with it a sense of peace, except I still felt like an outsider. As a result, I did listen more than speaking. Jeanette went out of her way to be friendly, and I gradually got over her initial bitchy attitude. I listened to more Julia stories, and that only fed my desire to get on with this search for her.

Later, Charles and I sat in his study, and he was drinking brandy. He put forth a question, "Jake, may I ask you a question?"

I replied, "Sure, whatever you want to know."

He began, "Why do you do this? I mean, why do you risk your life to find these missing people?

I said, "I really don't know, but I do know that someone has to care, a person who's not bogged down by the bureaucracy with its stupid rules that favor criminals. It's something deep within. It's more than logic or thought. I love my country, and I hate the idea that people like you and thousands like you have to go through these horrible feelings of hopelessness. We deserve better, greater, and we don't get it, so I try to give back a little more than was bestowed on me in my small way. Does that make any sense to you?"

Charles replied. "Jake, I think that's the noblest declaration I've ever heard in my life."

Chapter Three
Vermont

We arrived at Palm Beach Airport the following day at eight-thirty. The first thing Charles desired was to organize a get-together with the crew and introducing me to them.

We boarded his Gulfstream G550. I sat on one of the oversized tan leather chairs in the main salon. The two pilots and a younger woman in a blue-and-yellow uniform strode forward and sat down on the chairs opposing us to form a small semicircle.

Charles spoke, "Jake, this is Mike Nettles, our head pilot, and George McGreeley, his first officer. This attractive young woman is Regina Creminetti, our cabin hostess. Mike flew with the Navy before signing on with us at the firm. George was Air Force, so even though they were both hotshot fighter pilots, they handle this plane like a Rolls Royce. They know how I hate turbulence and bumps.

"Regina is an entirely different story. I met her in the first-class section of a United Airlines flight to China. I will let her tell you just how she comported herself and how I lured her away from her former employer.

"Jake, these are all exceptional people, and every day I trust them with my life and the lives of my clients and family. I allow a few people the use of this plane. People, this is Mr. Jake Reynard, and he is a former Force Recon Marine and New York City police officer. Henceforth, or until Jake or I call it off, this is his plane in every sense of the word. You are to take him anywhere; he wants to go, and if he wants it, he gets it. Also, he gets total access to all the money in the hide-holey plus the use of all your corporate credit cards. We have a rear cabin with a double bed and two couches in the back. Your feet might hang off the edge, but this should provide all the comforts of home for a fellow who lives on a boat. I'll tell all of you why I have asked Jake to look into the matter of Julia's disappearance. It's because I have it on the highest authority that he's the best there is in situations like these. The undertaking, for lack of a better word, is to find her dead or alive and return her to me."

There was a marked silence as he uttered those last words of finality.

He went on, "I know those are difficult words for any father to say, but I must be realistic. Jake is to receive all the resources at our disposal. Jake, is there anything special you need right now?"

I replied, "Yes, I have the right to carry a firearm in Florida. However, I'm not registered in these other states where we may be traveling too. That's why I was reluctant to fly in the first place."

Charles went on, "That's no problem. Mike, show Jake the hide-hole," and with that, the chief pilot motioned at me to follow him forward towards the cockpit.

As we stepped through the narrow corridor, he stopped by the forward lavatory and motioned me to look inside the compartment. He twisted the toilet handled to the left and pushed it in and down hard. With that, the toilet lifted six inches from its base and revealed a small compartment with a nine-millimeter Beretta and a wad of cash.

"Do you have your weapon on you?" he asked.

I reached back and handed him my Glock 27 .40 caliber butt first. "Nice," he said as he felt the custom grip and heft of my personal weapon.

We returned to our seats, and Charles spoke again, "It may be that you will be moving around in different places and confronting dangerous people. If any of you want out of this, tell me now. You will be paid and returned to working when this search is over. If you want in, you're on double salary for the duration."

Mike was the first to speak on the crew's behalf, "Mr. Alexander; I believe I speak for all of us when I say Julia was an exceptional person to us. I think you're not aware of how we all felt after her disappearance. She always treated us with the greatest warmth and respect. She never forgot a kind word or honored a personal occasion with a card or a small remembrance. We would be extremely proud to help

Mr. Reynard in any way we can. Please, sir, and no more talk about double pay!"

They all shook their heads as one. The old man's eyes began to mist over, and I knew that if he spoke again, he would start weeping.

I looked at all of them and said, "Well, it won't do at all for you to call me, Mr. Reynard. So, if you are under any false impression as to my pedigree, then I won't be able to bring any real fun and romance into your otherwise dreary lives."

They all looked at me at the exact moment and began to snicker. George, the first officer, was the first one to speak. "Well, Jake, we know, with a Marine, it's always a question of who gets the girl. I can't believe I'm saying this, but in this case, we all hope you get this girl."

There it was, and Charles began to laugh aloud. I put on my infamous gee-wilikers face.

A moment or two later, I said, "Can we get this crate in the air today or what?"

We were airborne, and a few minutes later. Charles turned

and said, "Every moment I spend with you, I sense your natural leadership skills. I have a feeling these people will be yours rapidly."

I replied, "It's easy to win people over to a cause when it's an honorable one, to begin with."

Charles said, "By the way, in that compartment, you put your weapon in; there are twenty-five thousand dollars. Use it as you see fit, and let me know when you need more. Please, be free with money, and bribe whoever you must. All the money in the world doesn't do me a damn bit of good without some resolution of this horrible event. Tell me when you're done in Vermont, and I will have all of Julia's friends prepared to speak to you in New York. I will also arrange for you to have your own driver in the city. Otherwise, it's a total mess getting around. I guess it's better to talk to them on their own ground. I hope you will take me up on my offer to stay at our home while you're in town. However, feel free to stay at any hotel you prefer."

I held forth, "I'd be delighted to take you up on your offer to stay with you and your family in New York, Charles."

"Good. Son, you don't know how much better I feel when you're near. It's as if a weight has been lifted from my shoulders. I no longer feel alone in this loss."
74

Those words made me feel worthy of this challenge. It's strange; I was so prepared not to like this rich Wall Street person. After being with him these last twenty-four hours, I've caught a glimpse of a completely different man than the one; I expected to meet yesterday morning. His people cared for him, and that's always a good sign. I'd been guilty of stereotyping again. It's a cop's most significant problem.

We sat back and were quiet for the duration of the trip. It wasn't an uneasy silence; it was naturally peaceful. The plane soared through the air effortlessly as I sipped gourmet coffee and ate fresh scrambled eggs with rye toast.

We landed at Teterboro Airport in New Jersey two hours and thirty minutes later, and I disembarked with Charles. As we walked toward his waiting limousine, he turned and said, "I almost forgot to tell you something. Mike was taken down behind enemy lines in Vietnam, and he survived three days without rescue. He's a good man when things get dicey. Every year he goes through a special training center to keep up on his procedures in a hijacking. I understand he's a crack shot with that gun he keeps concealed under the toilet."

"Good," I said. "It's always important to know you have some backup in a tight spot."

Then Charles made the most unusual gesture. He reached up to me and took hold of me. I wasn't prepared for this act of fondness. He said, "God's grace be with you, son, and stay vigilant. I don't want any harm to come to you."

With that declaration, he turned and got into his limousine and drove away.

Mike approached me and said, "I have to say, I've never seen the old man hug anyone except his daughters. You must be very close. Did you know Julia a long time, and was that the reason he gave you that embrace?"

I replied, "No, not a long time, but let's say this is really personal for him and absolutely vital to me. I hear you're a guy who can handle himself in a tight spot?"

Mike replied, "I assume the old gentleman told you about

my adventures in Vietnam?"

I said, "Yes, he mentioned something about that to me."

Then he asked, "Tell me, have you seen action?"

I looked back at him and nodded my head.

He said, "You were Force Recon. No kidding, it was one of your older brethren that found and rescued me from that shit hole."

I answered, "My partner, Duke, fought in your war. You'll get a chance to speak to him before this is all over. But who in the hell wants to talk about that kind of crap?"

We steered our way toward the coffee shop, where we sat in a booth and ordered two cups of coffee. Then Mike provided me with a background on all his people.

George served ten years in the Air Force flying F-15s. He's an excellent pilot, but I've never needed to find out about his abilities as to any rough stuff. Regina's an entirely different story. For starters, she's an international judo champion. Her father was her instructor and turned her into a star on the circuit. That's how the old man found her. He was on a United Airlines flight to China, and a drunk in first-class created a scene with his kiss-my-asses. Regina, as calm as can be, asked him softly to control his language. He wasn't having any of it and told her she was just like every other c*nt. That's a word in my experience one never uses when addressing a lady, no matter how drunk one gets.

Regina proceeded to take the guy's hand in her own. She did something to it that made him begin to cry and finally really sob. The fellow must have been at least six feet tall from what the boss told me. He was sitting there crying like a baby as Regina whispered something quietly in his ear. I have no idea what she said to this guy, but he shook his head and sat quietly, looking down at the floor for the remainder of the flight. When they arrived at their destination, he didn't register a complaint. He waited until all the other passengers disembarked and stood up to apologize to the entire crew for his offensive conduct.

"When she got off the plane, Mr. Alexander approached her and basically told her he would double her current salary to work for him. He said he would personally handle all her investments and get her a great apartment in Manhattan. The condo ultimately sold her on the job, but it was her relationship with Julia that had kept her flying with us.

Those two hit it off right away. Ever since this happened, Regina's been beside herself. You see, she was home with the flu on the day we flew into Vermont. She blames herself for not being with Julia. If you can get a handle on what happened, you will be taking a tremendous weight off more than a few sets of shoulders. Yes, Regina is definitely someone: you want to watch your back in a pinch. Never underestimate her abilities."

He'd just finished sharing his insights as Regina walked in and sat down. Then she signaled the server for another cup of coffee. Next, George strolled in and said, "We have our flight plan filed. The plane is topped off, and we're ready to fly when you are, Jake?"

I looked at their shiny blue uniforms. Then I asked, "Do you; folks have any jeans and sneakers or other casual clothes with you?"

They all looked at one another and nodded. I asked, "Could you please change? Because I want to arrive in Burlington looking like fishermen or students, and not corporate executives or cops."

Mike stood and said, "No problem. We'll change and be ready to take off in twenty minutes."

While they were changing, I called my office, and Brett picked up our phone on the second ring.

"Jake, we've been trying to get hold of you for the last twenty minutes. Was your cell phone turned off?"

"Yes, I've been around avionics, but now I'm in Teterboro, New Jersey. I'm leaving for Vermont in twenty minutes. So what have you got for me?"

She said, "I'll turn you over to Duke first. He's chomping on the bit already."

Duke said, "Jake, is that you, finally?"

I answered, "I'm waiting on you, Duke."

"Listen, I checked with VICAP for potential serial killers in the Vermont area and got negative responses from Florida to Montreal. So did you figure out a way to get your gun aboard his airplane?"

I replied, "Yes, Charles had everything figured out. I would hate to be the guy who tries to hijack this plane. I have some very decent people onboard with me. Listen, I've been thinking about this all night, and I'm beginning to form a half-ass idea. At least, it's somewhere to begin; on my desk is the phone number for Tony Camerato. You know Tony, he's one of my old team members from my days in Recon. Call and ask him if he wants to do some work for us. He lives in Chicago. Agree to his rate and tell him to get a flight to Burlington, Vermont, today. In fact, get Brett to set it up for him. I'll call you in two hours or so and tell Brett the hotel we will stay. Send him an advance as I know he's always short on cash."

"What's with that *we*? Have you given birth to a baby since you left here?"

I said, "Yes, smart-ass, the old gentleman wants me to keep his plane for the duration of my search. To tell you the truth, I think it's a more-than-satisfactory idea. All these people onboard have special skills. The head pilot, Mike, is a Vietnam vet like you, ex-navy jet jock, and a pistol marksman to boot."

Duke replied, "Well, that's all very good, but these people are pilots and amateurs. I guess you have a hostess on board as well."

I said, "Alexander offered to double their salary. They turned him down flat on his offer, so they're loyal. As to the plane's hostess, Regina, it turns out; she's a national unarmed fighting champion. You know this is beginning to feel more and more like a human trafficking situation. If it is, there's still a small chance she might be alive. Have Brett check on private flights in or out of Burlington on the day or days surrounding her abduction."

Duke claimed, "That's rather ironic because the FBI came to that same conclusion four-and-a-half months ago. Their report says the trail ran cold after leaving the hotel for her morning jog along Lake Champlain. No witnesses, no car tracks in or out of the park, no skid marks from any helicopter. The only hard evidence was a swatch of blue cloth found at Brian Leddy Park. It could be a potential match to a jacket she was wearing at the time. Hairs from that jacket had her DNA markers."

I said, "This means we can skip a lot of these interviews, except for friends she came up here with and that guy she came to see. When you speak to Alexander, don't mention this theory. He'll start making waves with the government people. We may need them down the road. Besides, there's no sense raising his hopes. I'll talk to you from Vermont after I'm settled in."

With that understanding, we said our goodbyes and hung up.

Chapter Four
Burlington

It was two in the afternoon when we arrived in Burlington, Vermont. George went ahead to the terminal to find a phone and reserve us rooms. I asked him to book them in the same hotel where Julia stayed. Mike arranged for the plane to be refueled, and Regina set off to rent a minivan.

At two forty-five, we pulled up to the Hilton Burlington Hotel and began our check-in process. George said, "I've got us four rooms with one by the name of your friend Tony Camorato. A one-bedroom suite for you in case you want to meet with all of us at one time, then you'll have plenty of room."

As the bellman opened the door to my suite of rooms, I was mesmerized by the effect of the floor-to-ceiling windows overlooking Lake Champlain. It was a bright March afternoon with light snow falling on the hotel grounds and the lake. The room faced west, overlooking Lake Champlain. I asked the bellman how far it was to the university and if there was anywhere along the lake, a person could run in the mornings.

He guided my eyes toward the window and pointed down five floors to a dirt path. I asked him, "How far can someone run northwards on that path?"

He pondered that a moment and said, "I don't run myself, but I've had guests tell me if you begin here, you can run north all the way to Brian Leddy Park. That's about four miles. I guess you could run even further south, but it's not quite as picturesque."

I thanked him and slipped him a twenty-dollar bill. It was time to call home again. This time, the phone was detected on its first ring, and it was Duke.

I queried, "You're picking up the phone now?"

"Yes, I have Brett going through all these FBI files to see if there's anything I might have missed. You, of all people, know it's better to have more than one person look at a record.

By the way, the complete dossier came by FBI messenger. I thought that a little odd, so I called my friend to thank him and asked how he could give me the entire contents of an ongoing classified bureau case.

"He told me word had come down from above that we were to be given any assistance required. That came from the very top. No one asked if we had any prior contact. He said, 'Whoever your client is, he has more juice than anyone; I've ever encountered before. Rumor has it that the director was called in front of himself at the large house on Pennsylvania Avenue. It seems the director had been treating this case like an ordinary snatch and grabs or run-away. As of this morning, the head agent responsible for the Boston office has retired, and I am to become your sole liaison with our agency."

I assured him that at no time did we mention his name, nor had we ever spoken to him about this or any other investigation. Duke went on before I forget, your friend Tony is on his way. He asked for eight hundred a week, if that was possible, and for a client. If it was for you, he'd require nothing. The guy sounded like he was having financial problems. I told him it was for a client, and the pay was two grand a week unless we had to go out of the country, and then we'd double it. I also wired a five-thousand-dollar advance to his account. I thought you would approve."

I responded, "That's great, because I know he always needs money. I know his former wife constantly busts his ass for money. It always keeps him totally tapped out. The guy has two little girls he worships, so he puts up with it. It seems my crew has corporate credit cards with huge limits. I don't anticipate we will have any other expenses. What time is Tony set to arrive?"

Duke said, "He should arrive at about ten tonight. I told him to call here first, and we'd give him the hotel address. He can grab a taxi from the airport."

I asked Duke, "If the bureau is going to be open with us, let's ask them if they have forensics or other pertinent photos. Did they check the area for all known rapists operating within a two-hundred-mile radius of Burlington? Furthermore, we need the names of any sex offenders living nearby. That would be helpful."

Duke stated, "Jake, I'm way ahead of you. I sent a package to FedEx to you for ten a.m. delivery. It will contain all the relevant forensics and names of the types of all the perps you've mentioned. The only thing they came up with was that torn piece of blue-jacket fabric bearing some hairs that were a DNA match to her gene type. It would have come from the ski parka her friends described. She was wearing that when she went off on her morning jog."

I asked, "Did you ask Tony if he had any traveling money? I once asked him to come down so we could take the *Switchel* out for a few days. He said he had to work, what with all those high child-support payments. He has to come up with a lot of money each month for his daughters."

Duke said, "I figured that out by his wavering about the immediacy of leaving. He waffled even after I told him about the cash deposit money. Jake, I don't think he even had any spare change. Duke went on; I thought it would be a good idea if we wired him some cash since the deposit might not be available until tomorrow. I had Brett send him a MoneyGram for five hundred, and I did it in a way that wouldn't encroach his pride. I let him protest a few times and finally told him, 'This was on your personal instructions." I've never met this guy. What's his story?"

I told Duke Tony's story. "It's simple. He was a born lifer like you. It was his old lady who insisted on him getting out of the Corps. She was pregnant at the time, so he did as she demanded. Like any former recon operator out on the street, the only job he could get was being a cop, driving a truck, or becoming a hitman. She nixed the police force, so he worked at security jobs for a while, but he couldn't make enough money to live on. He grew up with half the criminals in Chicago. He's a neighborhood guy. In a way, I was amazed; he didn't connect with them after his divorce. Nevertheless, he loves his little girls, and I guess that's what makes the difference.

He's someone who can sniff out a rumor on the street in any country or city. He has those street smarts you can't train into someone. The criminal elements have always looked at him as a player. He's Cagney and Bogart, all rolled up into one personality. We were in Chad once, and we needed some plastic as we lost what we took in on our drop. I sent him off with some currency. Three hours later, he shows up with two pounds of the stuff. I couldn't believe it! He's the guy we need if this is some kind of trafficking deal. I'll get him picked up at the airport. I'll wait for your package to get here tomorrow before calling you again."

After I got off the phone with Duke, I called George's room and reached him on the first ring. I said, "George, could you round everyone up and have them in my room at five this afternoon?"

"Sure," he replied. "No problem at all, Jake."

I spoke to room service and ordered some hot appetizers with a bottle of Chivas Regal and a bottle of Sancerre. Sancerre is one of my favorite white wines. I requested that it all be delivered to my room by five.

I laid down on that king-size bed and must have dropped off rather rapidly because the next thing I heard was a series of steady knocks at my door. I looked at my watch, and sure enough, it was five o'clock on the dot. When I opened the door, all three of them stood there with a waiter in the background. I welcomed everyone in, excused myself, went into the bathroom, and ran a cold washcloth over my face. I realized that all the flying had worn me out.

I walked back into the living room and asked what everyone would like to drink. I was told; the group all drank scotch except Regina. She only drank soft drinks or an occasional glass of wine. After preparing everyone a drink and telling them to dig into the food, I began, "It's become obvious to me this morning that you would all like to help me with this search. I'm going to fill you in on where I think we are going. You need to know how we're going to proceed for scheduling purposes. For starters, I don't know anything about this flying thing, but I know you have to follow the rules on how many hours you can fly without sleep and all that?"

Mike spoke up, "Jake, let me handle all that, and I'll make sure we always have someone ready to fly us out of anywhere. For example, notice George isn't drinking, and he loves a good scotch. When we have a long stay somewhere, we all go out together, and Regina's always the designated driver. We make sure those things are covered, and George, I, and Regina discussed all this in my room this afternoon. We are willing to bend, no, break any rules, and we need to be ready if it leads to you finding out what has happened to Julia."

"Well, there are three things you should know. First, I guess that Mr. Alexander has spoken to the President because we have full access to all their intelligence in this case as of three o'clock today. Furthermore, we can get any of the other agencies' assets we require. Third, I have a theory about her disappearance, and if it's correct, then I think there's a remote chance that she may still be alive. I don't want that spoken to anyone, especially Mr. Alexander. False hopes and all that it entails are not what's needed at this point. He's ready to accept her death, and I don't want to put him through all that heartache again."

They all nodded their agreement.

Regina said, "Jake, what makes you think she could still be alive?"

I began, "Let's go over the facts as we know them. The choices are kidnapped for money, but there's been no ransom demand. If Julia was murdered, it would usually be by someone she knew. Her friends and former boyfriends are all accounted for or have alibis that seem to stand up. The serial killers have been ruled out but not entirely by the FBI's Violent Criminal Apprehension Program database.

"There are no known murderous rapists or serial killers currently operating in this section of the country from what we've learned. They found no blood or tissue at the scene. In fact, no car or truck marks were found near the staging either. We're getting a list of sex offenders for this area. There is a slight chance that one of them may have graduated to kidnapping. As of now, there are no known active serial rapists in a two-thousand-mile area of Burlington. Rapists are like any other predators: they operate within a territory. It's usually; what leads to their capture? Serial killers are more challenging to catch because they kill not knowing their victims except for a quick study to get them isolated before they make a snatch and kill them. Today, because of something that's known as VICAP, the FBI has information on all violent offenders operating throughout the country at a single time.

"This doesn't look like a crime of opportunity. It seems to have had a clear purpose, and it lends itself to something called human trafficking. The concept derives from the fact that this was all accurately planned. Traffickers are highly organized. However, they usually work in larger cities."

George spoke up, "What in the hell is human trafficking, and why would they kidnap Julia?"

I responded, "After drugs' and Arms' sales, human trafficking is the third-largest source of revenue for organized crime. The reason is simple: you can sell a human being repeatedly. On occasion, there are cowboys in this business, people who operate on their own and fill special orders for wealthy people. Most of the time, these kidnappings are very organized. For this theory to be viable, several things have to be true. First, Julia would have to be desirable for men living in the Far or the Middle East.

She's very desirable. Her inner and outer beauty is always the aspect of her that has haunted me. When I first met Julia, she possessed an appearance of vulnerability. Of course, it's how beautiful she appears in person. I thought to myself at the time, 'She is no archetypal rich kid.'"

Mike spoke up, "Jake, you met the woman in question once

or twice. The rest of us will attest to the fact that Julia is the least typical rich kid you will ever meet.

Mike said, "Her sister, Jeanette, is another story, but Julia, well, we could sit here all night and tell you Julia's stories. I've been flying for the family for ten years, so I'm the senior person in this regard, and I first met Julia when she was fourteen. For starters, it is and has always been Mr. Nettles. Her courteous behavior doesn't do her justice. She was well-mannered and kind in a very old-fashioned way. Regina, I think of all of us; you were the closest to her. What do you have to add?"

I interrupted them, "Hold your thoughts, Regina. A minor point, and tell me if I'm crazy, but you all use the word *was*. In saying that, we create our own acceptance of the fact that she's not alive. You're all mistaken. I do know her. That's why I need to go to this full bore. I need to believe she's out there somewhere still alive. It serves my sense of resolve. I only lack a decent plan to find her.

If she's the victim of this type of crime, then every day, she's accepting any number of horrible abuses. She's being subjected to unspeakable humiliation. She is being held against her will and subjected to deplorable acts that you can't even imagine. Unfortunately, I'm all too familiar with this type of crime. However, on the brighter side, I know of some extraordinary people who can help her if we can find her alive. They can help her to get through all of this and become a more vital human being."

Regina looked at me. "How? Jake, can someone be able to recover from something like that kind of sexual abuse if that's true?"

I said, "She can adapt and heal completely in the right environment. I wouldn't sell the girl I met short on anything. Suppose a person can understand the emotions we experience during those dreadful events in our life. In that case, you can tap into the actual experience behind the emotions in a totally safe environment. You get hold of not only that experience also its effect on you. You can restore your spirit not to where it was but to an even higher plane. People in war see all kinds of awful things, and no matter how well they trained us. It always affects people in totally different ways.

"All of you people may know Mike was shot down in Vietnam.

He was behind enemy lines for three days. What you don't know is how he felt at the time that it happened. If he doesn't mind, I can speculate as to what was going through his mind."

Mike shared his consent, so I went on.

It's not easy to speak about fear, but that's bullshit because all people who have experienced war will tell you, fear is a constant. It only has its degrees. In fact, the ability to direct that fear in a crisis is what makes a great soldier or flyer. I'm familiar with fighter jocks, and I give them their due respect. They are always leading the way. In fact, they are controlling people who can accept orders from other take-charge types of people. That's a rare combination. Take them out of that control situation in a cockpit, and you have a fish out of water. He's a very disciplined fish, but a fish out of his element nonetheless.

"This lack of control comes about in its own inexplicable way. He, though independent, is now dependent on strangers to get him out of a tight spot. He's lost on the ground, and he recognizes his fellow aviators can't help him out. It's about non-flyers because unless he's close to a coastline, his carrier rescue team has to turn the rescue mission over to a ground unit trained for these types of extractions. Hiding in the bush was never his talent. It's not in his makeup or training to dig a foxhole and stay put during the day. Therefore, he maneuvers around, and in moving, he creates a trail for his hunters to track. The hunter becomes the quarry. Most times, they don't even shed those orange suits they wear so they can be spotted from the air.

They forget those suits can also be seen on the ground. They try hard, especially at night, to concentrate on home or their past. That's because if they can get their head into a specific place, a form of detachment sets in. That's good because the mind has to release its fears, or it can self-destruct. The only people who can survive in that environment and get out intact are those with immense reserves of self-discipline. When they get back home, they incur feelings of exhilaration, followed by depths of depression. People who identify the emotions involved from that specific experience must be dealt with that guilt and not from some book. If they delay getting help, over time, it becomes more and more difficult for them to deal with."

I'd finished, and everyone was quiet. I looked at Mike to see if I had overstepped any of his boundaries. He looked over at me, and a small smile appeared at the side of his face.

He said, "I see I have a younger and brilliant brother here with me."

George stood up. "Now, I understand why you never wear that Distinguished Flying Cross; you earned."

Mike looked at him and said, "Medals are given by older statesmen to grant younger men some form of recognition. It defends their self-righteous, moronic, and egotistical decisions made during their own self-created, pointless wars. It assuages their guilty conscience from having so much blood on their hands. Besides, a lot better men than me were shot down and never lived to tell their tale."

Regina looked over and spoke, "I know Julia better than anyone here. Maybe I knew her more than her own sister. We hit it right off on my maiden flight. She asked me to sit down and chat with her. Two hours later, it was as if we'd been best friends for years. When we disembarked, I thought perhaps; she was only lonely. I questioned myself. I should have known better than to become intimate with my boss's family members. Then the next day, she phoned me. I was unpacking my clothes in my new apartment. I was all of three days in New York. She insisted that I come to lunch by saying she'd already sent a car for me, and we were eating with a few of her close friends.

"She never gave me a chance to answer before hanging up the phone. Twenty minutes later, a driver shows up at my door. We drove to a small restaurant in Greenwich Village called El Faros, a terrific Spanish restaurant. When I walked in, there was Julia with two of her best friends. She introduced me to Shawna, a friend from as far back as preschool, and Patty, her best friend from college. I sat after the introductions, and she announced that I, Regina, was to be afforded all the gossip-mongering and girl secrets from their group. Everyone laughed as I sat there, stunned. I thought, 'What would I possibly have in common with all these wealthy females?'

"It wasn't until three or four additional lunches and a few rounds of club crawling that I found out the truth. Shawna was a schoolteacher in Bed-Sty. Her father is the captain of an excursion fishing boat on Long Island Sound. Patty and Julia worked together at the Twenty-Second Street Shelter that they created to house all those homeless people. Patty's parents have money, but you'd never know it from the way she lived. She possesses a trust from her grandmother, like Julia, that pays out a substantial income. They spend most of their trust incomes on that shelter.

"Patty keeps the shelter open today as a tribute to Julia. She works there and is engaged to a social worker who hails from Wisconsin. Tom Becker, her fiancé, is a terrific guy. That was a fix-up by Julia. Because of Julia's influence with Patty's dad, she even got her dad to accept Tom's seemingly meager avocation. You see, Patty's father is a wholesale banker, and Mr. Alexander runs all his brokerage cash accounts through his bank. Anyway, let's just acknowledge the fact that Julia never fit her pedigree like her sister, Jeannette."

I asked, "How is Jeannette dealt with in a normal situation?"

Regina spoke up, "For me, it's difficult. I believe she resented the friendship that developed between Julia and me. She can be a cold bitch at times." With that statement, they all nodded affirmatively.

Regina went on, "I guess, to be fair, it's somewhat challenging to live up to the type of passion and sincerity that Julia chooses to lead her life. Even Mr. Alexander couldn't help but show his love for her as his favorite. Jeannette, for all her faults, has always protected Julia like a lioness watches over her cub.

Julia was the youngest, so Jeanette had to become the mother, and as a result, Julia is unselfish. She always wants to see everyone else happy. I've traveled a lot and met many people, but of all of them, I'd have to say Julia Alexander is genuinely unique. Especially if you understand the environment into which she was born, and that consumed her life. By the way, Mr. Jake Reynard, I know how you fit into all of this, and you hurt her terribly."

I returned that comment with, "Then you must also know it was the biggest mistake in my life."

With that statement, I suggested we adjourn for dinner.

Over a steak dinner, I filled everyone in on my friend Tony

Camorato. Regina volunteered to pick him up at the airport. I told her she didn't need to, but she insisted. They all asked me about Tony, and I responded with a typical Tony story. I thought it summed up my dearest friend.

I began, "Once on a mission in Africa, we were sent into the bush to gather some intelligence on troop movements. Our main objective was to avoid this country's soldiers. It was a three-day mission involving a four-man team. The purpose was an in-and-out with pictures, but no physical contact to be made. We came in at night by parachute to a remote landing zone and encountered no problems on landing. Then we had to hump in twenty clicks and wait for daybreak. The most terrifying thing about Tony is his inscrutable smile.

I've thought about this for years, and given Tony's difficult childhood, it's a wonder; he withstood it at all. I have never figured it out. Two days in, we found ourselves in an unbelievably bad situation. We had moved into an area where there was only a light brush covering, and around dusk, here comes a fully armed company of soldiers setting up camp, with some of them no more than five meters from our own position."

Regina jumped in, "What did you do then?"

I said, "Before they set up, I signaled for my team to dig in. We'd have to wait for nightfall and then try to sneak out undiscovered. We were all in heavy camouflage suits consistent with the terrain, similar to a sniper's suit. We dug in with our combat knives and attempted to use the ground to our advantage. We were trying to stay as motionless as possible. We even slowed down our breathing when somebody started to move toward us, taking out his John Thomas along the way. He moved to within a foot of where Tony was lying and began to piss. He's pissing on Tony's back while he's looking up at the night sky and talking to his friend.

"In the middle of all this, I'm watching Tony, as he knew I would. He raises his head, puts out this smile like, 'Isn't this great? It's like a day at the beach.' I had to stifle my laughter by jamming my T-shirt in my mouth before I went into even great fits of laughter. The soldier finished and moved back to his cook pot. Tony knew the effect; this would have on me, but he did it anyway. He's utterly crazy at times. That's my Tony, but there's no better fellow to have with you in a tight spot."

Toward the end of my story, they all were laughing like hell.

Regina popped up with, "So, he's into golden showers, huh?"

Her remark provoked another round of hilarity. We finally agreed to get some sleep and meet up early in the morning in my suite of rooms.

Chapter Five
The Run

The following day, we met for breakfast, and I made introductions all around. I decided to break up our group in a more efficient way. I asked George if he could assume the duties of logistics and support? He said he could, so I gave him some minor tasks to perform. He would stand by in my room to take calls and make the necessary arrangements. He'd also serve as our checkpoint while we were in Burlington. My suite had a large table to set up on, and I told him the first thing I needed him to do was call Duke or Brett and coordinate some searches and appointments. I wrote down my requests late last night. I handed him my notes and turned to Tony, who was to tap into the local bad-guy network and stir it up a little.

I asked, "Tony, see if any known traffickers are operating within the city or reports of snitches with information."

I asked George to give Tony a few thousand dollars for snitch money. Mike, Regina, and I would retrace Julia's route on the morning of her disappearance. There was a very remote chance that we would discover anything new, but you can never tell. We put on running gear and began walking north along the lake by the side of the railroad tracks. It was cold as hell at this time of the year. The first place we came to was North Beach Park.

Mike asked, "Is there a possibility she could have stopped here? We've come almost two miles."

"No," said Regina. "That wouldn't even be a sprint for Julia."

I said, "Besides, this isn't where they found that piece of blue cloth."

That said, we decelerated our speed significantly. I told them to begin a sweep with their eyes from left to right along the shoreline. There was no way to alter a jog this far north along the path to Brian Leddy Park. At four miles in, we wuere in the park, and I noticed the water depth by the shoreline was more in-depth, or at least; it appeared to be under the thicker, darker black ice. It meant even if someone was this far away from the main inlet, a decent-size boat or plane with floats could land here.

It looked to have at least a four- to five-foot bottom. I wasn't sure because of all that dark ice. The problem was, this was the wrong time of the year. There was still a lot of ice and snow on the lake. My sense of depth was a guess at best. I decided to consult the nautical charts for the correct explanation.

We stopped at a bench to sit down, and I said, "You know, we've come about four miles, and that seems a stretch for a morning run."

Regina said, "Wrong, Mr. Marine. In the city, when we ran together, we'd do four miles every morning. That's on hard city streets. On dirt, I could see her doing an easy five. If she stopped here, she would have rested a few minutes before starting back, not long enough for her to cool down."

I let her comment sit with me for a moment. Then I began to look around. The first thing that hit me was the total remoteness of this park. Mayhem could have ensued here, and no one would be the wiser. It was isolated, and the trees blocked everything behind us but the water facing us.

As trusting and naive as Julia was, she might have grabbed a line from a boat and aided her own captors by securing their vessel to land.

I said, "This is getting us nowhere. Let's start back to the hotel."

Mike spoke up, "Are you telling us this walk has been a total waste of time?"

"No, on the contrary," I said, "you see the depth of the water here? I can't say for sure, but I bet it's at least four or five feet deeper than near the hotel. Down where we began, the water was only a few inches at the edge, and it remained shallow for some distance past that."

He asked, "What does all that signify in our search?"

I said, "It means, if you follow my theory, she could have been grabbed and transported by boat or some other waterborne conveyance. These are only speculations at this point, but some things are pretty straightforward. Whoever took her didn't know who they had, and she didn't tell them. Maybe she couldn't tell them in the beginning. That's when she would most likely have tried to reason with them. Otherwise, they knew exactly who she was, and someone specifically sought her out. You usually don't run around lakes in your own country with ID on you. So again, they would have no way of knowing who she was unless they knew beforehand. No, I believe she was chosen for a specific reason, but not for who she is as an Alexander. The only way to snatch, grab, and keep the subject quiet is with drugs or a blow on the head. Some strike on the head seems out of the question. That torn piece of her coat signifies some struggle. Drugs could explain her not saying anything about who she was after that.

"Later, she might have surmised there was no advantage in allowing her captors to know who she was. Better to be a nobody until you figure out a way to break away from your captors. If they seized her by boat and wanted to leave the country, then Canada or New York appears to be the way they might travel. In a heightened state of alert, ships would be moving south in September. The border control people would be overwhelmed with southbound traffic from Canada. A boat traveling north during peak traffic hours, especially one with a Canadian registration, could be waved right through at the border.

"The obvious problem is that a boat would require someone knowing that she would be here in advance. No, a boat, though a logical choice, would be out of the question unless they knew about her trip to Burlington. If they were inspected, it would be rather cursory. Depending on the type and size of the boat, there are plenty of spaces to hide someone on a boat, especially a dormant human being."

By the time we hit the hotel, I felt I'd had a workout, not being used to this cold Northern weather. George was in my room and said he had connected with Brett and Duke, who were both anxious for something to do on their end. He said he'd set up a meeting with Peter Osterhaus, the friend they all came to visit, for 3:00 p.m. today.

Then George told me the FBI package had arrived. I asked Regina if she could take the envelope to the office center downstairs and make three copies. She replied, "Okay," and left. Forty minutes later, she returned, and I asked her to dispense the copies to everyone.

I then asked, "I'd like you all to take a set to your own

rooms and read through them carefully. We'll gather here and trade our thoughts on what we have learned and thought about these reports at two o'clock. This is referred to as an intelligence circle. We all get an opportunity to have eight pairs of eyes and two different genders looking at all these reports. Then we can conjoin all of our ideas.

"Regina, as a woman, you are the major player in this process. I know Duke will have Brett read these reports also because we both value her collaborating skills. If you want to trade thoughts with her, then please do so. If that's it, let's get on with this, but try not to allow any of my theories to invade your thought processes. We don't want the donkey to design the cart."

After they left, I dialed our Florida office and spoke with Brett. "Brett, I've got some research that I need you to do for me."

"Okay, Jake, cough it out. What do you need?" she replied.

I said, "I need you to get a maritime chart of Lake Champlain with particular emphasis on the Canadian and New York sides. Then check for any charter companies that did a bareboat charter or rented a seaplane or helicopter with pontoons within the week of Julia's vanishing.

"I want you to concentrate on Canadian- or New York–registered planes or boats of thirty feet and longer from towns accessible, having their own airport. Then check the charts around Brian J. Leddy Park for water depth. If you can develop any charters, get Duke to perform a time-travel study from the point of origin to Burlington and back. Emphasis should be on any returning charters that checked in at odd hours or at night."

Duke piped in, "I'm on the extension. I guess you have a theory?"

"Let's say I'm eliminating some alternatives. I would like you to help with this check of the water depth in front of Brian Leddy Park. It's critical to my theory. My first thought was a boat might be used in this kidnapping. That conflicts somewhat with my time theory, but we can't leave any stone unturned. I thought about the preparation for the grab, and I realized that there wasn't any way to plan so far in advance. On the way back from our run, I looked up and saw a small plane.

It came to me if a pilot is involved in any of this, and given the time of the year, it could have been a small waterborne aircraft or helicopter fitted with pontoons. Even a small boat can be rented fast with few questions asked. Anyway, we have to nail down their method of exit."

Duke went on, "Have you spoken to Charles Alexander yet? He called me twice today."

I replied, "No, I want to get through this FBI package first. Everyone has a copy, and we're going to do an Intel circle at two. I'd like to have you guys on a speaker hookup. We can; all participate in the circle. Will that be acceptable? I'm assuming you both went through these files already, correct?"

"Absolutely, and we haven't discussed it yet, as per your instructions with Duke," chimed in Brett.

I said, "Well, I've given you guys a lot to do, so I'll let you get to it."

At two o'clock, we met and sat around the dining room table in my room. Duke and Brett were on a speakerphone situated in the middle of the table.

I said, "Who wants to begin? I need to speak last since I've already started a theory that may be off-target."

Regina began first, "That photo of where the piece of material was found is within a few yards of where we stopped our search this morning, between the bench that overlooks the lake and the water where you made your comment about water depth. When they surveyed the scene, the forensics' people found that the grass in that area was trampled as if there might have been a scuffle. The odd thing is, they never mentioned the possibility of an escape by water."

I said, "I live; aboard a boat, so it's something a mariner might think. Maybe the FBI team had nobody familiar with that type of setting."

She continued, "It does seem they only pursued the theory of a ground escape. With the amount of interstate traffic that was scrutinized, it really makes your idea seem better. The struggle doesn't surprise me either, as Julia has taken self-defense lessons with me for the last two years, three times a week. I don't believe for a minute she would let anyone abduct her without putting up resistance."

George added, "Someone had to be waiting and prepared for this assault. That meant someone was planning this beforehand. The FBI interviewed all the people they could reach during the day in question. They didn't pursue anyone from the day before, and we all know Julia ran that day as well."

I asked, "Mike, you've been silent so far. Do you have anything to add?"

He answered, "I noticed in one interview. Someone said, 'There were usually a lot of people who run in that particular park," and yet no one has come forward since the kidnapping. Enough time has passed that maybe we should be able to spot and question one of them. I mean, if a boat or a guy was hanging around, it should have been seen by someone. This town is small. The trouble is this time during the year. It's too damn cold to run for most people."

I said, "Duke has had Brett working up hits on the profile I gave her before we began this report. I know it's not much time, but I'm wondering if we could be on the right course with this water-escape concept."

Brett spoke up before I was finished, "Yes, as a matter of fact, I've come up with two profiles that fit. I have eleven more to follow up on. Jake, it's my number one priority."

Duke spoke again, and all attention turned to the phone. "Jake, I think from what I've read, your theory is beginning to grow legs. Besides, it's all we have now. When you read the FBI report, they had their Boston people in this small town, and they moved around with somewhat clumsy feet as far as the local cops were concerned. We have the advantage of not being cops, so maybe there's something they are holding back, and we need to explore that line of thinking. At that point in the park, the water depth is considerably deeper than the rest of the shoreline moving towards the hotel. Anyway, how much longer do you intend to stay in Burlington?"

I said, "Another two or three days should wrap it up. That is unless Tony comes up with something noteworthy. When you said the depth difference was significant, what did you mean exactly?"

Duke restated his opinion, "I meant the water. Above that point, it's six to seven feet all the way out to the channel marker. It's pointedly lower, say, one to two feet near the hotel. There's a trench of sorts at Brian Leddy Park. Excuse me for disagreeing, but speaking with the locals is a waste of time since time is of the essence. I believe you run with the theory you have until it repudiates itself. Personally, I like your idea of a water escape. It sounds highly plausible. There's a series of locks you would have to pass through. Nevertheless, you can literally go to Quebec, Ontario, or even up the St. Lawrence Seaway in a powerboat with a shallow draft. We have to expand our search for charters because we can't assume there was in any critical time factor."

I returned, "I've sent Tony on a mission, and I've yet to hear back from him."

Duke replied, "I want in on this search, Jake, and Alexander has welcomed me aboard. In fact, we are both to stay at his apartment in New York if we meet up there. I know this is your baby, but I had to ask. I realize you don't think about this business as such, but this could be a major success for us all."

I came back really strong. "Yes, I guess it would. However, I have a missing girl out there in unceasing danger, and you were right with your first assumption. I could not care less about our business right now. My mission is to find and return Julia to her family. If Brett comes up with what I've asked for, then I need to be in Canada, and you need to be in Washington. You can get us what we need there and do what's required with these government people. Nobody else can do that but you. Are we clear on my position in this, Duke?"

He replied sheepishly, "Yes, I am, and as always. You're responsible for all field operations, Jake."

I replied, "Please ask Charles's secretary to set up accommodations for Tony in New York."

"I can handle that, Jake," Regina said meekly.

"We should be in New York no later than Wednesday or Thursday. I can't stress enough the importance of this search that Brett is conducting. I think our next move will be on to Canada or upstate New York to follow up on any boat or float-plane rentals."

With good-byes all around, we stood, and I told everyone I had a meeting with Peter Osterhaus in four or five minutes.

I asked Regina to stay after the rest of them filed out of my room.

I turned to Regina and said, "Don't be afraid to jump into the interrogation with this fellow. I know you're a lot sharper than you let on."

She smiled at me with one of her rare grins and said, "Jake, I feel terrific about what you said to your partner. I'm pleased about your motivation regarding Julia's disappearance. I know all about you from a conversation she and I had some time ago."

Peter Osterhaus showed up at three on the dot. We made introductions all around, and it seemed he knew Regina. His manner in looking at her begged the question, why was she here? So, I began, "What was the extent of your relationship with Julia?"

He looked at me. "What kind of question is that? If you're really from her father's firm, then you already know all about our relationship."

I said, "Well, let's pretend for a moment that I know nothing."

"All right, what do you want to know?"

"I want to know everything about you and her."

"Jules and I used to date in college. However, that changed later into a kind of friendship."

"What made that happen, and at what particular point in time did it change?"

He thought about that for a moment. "I guess it changed after I asked Julia to marry me last year. Until then, we were always paired together among our group of friends, as Regina can attest. When I asked her to take that next step, I imagine she must have examined her feelings about us and found me wanting as a desirable life partner."

I asked, "Did that upset you? Were you very angry with her response?"

"Of course, I was upset. You know the cops and the FBI asked me these identical questions, but I was with Patty and Tom having breakfast at the time of her disappearance. Plus, you couldn't stay mad at Julia. She would never allow you to express complex passions or emotions."

"Is there anything you can recall from that time that perhaps you didn't then?"

"I've thought about that night before she went missing continually. Something did come to mind recently. We all ate in the hotel the night before, and I noticed some foreign nationals in the dining room. I didn't think much of it at the time, but this place is real Americana, and the only foreigners we see are visitors at the university."

I asked, "Peter, why does it seem so odd now?"

Peter said, "First of all, most of our visiting professors never eat at expensive hotels like this one. Unless someone on the staff or a parent is paying for it, it's extremely pricey on a teacher's salary. When I knew we would meet here today, I checked with the registrar's office and found we had no visiting guest lecturers at that time. It was too early in the semester."

I asked, "How did you know we would meet before George called you this morning?"

He said, "Regina called me last night and told me."

I asked, "Can you remember anything about the way these

people looked or some features that made you consider them foreigners?"

Peter said, "Yes, they were dark and had semantic features, like someone from the Mideast, and when I passed their table, I heard one of them speaking Arabic."

I asked, "How did you know it was Arabic; they were speaking?"

Regina jumped in, "Peter's field of study is ancient history, and he knows many ancient languages." She turned and asked, "Peter, why didn't you tell the police about these people at that time?"

Peter said, "These cops thought I murdered Julia. That was obvious from the beginning. They beat the hell out of me in the basement of their jail. I was hit with a phone book and held against my will for eighteen hours until they finally allowed me a phone call to an attorney. They were brutal in their conduct towards me. I still have a lawsuit pending against the town of Burlington. Later, I didn't think much about it. As I reflect, I accepted that Julia was dead somewhere. Could I have been mistaken? Is there any chance that I've been wrong after all this time has elapsed?"

My observation is this kid acts rather tortured. However, I sense there was more than he wasn't telling us.

I said, "Yes, there's a slim chance she's still alive. No one has found any motive for her abduction yet. I asked, Listen, Peter; I want you to do something for me, all right?"

He replied, "Sure; I'll do anything if you think it would help find Julia."

I said, "Close your eyes and relax, Peter. I'm going to guide you through that last evening. You will attempt to recall anything significant. For this to work, you need to relax completely. Sit down in this easy chair."

I motioned for Regina to move into the other room. I said to her, "Listen, I said in a hushed tone, I'm going to start him off in his room and attempt to guide him through that night. I'll ask him what he was feeling and what the surroundings looked like. We used to do this after a mission, and you'd be surprised: what comes out of the subconscious mind? If you have something to add, write it down in a note, but don't speak at any point during this exercise."

We went back into the room, and he was dutifully sitting in the chair with his eyes closed.

I began slowly, "Peter, where did your evening begin that night?

He replied in a soft voice, "I was in my quarters at the school."

I asked, "What were you thinking about before you came to join the others?"

He said, "I was wondering if her trip up was her way of telling me she'd reconsidered my proposal. If we had a moment alone, I would ask her."

I asked, "What feelings did you experience after that thought?"

He said, "I finished dressing and noticed I was running late. I hurried over, but those thoughts of Julia's objectives weighed heavily upon my mind. We hadn't seen each other for three or four months, and I had no intention of going down to New

York to speak to her. I was upset, and she knew I was angry. When I walked into the dining room, only a few people were sitting at the tables, but I saw those two foreigners right away. I sat between Julia and Tom, and then a vodka martini was placed in front of me.

"Julia asked me, 'We ordered a rib-eye steak for you, medium-rare. Will that be satisfactory?' I said, 'Sure,' and the introductions began. I'd never met Tom before. Then we toasted to their engagement, Patty and Tom's, and the conversation turned to where they would live after they married. We took a minute to order some wine, and the conversation continued along in that vein."

I asked, "Describe the dining room and the people who were present that night."

Peter replied, "Well, I soon grew tired of all that wedding conversation, so my eyes and attention began to wander around the room. Two tables down, there were a father and daughter. She had to be a student, as they were having a heated debate over some frat party she went to and had somehow come to her father's attention. Three tables on the other side of them were these three Arab guys."

I asked, "What did you notice about the way they appeared? Did any of them have any marks or unusual scars? In point of fact, why did you notice them at all?"

He said, "The guy with his back to me turned at one point, and he had a long scar running down the right side of his face. It wasn't unsightly, merely somewhat sinister. They all had black hair and brown skin with pronounced semantic noses as to the rest of it; I noticed them because they kept glancing over at our table. When they saw me looking back, they turned around, then I turned away. You know, we're all like children when it comes to those types of things. I did notice that occasionally they continued to stare at our table. I thought at the time that perhaps, I had offended them in some way.

"Later on, I went to the men's room. I was mindful they might follow me, but they didn't, so I put it all down as nerves about Julia being here and all these emotions I was experiencing. On the way back, I did overhear them speaking in Arabic, but the only word I caught was *Tey... Teyyara* or 'flying vessel.'"

I said, "Plane? Are you sure that was the word used?"

"Yes, I heard a *plane* or as they say it, *Tey, Teyyara*."

I took him through the rest of the evening, but it soon became apparent that Julia's coming here had nothing to do with anything other than an attempt to recover their long-held friendship.

After an hour of this, we headed down to the bar to meet everyone else. We asked Peter to have a drink with us.

All this time, I think that something doesn't quite jell in the way it should have. I would love to put this guy Peter on the machine. This lawsuit—maybe he missed his big crack at the heiress, and that agitated him.

Tony was there when we arrived. I asked him, "How was your day? Did you get to meet the franchised gentry in this burg?"

He told me, "Yeah, but we need to save that particular discussion for later."

I said, "Acceptable," and we all ordered drinks.

When we finished our drinks, I asked Peter if he knew of someplace other than the hotel to eat and if he could recommend a restaurant for a warm meal.

He recommended an Italian restaurant in the downtown market called (The Three Tomatoes). I looked at everyone, and they all said yes at once. We asked Peter to join us, but he begged off. You could tell. He felt weary and out of place even though he knew everyone here except Tony and me.

There was more to this guy than this current story. Nobody accepts rejection this well.

After he left, while George was settling the bill, Mike commented, "He's taking this whole thing really hard. He's blaming himself, and he had nothing to do with any of it. That youngster is only guilty of being infatuated with Julia."

I rejoined, "He lost at love, and then this kidnapping was his final loss. I feel sorry for the guy, and I hope I didn't add to his misery." I kept it to myself that I had my own doubts about Mr. Peter Osterhaus. His story didn't quite ring true. Sure, the pressure would have been on these small-town cops, but before they got to any rough stuff, he could have shifted the investigation by being more forthcoming about who he saw the previous night."

Regina jumped in, "You didn't, and as a matter of fact, I think you went a lot softer on him than the local cops. He and I talked over the last few months, and I'm glad you let him do this himself. Reliving that night with a little of your guidance, even though I didn't know what you were doing, didn't seem intimidating."

At this point, Tony jumped in with his big grin and said, "You don't mean he's your type—a preppy professor and not-a-good-looking Italian boy with a smile that could bring joy to your heart forever and music; to your soul never-ending?"

Regina turned to me, laughing, and said, "Where did you find this guy? He never stops pitching."

I grinned and said, "That's because what you don't realize is you are under a full-frontal assault, Marine Corps style."

Tony piped in, "Yes, you have to understand that aspect of it. What's more, you're going to love it. There's only one thing better than an Italian boyfriend, and that's a bona fide Marine

Corps Italian lover."

"Okay," I said. "Ease off, and if Tony offends you in any way, Regina, show him what your father taught you. You have my permission, but please, no permanent damage."

With that stated and me savoring Tony's bewildered look, we set off for the Three Tomatoes. We enjoyed a great Italian dinner of stuffed manicotti served with a great bottle of Chianti Classico.

When we returned to the hotel after dinner, Tony came up to my room. The first question I asked was, "What's all this with you and Regina?"

He replied, "Isn't she something else?"

I said, "Yeah, she is, but I guess what I'm asking is, how did you get to know that?

He replied, "When she picked me up at the airport, I hadn't eaten all day. So she took me to get a pizza, and we began talking. I guess we gabbed for about three hours. Mostly about you at first, but then about each other, our families, and she's a wonderful listener. Hell, she's a great woman. She's kind of old-fashioned. You know, she still speaks to her father every day."

I said, "I see. Do you think there's some mutual interest going on here?"

He answered, "I don't know. I only see this girl is wonderful, and I could gaze into those eyes of hers all night. Unbelievably, since my divorce last year, that was the first time I've even had dinner with a woman.

Anyway, I found out. There's a guy here, like in every town. He pretty much runs all the side entertainment, if you understand. His name is Johnny-Boy De Lucchi, and most of his crap is relatively petty. I mean, it's a small town. I got some info that he reports to someone higher up in Boston. I told him I was from Chicago and gave him some street references. He could check me out. I said my reason for being here is that my niece will attend school here in the fall. I heard about the disappearance of that rich, broad six months ago, and I was concerned."

"He said he understood what I meant, and they were all distressed at the time. Mostly because of the heat, it drew down on all of them. Of course, the reward made it very enticing, so they made inquiries on their own."

"What came up?" I asked. "Could it have been a local thing?"

He said, "No way. As a matter of fact, he said they think it was an actual kidnapping, but not a sanctioned one, not even from any out-of-town lads. With that kind of money on her head, you wouldn't be able to trust your own mother. You know these guys. They don't get involved with civilians unless it's something for ransom or revenge. If it was, he said the perps couldn't hide within a thousand miles without someone knowing. Did you know her old man posted a ten-million-dollar reward within a few days of it happening, and then he upped it to twenty million two days later?"

I said, "Yes, I did, actually, and it doesn't surprise me that he did. So what you're saying is, they had a double interest in finding out what happened to Julia, and they came up empty."

Tony said, "That's about all there is to this part of this puzzle. She was here and gone without even a strange car in town."

I then filled Tony in on my working theory. After ten minutes, he looked at me and said, "You know, that makes the most sense of all. Whoever did this, it was for a reason the cops didn't comprehend or perhaps the boyfriend?"

I said, "I think I know why." I flipped her picture across the table. "*Capisce?* On the other hand, am I too easily overly impressed?"

Tony said, "No, you're not. She's a beautiful girl, especially if you like that aura of purity and untouched innocence. Many freaks live for this type of look, and I hope he's the more benign type. The one who wants to use and not destroy, because if he's the other kind, then you know we're already way too late."

I said, "Yes, well, I have Brett checking all boat charters, and tomorrow I've got to get someone working on the private plane traffic and routings. Then maybe we can find a place to begin our search. We're going to New York tomorrow, and depending on what Brett comes up with, it's on to either Canada or upstate New York. By the way, are you carrying?"

He replied, "If you call my baby Glock carrying, yes, without the rounds, I can go through any metal detector."

I said, "Listen, I interviewed this guy she came to see, and suddenly he remembers two Arabs in the dining room that night. Something about this guy doesn't ring true to me. I mean, after six months, he remembers these guys in great detail. I want you to check with the night manager and see if two or three guys with that description stayed here at that time."

I then handed Tony the piece of paper with the description as Peter had given it to me.

"Tony, Duke, and I have been doing pretty well at this business lately, and I believe we're at a point where we could use more permanent support. I want you to think of joining us on a full-time basis?"

He said, "Listen, Jake, I'm not looking for handouts. Besides, my girls live in Chicago."

I replied, "Hey, pecker head; this job allows you a lot of downtime. As far as that goes, this money alone would allow you to go to Chicago or bring your daughters to Florida anytime; you want. I also believe that if you and the ex-wife were to put a little distance between yourselves, it might calm things down. If you don't mind my saying it, that would be a lot better for your kids than anything else. I'll have to speak to Duke, but with all the jobs we're turning down, I know he'll go along. Besides, you two would get along famously."

Tony said, "You're talking about a former officer and me, the baby Piason?"

I said, "Yes, but he was a mustanger, so he's really one of us. All I'm asking is give it some thought."

He said, "I will, and I didn't mean to sound ungrateful."

I said, "I understand, Tony. Of all the things in this world, I know; I understand that. Let's grab some sleep, and I'll see you in the morning."

Before he left, he asked, "Regina told me this was pretty personal for you. Is that true? And how are you connected to this girl?"

I told him that would require a really lengthy conversation, but I would fill him in along the way.

After he left, I sat with my last glass of Sancerre, looking out into the night sky, and thought to myself, *If you're still alive, Julia, I'm going to find you. It's in my bones, and I can't shake this feeling loose, so hold on. It's only a matter of time, and I'll be coming for you.*

Tony and I spent the next day looking for that night manager on duty the evening before Julia's abduction. He no longer worked here, but the old register showed no Arab-sounding names booked into the hotel that night. None of the other people seem to remember these two until we met Clyde Clement, the concierge on duty that day. He confirmed that three Middle Eastern types had been loitering around the hotel all day, but they never checked into any rooms. It seemed he saw them speaking to a white gentleman that same day in the lobby, but he couldn't describe him.

We asked Clyde if he could remember this white guy in a photo. He couldn't, and that brought us to another dead end.

I said, "Tony, those guys had to be staying somewhere in town, so check all the hotels and rooming houses you can locate in Burlington and the nearby suburbs."

After he left, I thought it was time to call Charles. I got him at his office, and his first question was, had we found out anything new. I told a little about the continuing theory of water or air escape, and he seemed pleased. I also mentioned that it was too early in the investigation to speculate any further.

I continued, "Charles, this is only the beginning. I don't want you to get too far along in your thinking."

He replied, "Jake, as far as I'm concerned, this is your investigation. I'm very grateful that you called. Is there anything I can assist you with at this point?

I said, "No, but I appreciate this use of your crew, as they are turning out to be reliable and very useful."

He said, "As I said before, son, you take care, and I will look forward to seeing you at our home in New York when you return." Those last comments made, I disconnected with a warm goodbye.

The next day, Tony did his magic and found a small motel located three miles out of town. From there, he tracked the three Middle Eastern guys to a local Hertz agency from the plates on file at the motel, and that's where the trail stopped as they rented a car and returned it two days later. Tony could finesse one name from the Hertz agency by flashing his phony Homeland Security credentials. The driver's name was Karīm Hiaasen Abdel Massih, and he had to show his passport to rent the car.

I told Tony that he put in a great day's work. He was created to do this kind of work. Now, we had a name, and this was a great beginning. I called Duke with the name and asked him to let Brett find this guy's entry point into the United States.

Now, it was time to go to New York and elucidate my thoughts to the old man. The decision was made. I said "Good night" to Tony, turned down the bed, and had a second night of restless sleep.

CHAPTER SIX

NEW YORK

We got off the ground at eight-thirty. Mike told us the weather in New York was cloudy and rainy. I asked Regina if she knew of a moderately priced hotel for Tony, and she said, "That's already been taken care of, Jake."

There was something about her smile and the way she said it that gave me pause. I thought about the way these two had been jabbering all morning. Perhaps there was something in the wind. I wouldn't be surprised if she put him down in the Bowery to calm his hot-bloodedness.

Tony stood six foot one with one hundred seventy-five pounds of muscle and was the total package when it came to the women we met over our years as friends. He had dark hair and movie star good looks with an undeniable charm. That was until he met his wife, who totally dominated him. It only took a year for her to cower to him.

Mike came back from the cockpit and took the seat next to mine. He said, "Jake, when we land, there will be a car for you. Mr. Chapman is picking you up, and the old man requested you to go to his office first if you didn't mind."

I said, "That's good. I believe it's time to fill Charles in on my working hypothesis. By the way, who is this, Mr. Chapman?"

Mike said, "Oh, I guess when you were in Palm Beach, Mr. Chapman was back home attending to the funeral of his mother. Let me think about this. How can I describe Mr. Levi Chapman to you? First of all, he's a Marine like you. Mr. Chapman has been Mr. Alexander's, I guess you'd say, the man for all seasons, best friend, and surrogate mother to the girls for over twenty years, but he's far more than any title merits.

"He also provides security and is responsible for the household staff and has bought those girls up since their mother's death. He's the only one I ever heard, tell Jeanette to be quiet beside her father and had her comply instantaneously.

"It has always been Mr. Chapman and never Levi, which is his first name. Only the girls or Mr. Alexander are allowed the privilege of addressing him as Levi. If he likes you, he's evenhanded, but if not, or your profile, let's say he is the most imposing man in both size and character. He is loyal only to the interests of Mr. Charles Alexander. Julia's disappearance might have hit him hardest. I credit Mr. Chapman for holding the Alexander clan together and saving Charles Alexander from falling to pieces. He's never married, and he treats this family as his own."

I thanked Mike for his input, and ten minutes later, we were taxiing on the tarmac at Teterboro. We descended from the plane to be greeted by the most significant African American; I've ever met besides once seeing Shaq on the sidelines at a Knicks game in New York.

He walked over and said, "You are Mr. Jake Reynard?" All six foot eight or so leaned towards me with an extended hand the size of a baseball glove.

I said, "Yes, and you must be Mr. Chapman," as I took his proffered hand.

"I am, Mr. Reynard, and I am to drive you to the offices of Mr. Charles Alexander. Then I will take you to our home in New York."

In the next moment, he went over to the plane, and after Mike pointed them out, plucked up my duffel as a child would pick up scattered toys.

I looked him over at that distance, and after you'd get over the initial shock of his enormous size, you'd notice he is an extremely handsome man. It was challenging to peg his age. There was a slight edge of white to his full head of closely cropped hair, but he moved with the agility of a much younger man, especially if he was in his fifties or sixties.

We then got into an older but beautifully maintained Mercedes 600 Limousines, and I chose to sit upfront with him.

I attempted to open a conversation by saying, "Since we're both employees, I wouldn't feel right sitting back there."

He gave me a stern glare from the driver's seat as we began to drive away and said, "I understand you're a Marine?"

I replied, "Yes, I served in the Corps."

He said, "Then, that's the only thing we have in common. I read your dossier. I sat across the room when Charles made his Washington calls about you. He's a man who is used to being in control over his world. When this incident happened, he forfeited all that. I believed at that time we might lose him."

I said, "I guess you have a point to make with this negative tone of voice?" I didn't like the tone of his voice one bit.

He said, "My point, Mr. Reynard, don't do anything to hurt this family or take advantage of our grief in any way. Are you absolutely clear on that point?"

I said, "I'm awaiting the threat! I love taking a pleasant plane ride, meet a fellow brother in arms, and then receiving a half-baked ultimatum."

He peered at me and said. "I guess you're a bad-ass as well?"

I replied, "Mr. Chapman, before we get any further off on the wrong foot, I was in the middle of a long-overdue vacation when this situation came up. That's one. Number two, I don't take every job; I'm offered. Number three, and most important of all, I never accept anyone's crap whatsoever. I happen to like this old man, and I took this on because, well, never mind why. I have personal reasons for doing this. Perhaps you should take me to a hotel as I don't think living with you and Jeanette Alexander over the next few days will suit my disposition."

He pulled the car over onto the shoulder of the road, stopped, and turned to confront me. He said, "Look here, you have to admit that five million dollars are a lot of money to pay someone for what in every likelihood is a corpse. Besides, what can you possibly do that the FBI can't or didn't do previously?"

I said, "All right, I'll go over this with you one time. Who said anything about five million dollars? Second, normally you'd be correct about the FBI, but ever since 9/11, they have been stretched out well beyond their assets. They are strained to a point beyond any normal limits. And last, of all, I happen to be damn good at what I do in these types of cases."

He said, "Mr. Reynard, Mr. Alexander told me, dead or alive, he planned to pay you five million dollars. If by some miracle, Julia is still alive, he said he'd pay you a hell of a lot more money than that."

I said, "Mr. Chapman, Mr. Alexander, and I never discussed fees. I told him my partner, and I would never expect or accept a fee like that. We don't exploit people in their time of grief. We bill a daily rate with expenses similar to his attorneys and probably a hell of a lot less than any New York attorney. As for myself, for purely personal reasons, I won't accept a fee or reward regarding Julia."

He looked at me for a moment as if measuring the sincerity of my words. Then he said, "Mr. Reynard, possibly I owe you an apology. I did hear you are exceptional at what you do. I can make no further excuses for my poor behavior. I have been with these girls since the beginning of their lives. Protecting this family has been my life ever since I left the Corps a long time ago. I have also done some checking through my grapevine, and you came up as a top Marine. However, I know money brings out the worst in people."

We sat there quietly for a minute, and since he was the elder, I felt it was incumbent upon me to re-break the ice.

I said, "Mr. Chapman, with all due respect, you're correct, except I knew Julia. I would appreciate it if you call me Jake, and I will address you as Mr. Chapman, as is your due being the senior member of this group."

He continued to study me, "This group? What group are you referring to exactly?"

I said, "I have put together a small team. If my working hypothesis is correct, I will need all the help I can get in this case. Now, I'm going to share an idea that I have with you. I want you to give me some insight into what I should and should not share with Mr. Alexander at this point in his grieving process."

He said, "All right, but there will be no more talk of hotels. It would upset him no end. He's completely taken by you. Now, I understand. H surrounded by people who are constantly attempting to placate him. I see you're a different cut of man. Hell, that only means he has someone else he can discuss this with."

I said, "I respect him, and I wasn't prepared to feel this way about him. I promised him I'd work out of his place as long as I stayed in New York City."

I then laid out my theory in detail, and he listened with a concentration on everything I had to say.

We pulled back into traffic, and a distinct impression went through my mind. I had to have Duke look this person up. I had an idea: there was more here than met the eye.

We pulled up to One Hundred Wall Street, and Mr. Chapman told me to proceed to the top floor, where Mr. Alexander would be waiting for me. After I had spoken to him of my hypotheses, his mood had lightened.

He said, "You should share everything with Charles. He needs something to cling to now more than ever. If we are going to worry about his feelings and the possible disappointments that may come later, it will have to be dealt with somewhere down the road. Besides, your idea explained things that hadn't even been considered by the police or the FBI."

I was greeted on the top floor in the foyer by Charles himself. I saw immediately from the looks on the faces of his people that this was a profound breach of protocol. With my hand still in his, Charles moved me from one desk to another and introduced me to his entire private staff of sixteen. He turned, with me in tow, ordered coffee, and asked if I had eaten breakfast. I replied, "Yes, I had something to eat on the plane." He instructed Rhonda, whom I guess was his top gal, to send Mr. Chapman into his office when he arrived on the floor.

We entered what could only be described as an ample office space even by New York standards. Charles looked at me and instantly surmised what I was concluding.

He said, "It's meant to look imposing, Jake. You have just entered the greatest bullshit arena on this planet. On this street, fortunes are made and lost every day, and a lot of posing went on, but the strange thing is, there is a code of honor here. When you buy or sell millions of dollars of securities, you are completely at the mercy of the other fellow's word. I meant before taped conversations. I might add that nothing has changed besides some of the more personal dialogue from our conversations. Now, all you get is a quick restatement of the order at a stated price, and you have to trust that the other guy will pay on settlement day."

Charles had just finished clarifying that bit of his daily life when Mr. Chapman came walking into the office. His secretary followed us with three coffee cups in a beautiful porcelain coffee pot and a blue-and-white sugar bowl and creamer. She placed them on a small coffee table surrounded by a sofa and two love seats at the back left corner of his office. Everything was decorated in an English motif with oversized comfortable chairs and warm dark wooden side tables.

He said, "Thank you, Rhonda. I think we'll be comfortable here. Please hold all my calls, and I mean every one of them. Jake, since you returned so soon from Vermont, I gather you either have some new insights, or you're convinced that it's hopeless."

I said, "Charles, indulge me until I'm through speaking. Then I will answer any questions you have."

He said, "Yes, please, son, go on with what you have discovered."

I said, "I have a theory. It may or may not be correct. I may be way out of bounds here, but certain truths led me to this concept."

I then filled him in on my entire thought process from

beginning to end. I left out nothing as Mr. Chapman had instructed me to on the ride into town.

Charles turned to Mr. Chapman at that point and asked, "Levi, what do you make of this trafficking theory?"

Mr. Chapman hesitated for a moment and said, "The way Jake explains it; I think it says a lot about why the FBI hit a dead end in their investigation. Those people in the dining room, that piece of her jacket, the water route for an escape, it fills in a lot of missing holes and most of all, Tony finding that name."

Charles said, "That's what I'm thinking. Jake, do you think there's actually a chance she could still be alive?"

I said, "If my theory is correct, and they don't know who she is, then that's a strong possibility. However, make no mistake about it if she was trafficked, and they find out that we are looking for her. They will eliminate her immediately. Now, if, and this is the big if she's alive, then we're going to have an extremely damaged girl on our hands. She's going to need a lot of help restoring and healing herself from whatever tortures she has experienced."

Charles replied, "Yes, of course, you're correct, but never sell Julia's resilience short. You know, of course, about her and Patty's shelter down in the Bowery?"

I said, "Yes, I did a security job at her charity event to raise money for that shelter. Do you remember me say I did some work there? I never connected it with hers until Regina told me about her and Patty. Do you remember me telling you how I first met Julia?"

Charles said, "Yes, I do, but what you probably didn't know is that she, Regina, and Patty had been accosted there twice. Both times out of her fear that Regina would kill the attackers, she talked to those would-be attackers in a way that was both daunting and, at the same time, kind and reassuring in both instances, and in one, there was a knife involved. Julia managed to defuse the entire situation. I think she and Patty actually took that individual out for breakfast. He still resides at their shelter doing the custodial work. She never told me about any of this, but I had Levi pumping Regina for that story. It scared the hell out of me when I found out.

"I wanted to pull the plug on this entire shelter, but Levi

talked me into backing off from that course of action. This brings me to my people. How did it go with them?"

I told him how we'd formed a small group. How dedicated they were to the entire investigation.

He said, "I expected that from Regina. You know, she and Julia were very close friends. Levi has been teaching both my girls self-defense since they were pint-sized. Julia of the two got the biggest kick out of it. Levi let her throw him to the canvas when she was about eight years old. That incident sealed her interest in the martial arts forever.

"When she found out Regina was a judo champion, she went out of her way to befriend her. If Regina wasn't flying, she and Julia did everything together. It was an uncommon occurrence that Regina was homesick on that particular day. They would have been running together, and stupidly I called the plane back to New York the day before. Even Mike wasn't there. He often runs with the girls. I loaned the plane to a customer to fly to Nassau to be with his mistress. I've lived with that decision ever since. I can't even look at that bastard today when we attend functions."

I said, "Charles, if for a moment we believe in this idea of her being trafficked, then you must realize we are dealing with professionals. We are not talking about muggers or boisterous passengers in the first-class section of a commercial airplane. If Regina was there, chances are, we would be looking for two missing women now."

Charles asked, "Jake, how do we bring these people to justice? How do we get them in front of an American court?"

I said, "Charles, we don't, because these individuals are not people in what you think of, in normal terms."

He asked, "What do you mean by normal terms, son?"

I looked over at Mr. Chapman. He shook his head up and down, expressing for me to go ahead, as if saying, "Tell him what must be done."

I said, "I mean, it's dead or alive. If we have irrefutable proof as to who did this to your daughter, then we will have to deal with them personally and on their terms."

He went on, "How, Jake, how can you deal with people like that?"

Thank god Mr. Chapman interceded at that point. "I consider; Jake means that he would have to eliminate them with extreme prejudice. It must be their deaths and, along with that, all future threats to our family. This is essential for your and Julia's peace of mind and our family's impending future."

Charles spoke, "Is that the only action we can take, son?"

I looked at him and said, "Yes, absolutely. I can assure you of that, but I never wish to have this particular conversation again. I knew this going in. It's no surprise to me. I took the liberty of hiring an old Recon team member of mine. Tony Camorato will assist me in any situation that comes up that would require our special mutual skills."

I told him about the financial arrangements I made with Tony. "He said anything I wanted is okay with him."

Then he started the five-million-dollar conversation, and I stopped him cold.

I said, "Charles, I've told you my personal reasons for doing this search. I don't work for reward money, and I'm not a bounty hunter. We work on a day-to-day-fee basis, which I thought Duke would have gone over with you by now. We have gotten bonus money in the past, but I am not an assassin for hire. I am willing to do this because I believe in what we are doing here. I know what is required and necessary to live with peace of mind in this world. If I find Julia alive, I will take steps so you, she, and I can sleep peacefully at night. If I find her dead, I will give the people responsible, my type of justice, because of my previous relationship with her, but never would I take any money for this. It's all too personal for me."

Charles said, "Please, Jake, do whatever you think is best, and I will be judicious. I only thought some form of incentive was required."

I said, "Mr. Alexander, since I met your daughter, and with all the following facets of her life, I've learned up to now. I'm having great difficulty sleeping at night. I find myself totally resolute in this undertaking. It's not right, but it's there, so I'm coping with it as best I can. If Julia is alive, I am going to find her and return her to you. I need no further encouragement in that undertaking. The FBI's people did an excellent job of ruling out any other possibilities. I'm sure if they had a stable team left in place to complete their investigation, they might have come up with the same findings we have. They were not left alone. I repeat, no one allowed them to complete their job. People were pulled off. New people were reassigned to other tasks. As a result, everyone has laid their hands on that original investigation file.

"While I'm here, I want to talk with Patty and Tom. Then, I'll await the results of this boat or plane search from Brett. She is searching for all the various boat and plane charters from the Canadian side, and upstate New York has done in the time we're talking about. I have one big hole in my theory. I mean, these types of crimes are highly organized, and by the location, it would have had to be someone who targeted her specifically. Human traffickers don't go to places like Burlington, Vermont, looking for stray isolated joggers. She was under observation long before this happened, and it was too preplanned. If she was trafficked, then she's out of the country, and that has got to mean a couple of different things."

Charles spoke up, "What are the various likelihoods, son?"

I said, "First of all, we must be lucky to find out how they took her out of the country. I mean, what method of travel? It would be easier if all pilots must file flight plans if it was by a private plane. If it was by ship, that makes it more difficult, especially if they took her out through Canada."

Levi said, "What's the difference between these methods?"

I restated, "Outbound traffic doesn't hold much interest for Canadian shipping customs officials. They get a manifest and destination and, more or less, accept it at face value. There are hundreds of ways a ship can divert from its destination en route and a hundred more ways to debark from a ship before ever even reaching a port. No, a ship is still the best way to smuggle cargo, especially human cargo. Canada is more concerned with people bringing things in that are dangerous or injurious to their own people."

Charles looked at Levi and shrugged. "I predict we have a long way to go before we see any conclusion to this undertaking."

Levi looked at him and said, "Yes, it seems, except for the who. Jake has come up with the perfect viable working plan as to the how and why, and wasn't that what we required most?

We needed a little hope that she might still be alive?"

Charles said, "Yes, Levi, of course, you're right. Son, you have done far more than a commendable job. I hope you don't think I was trying to bribe you with my money again. We believe in the world I operate in that financial inducements are always necessary. You've explained your motives, and they're a lot more admirable than what I'm used to dealing with. So again, please accept my apology if I have offended your sense of honor in any way."

I replied, "Please, Charles, there's no need to apologize. I work for you and your family, and as that is the case, we must always speak to each other with candor and openness. You know, I didn't realize it before, but you now have four Marines involved in your cause. With that many members of our brotherhood, you could conquer a small country. I don't contemplate anyone has ever attempted that before."

Charles looked over at Mr. Chapman with confusion. Levi and I burst out laughing. A moment later, he caught on and began to laugh along with us.

Charles said, "Well, I can tell you two are going to get along fine. So, if I may excuse myself, Jake, Levi will take you home and get you settled in. Oh, by the way, do you have a dress suit with you?"

I said, "No, I don't. I've never had any use for a suit."

He said, "Levi, please go and see Mr. Gianni on the way home. Tell him to put six people on two suits, but I want his best by six tonight."

I stated, "There is one other thing. I heard you had a conversation with the man responsible in DC."

Charles replied, "Yes; I did if you want to call it a conversation. It was more as if I threatened him, and believe me, with the amount of support I could pull from his election this year, he'd spit nickels out of his ass for me if I asked. Do you have any special requests?"

I asked, "I need to know if any of our satellites were operating over that part of Vermont at the exact time of her abduction, and if so, do they save the photos. It would be the same on the Canadian side, either Quebec or Ontario. I also know they monitor all outgoing calls to other countries. Do the Canadians monitor cell- or ship-to-shore calls as well? If they do, we need them to look for any calls from the night before Julia's abduction that were made to either the Far or the Middle East."

Charles asked, "Do you have an idea as to where exactly?"

I said, "I don't know, but Japan or any of the Arab countries would be a good place to begin."

Charles said, "I have a liaison with the president's deputy chief of staff. He has been told by the president that I am to receive whatever I ask from any agency. Even so, it would be better if you run all your requests through me. That was his only demand. They are concerned about the use of government resources by private individuals. He even tried to talk me into letting the FBI back in on the disappearance. I said no, I wanted their work product, but that was all. Jake, I had to give him your name. I hope that was all right?"

I nodded affirmatively as he continued. "He called me back that afternoon and said his people had assembled their own report on you and stated that with the possible exception of your healthy disdain for authority, your job performance had always been superior. Your service record was rated far above excellent. In fact, he told me he couldn't understand how the Marine Corps lost you. You should be working for him as an officer on his intelligence team. I reminded him of his own early days before holding public office and how much he enjoyed working under people with an inferior intelligence and disagreeable manner.

"The president laughed and said. 'He's right, Charley. Listen, you have Reynard run all his requests through you. I will get him everything he wants. You tell me if anybody screws around with him. Call me back, and I'll have his or her ass. Charley, it's not that you threatened me, but you did remind me of how I got here. Sometimes, in the middle of the day, I need to be reminded of my true friends. You could put me against the wall if you wanted. I mean this from both Marge and myself. We hope this fellow finds Julia, and we will both; pray for her safe return."

"So, Jake, that's where we stand. If any of what you requested is available, I feel confident we'll get it."

Mr. Chapman and I exchanged looks at each other with a

similar expression of skepticism at Charles's comments. As we turned to exit at the same time, Charles said, "Levi, set Jake up in my office at home. He'll need some workspace and Jake; we dine at seven. If that's all right with you, and I hope you'll join Levi and me for cocktails at about six?"

I looked at Levi. He nodded, barely detectable with his eyes, and I said, "I would be delighted."

We stopped on the way to Charles's apartment at the shop of Mr. Alberto Gianni, tailor to the stars or whomever. I was hastily measured for two dress suits. I asked Mr. Chapman about all this, and he stated, "We always dress for dinner, and he wants you to feel at ease, and this is only a small present from him to you, personally."

I replied, "I never wear suits unless I'm going to a funeral or a wedding."

Levi said, "Indulge him and believe me, in New York, you'll feel a lot less conspicuous in a suit. That reminds me, do you have any dress shoes?"

I answered, "Yes, I have a pair of Italian black loafers. Will they suffice?"

Levi said, "I expect they will have to suffice," and we both began to laugh again.

Chapter Seven
Park Avenue

By the time we parked the car and rode up on the elevator, Mr. Chapman had begun to brief me about all the security measures to get in and out of this building. The lift we were in belonged to two families who occupied the thirty-first- and thirty-second-floor penthouses. Each family needed their own keys to run the elevator. He handed me a copy of the keys.

He went on, "Try not to lose this elevator key. Because then we would all have to get new ones made for everyone."

I put the elevator key on my key ring, as he suggested. He said, "You are to come and go as you please and treat this as your own home. Charles stressed that to me, above all else. Since no one has ever stayed overnight in this house, I know he thinks rather highly of you. I didn't miss it when he addressed you as 'son.' Don't be put off by that, as I believe he feels that way about you. I have never heard that particular expression from him before. He treats you as an equal, and that is most uncommon in this world, Jake. The two of you have bonded quite rapidly.

"By the way, I appreciate the way you got him to laugh today. I haven't seen him laugh since this entire abduction began. Now, if you want to make my day at dinner, you can extract that stick from Jeanette's behind with your charm."

I looked at him and said, "I don't think I have enough charm or patience to take that task on."

He looked at me and smiled. "I understand what you mean. Jeanette can test your patience, but underneath she has a significant heart. I think it's terrific that you're so noble. I mean, we don't see that often. Charles, another first, is worth about four billion dollars as he allows you to call him. I say about, because who knows what he did down in that office of his today. I'll let you in on something: everyone here is wealthy, including the housekeeper, the cook, and myself. Each of his daughters has a hundred-million-dollar trust, which, of course, is managed by Charles's firm. I have a current net worth of around seven or eight million dollars."

I looked up at him and asked, "Then why do you continue to work?"

Levi said, "It may surprise you, but I have never needed money. I receive a little check from the government for prior services rendered. When I came aboard, I asked Mr. Alexander if he could invest my salary, and he graciously did so.

Why do I continue to work here? For starters, these people are my family. Secondly, Charles and I remain the closest thing to real friends either of us has ever known. I give him his respect and mind you; he gives me mine. We trust each other completely, and that is, as you know, a rare thing.

One last thing, and I'll leave you to rest before dinner. What you said, in the office, about what you would have to do when you find out who is responsible for Julia's kidnapping. We both know what must be done, but you must promise me I'll be present to assist you in introducing these people to the Almighty.

Before you say anything else, ask your associate Duke who I am. Then you can come to that decision on your own. If he doesn't recall me, he can make one phone call and find out all you'll ever need to know about me."

Something was daunting in his eyes when he expressed that bit of information. It prompted me to surprise myself by agreeing to speak to Duke.

That understood, he left, and I sat down at a small desk in this beautiful room I was provided. It was all done in a French provincial manner with deep greens and whites. You couldn't help but notice the ceiling. It was layered upward into a dome, giving you a sense of being in a cathedral. I dialed the office and asked Brett how she was progressing in her investigation.

She said, "I think I'll have the boat part of it narrowed down today or early tomorrow, but the plane thing will take a little longer."

I said, "I can assist you with that as the plane will be a rental and has to be something that can land and take off on the water. Ask Duke about what types of planes can do that as I'm sure he'll have knowledge of all the categories of aircraft that can operate on a lake of that size."

I implored her to call me no matter what time she finished her research. I gave her Alexanders'' home phone number and asked her to put Duke on the line.

After he picked up, I filled him in as to where we were on my end. I told him about the intelligence I'd requested from Charles and the suspicions I had about Osterhaus.

When I finished recounting Charles's phone call to the president, he began laughing like hell. He said, "I'm beginning to like this guy, and you know how I despise rich guys."

I replied, "Hell, Duke; you're the richest guy I know." Then I enquired, "In all your comings and goings in the Corps, have you ever heard of a giant by the name of Levi Chapman? He's a huge African American who's about as large as a small apartment building."

He asked, "You wouldn't mean Marine Gunnery Sergeant Levi Chapman, would you?"

I said. "Yes, that's the name, and he said I should ask you to fill me in on him. He's worked within the Alexander family for more than twenty years and has been solely responsible for raising these girls. Furthermore, he's fiercely loyal to Charles Alexander. He knows if I find out who did this, I will have to sanction them to ensure our mutual peace of mind. He wants in on that, and I don't know what to make of him."

Duke replied, "Well, my friend, if he is the *real* Levi Chapman, I met him once at the very beginning of Vietnam at the NCO club in Camp Butler on Okinawa. I will confirm what I am about to tell you, but I find it hard to believe that God made two men like Gunnery Sergeant Levi Chapman. First, your large friend is a holder of the Medal of Honor given for his feats of heroism in Vietnam. He possesses two Silver Stars and three Purple Hearts as well. There was a story that they would award him a Navy Cross, but rumor had it that he turned that down. He said it wasn't warranted, but his collaborator on that particular foray should receive it instead, which he did, and that was how Levi acquired his second Silver Star. It's said that Levi told the brass he'd won more honors than he deserved for just doing his job. He completed three tours. His company encountered a North Vietnamese battalion, and his captain and lieutenant were severely wounded in the initial exchange of fire. Since he was the top-ranking soldier, he took command under feverishly heavy fire. He rallied his company into making a frontal assault. He was wounded through the thigh and arm but continued moving forward, which inspired his fellow Marines to drive on, despite the obstacle of being severely outnumbered. They say he was directly responsible for killing twenty-two of the enemy and wounding ten more in what ensued. He picked up enemy weapons, exhausted them of ammunition, and kept gathering up new ones along the way.

"The story goes on that after two and a half hours when the initial bite of the enemy's first assault had abated, he was seen carrying his captain on his back and ordering everyone onto choppers back at the evacuation LZ. He was the last one to board that remaining chopper after returning a second time for his lieutenant. The enemy had regrouped and sent a platoon-sized unit to block the helicopters from leaving by that time.

"He mounted another counteroffensive with the ten troops he had left at the landing zone until those choppers with the wounded were away. It's said by the pilot of that last helicopter that when the smoke cleared, our side had two injured, but the Cong lost twenty-two. On the citation, the word 'Inspired' was used twice, and that's a first, even for a Medal of Honor recipient. I'll find out what Levi has been up to since he got out of the Corps, but if I were you, I'd never mention his accomplishments. They say he left the Corps because he was a modest man, and you know what follows you when you become a legend in our Corps. Believe me, if we're talking about the same man, he is a legend right up there with Puller, Butler, and Daly.

"When Vietnam was over, he was our most decorated Marine on active duty. I'm not even telling you about all his other awards. He is entitled to wear six rows of ribbons and, of course, the big one around that massive neck."

I sat there thinking about that for a moment after hanging up the phone. My whole sense of Mr. Chapman completely transformed. There are certain things in this world they don't give away. A holder of the Medal of Honor receives a life pension plus whatever disability he would have earned from his wounds. All holders of that medal have been wounded horribly, and most of them fatally. If you're an enlisted man when you wear the award, officers must salute you instead of the opposite way, which is our custom. We salute this medal in every instance. I believe, like every honor, it must give its burdens, especially for a man of size like Levi, who never had to impose himself on anyone. He was a modest man, and that medal must have become a weighty burden. Believe me, if he were five feet four, he'd crow like a rooster and have no hesitance in telling me who he was when we first met.

I decided to take a power nap and awaken at five. When I awoke, I went to the door, and as I opened it, I viewed two suits in a garment bag hanging on my door. There was an additional bag with what I soon discovered there were supplemental shirts and ties.

I stepped back into the room and opened the garment bag to view two custom-made suits, one a charcoal-grey pinstripe and the other a beautiful soft–navy blue. I felt the material and understood what a friend had once said about certain fabrics feeling buttery. Where the maker label should have been, it merely said Jake Reynard in scripted hand stitching.

I took a quick shower, shaved, and donned the new grey suit. I discovered I was sleeping in a female's room by the various shampoos and cosmetics in that bathroom. I wondered if the old man had put me in here on purpose.

I picked out a dark-green shirt with a lime tie and felt like a real man about town. Luckily, I had bought my black Italian tassel loafers, so as I left to join the others, I felt prepared to have a drink with the upper classes of Park Ave. I went to put the other one away in the closet, where I saw female dresses. I held one up and smelled it—this was Julia's room. There was no mistaking that sweet leftover odor of her.

The apartment was initially the only thing I noticed as the elevator opened; you were in a large interior hallway. A swift left, and I had walked down a long corridor to my room, which was the last door, on the right. The room itself was approximately the size of a double suite I once stayed in at the Beverly Wilshire Hotel. Now, as I retraced my steps, I realized this apartment was really huge. It was most likely an entire floor within the building. I wondered again whose idea it was to put me in Julia's room. There had to be other guest rooms.

I made a left at the front door and entered a grand hall with open rooms adjoining each side with what looked like a glass conservatory at the end of the corridor. It overlooked the East River four or so blocks away.

As I moved on, Mr. Chapman came out of a room to my left and ambled over to me and said, "We're in the library over here, Jake."

I saw Mr. Chapman and said, "Thank you, Mr. Chapman, or may I now address you as Gunny?"

He stopped mid-stride and said. "When we're alone, you may address me in any manner you please. Here, there will be no talk of former exploits. Will that be satisfactory?"

"Yes, and by the way, my partner Duke met you once in Okinawa."

He said, "Yes, I know all about Major McGarrity, and you for that matter. Now that we understand each other, will you honor my request this afternoon?"

I saw that look, at his eyes again, that single-mindedness of purpose. I said, "Yes, if it's possible, I will honor your request under one condition."

He asked, "What would that condition be?"

I said, "In the field, you must take direction from me. I would bet you haven't taken directives from anyone in quite a long time."

He replied, "Jake. You will find out; I'm a team player. If we have any possibility of finding the ones responsible for Julia's abduction, I promise to bow to all your demands on all tactical issues. You're this operation's leader.

"One last thing, I know the Major has contacts in intelligence. I have retained a few vouchers among the enlisted ranks and a certain officer who has risen very high. Believe me, if I wanted a platoon with full armor on Park Avenue tomorrow, it would be here. I've never used up any of my chits, so I'm long overdue."

I said, "Okay, I'll remember that whenever we need something."

As we entered the room, Charles stood up and walked over to me. "So good to have you in our home, Jake," he uttered those words with his arms extended.

I stepped into them and said, "It's good to be here, Charles," and returned his fatherly embrace.

He said, "I've taken the liberty of pouring you a glass of fairly decent Graves."

I said, "I see you've spoken to the rest of your crew, Charles. You don't miss a trick."

At that moment, Jeanette, who was sitting, in a corner next to a marble fireplace, spoke up, "Jake, you'll soon learn that father never misses any details about people regarding their wishes or desires."

Charles spoke, "I hope that didn't put you off, Jake. They called to check-in, as they always do. I asked how it all went in Vermont. They were very enthusiastic about your theory." I hope you don't mind, Jake?

I said, "Not at all, Mr. Alexander. You're entitled to have everyone's point of view. I'd like to know if you made that call that we discussed this afternoon."

He replied, "Yes, I did, and they think they may have everything you asked for at NSA. It all has to be retrieved from their archives. It might be a good idea for you to go there and look at them yourself. They won't permit the photos or Intel; we want to leave the NSA building."

I said, "That makes good sense, but I think I'll ask Duke to go. He's spent years working among these people. Reading intelligence is right up his alley. Mine was always gathering it. Besides, I believe he still maintains the proper clearances to view all this material we want. I believe they could only curtail my investigation with red tape. Duke and Mr. Chapman share common friends who can spare us a lot of difficulty in our efforts."

At this point, Jeanette spoke up, "What is all this talk of Intel and Duke and the NSA, Daddy?"

Mr. Chapman, who was sitting quietly on the couch, chimed in, "Dear, this is about the investigation into your sister's disappearance. There's a chance that she might still be alive. We are using some of your father's connections to develop our efforts in finding out."

She expressed in another one of her sarcastic tones, "Do you mean Jake in three days has discovered something the FBI and everyone else couldn't find after six months of investigations?" This was all started with her standard fierceness of tone.

Mr. Chapman spoke in a manner equal to her own, which could only be described as stern and corrective. "Yes, that's what it means. Furthermore, I received word, you were very impolite to Jake in Palm Beach, and I didn't hear that from him. You know that kind of rudeness directed towards a guest in this home is inexcusable. You were taught better from the time you were a child. Jake has the full confidence of your father and me. Do you understand that?"

She said, "Yes, Levi," in a feeble mousy voice. I didn't think her capable of displaying this level of humility.

I was stunned for a moment when Mr. Alexander spoke up, "I believe that's enough unpleasantness for this evening."

Jeanette looked over at me, and there were tears in her eyes. She said, "Jake, I apologize," and moved toward Mr. Chapman and walked straight into his massive arms. "Levi, I'm so sorry. I hope I haven't unduly upset you."

He held her in those massive arms for what seemed an eternity, but in reality, it was only a few moments.

He said, "That's all right, little girl. We all slip up in our manners sometimes. We are all under tremendous pressure. However, you must try harder to give people an opportunity. Not everyone is out to hurt you or our family."

We entered the dining room, and everything was set up on the sideboard. Charles told us to serve ourselves. With that, we all sat down to eat. Dinner was a simple fare of roast chicken with oven-roasted potatoes and onions surrounding the bird. Fresh snow peas and yellow squash were served as well as the best gravy I believe I've ever tasted with roast chicken. It had a hint of port wine with a touch of sage also. The squash had been baked and contained allspice, cinnamon, and brown sugar, a recipe with which I was pretty familiar.

"This dinner is delicious," I said. "Whoever the cook is, I applaud them enthusiastically."

After I made my comment about the meal, everyone smiled, including Jeanette.

Charles said, "Jake, it's the cook's day off, and Levi prepared this meal. If I'm not mistaken, there's a great desert somewhere as well. He also picked out this wonderful Grand Puligny-Montrachet; we are drinking."

I said, "Well, the wine is excellent. Mr. Chapman, all I have to say is, in the short time of our acquaintance, you have astounded me."

Jeanette, who, for some reason, was seated next to me at the table, said, "Levi amazes everyone who meets him."

I said, "Yes, he does, and that brings me to something else, Mr. Alexander. When I leave for the next leg of my trip, I would like to have Mr. Chapman accompany me. He has some special talents and connections that could possibly assist me in our mission."

Charles spoke up, "Well, I don't know about that, Jake. I know you and Levi share a certain bond, but he's a little advanced in years to go off gallivanting abroad."

Mr. Chapman turned and looked him straight in the eye. He said, "If we're talking about being aged, then speak for yourself, old man. If I choose to go, I will go, and I don't require your consent or funds to go with him. If it's necessary to get your blessing, I will simply resign from your employment and go independently. You know, I have more than enough assets to handle this without problems. You forget, Charles; we raised these girls together. If Julia is alive, she's going to require a familiar face. A face she knows and trusts that will protect her no matter what happens. I know Jake will do that, but she doesn't know him that well, after so much time has gone-bye."

Charles replied, "Levi, I've never seen you this upset. Please, for the love of God, calm down."

Levi said, "Well, I'm upset. I wanted to go up there initially, and I allowed you to talk me out of it. Now, we find out these damn fools missed some important evidence. Evidence that could have led us to Julia's captors. Charles, I'm not blaming you. It was my fault for not insisting we go private at that time. This time, I will go. Do we understand each other on that point?"

Charles said, "Yes, yes, Levi, you're right. Someone from the family should be there if Jake finds Julia alive. Jake, you realize we're only two old men who were waiting for grandchildren when all of this happened. Levi and I have shared every moment of these girl's lives together. Levi, you're my oldest and dearest friend, and I don't want to see you injured again. You know exactly what I mean."

Levi said, "Charles, we can't exist with fear. It's the one thing God won't tolerate, and those who do so suffer mightily for their uncertainty."

Charles looked at me and said, "Jake is at a disadvantage as he's not aware of all the pain you've gone through in the past—your own rehabilitation and that long road you had to travel from your injuries."

At this point, I interrupted, "Excuse me, Charles, but I'm completely aware of who and what Mr. Chapman is. We are both Marines."

Charles said, "We never speak, about those things in this

house, Jake."

I said, "It seems my partner and Mr. Chapman share a common history. In fact, the entire United States Marine Corps knows who Mr. Chapman is, which is exactly why I need him with me. As far as anyone getting hurt, I can assure you that he will be well protected, knowing in the end, he will probably be the one protecting me."

Jeanette then came out of her stupor and probed, "What is this all about? I'm totally confused by this entire conversation."

Her father replied, "It's about some things that happened a long time ago. It's also something Levi does not wish to discuss. Is that satisfactory for you?"

She replied, "Yes, Daddy. Whatever you say."

Charles asked, "Now, Levi, what's for dessert?"

"I believe there's a baked Alaska in the refrigerator."

After dessert, we all retired for the night, and I lay dreaming about Julia lying in this bed.

Chapter Eight
The Charters

I awoke to the phone ringing next to the bed—God, how, I hate the sound of a ringing telephone in the morning. On the other end, Brett's voice gave me a sense of relief, as I knew she'd have something important to communicate.

I said, "What's the scoop, pretty girl?"

She replied, "Good news. I found two charter companies that rented large boats and a seaplane called a Beaver on those dates. They all match within the days and dates of your possible return scenarios. One arrived in Toronto during heavy nighttime traffic, and the plane was rented and flown from Mt. Hope in Canada. They both have smaller airports, and I've begun to check outgoing private flights within our timeline."

I asked, "I was waiting for you to call last night when you

finished."

"Jake." It was Duke on the extension, as usual. "She was here until two this morning, so hold on to your drawers."

I measured his tone of voice, and it was ill-tempered.

I said, "I'm sorry, Brett. I'm pretty wound up on this particular case. You're doing a great job."

"No problem, Jake," she said. "The bad news is Toronto. There is a lot of international shipping, and a few big ships left port for overseas destinations on the days surrounding the week of her disappearance. I'll fax over the names and addresses of the people I spoke with at all these locations. I'm sure they will cooperate with you. I told them all this might involve the kidnapping of a young girl, and they all sounded eager to help."

I said, "Thanks. Now I need to have another conversation with Duke."

Duke grumbled, "What did you think; I went to have breakfast at the yacht club?"

I said, "Sorry, Duke. I need you in DC today, and it would be great if you could get a shuttle ticket and arrive there by twelve noon."

He asked, "Sure. What's happening in DC?"

I said, "When you get there, they should have some satellite stuff from the NSA and the date and place of this guy whom Tony found. Call Charles's office and speak with a woman named Rhonda. She will have it all set up for you, including where you're going to stay. I want Brett to continue her search. If Julia's still alive, you can't imagine what she is enduring each day."

Duke said, "Yes, I know, Jake, and by the way, our mutual friend Gunnery Sergeant Chapman is one in the same person. You wouldn't know this, but there was very little work for returning soldiers after Vietnam. That's when he joined up with Alexander as a kind of driver and security personnel. The scuttlebutt has it that their relationship goes a lot deeper than employer and employee. During that time, Mrs. Alexander was dying of cancer, and a powerful bond developed between her and Levi. Gunny was her confidant, and before she died, he made her a promise. He'd look after her two girls. I spoke with a friend of mine from the Marine Corps League, and he said the Gunny makes a rare appearance at some of the reunions. He said, 'He still fits in his original dress blues, which, of course, had to be custom-made from the onset."

I replied, "I viewed the uniqueness of that relationship last night at dinner at the way that he told the old man he was leaving with me no matter what Charles thought. He certainly doesn't speak to Alexander like any employee or lackey. However, when the other daughter, Jeanette, began to speak in her usual sarcastic manner, his chastising set her to tears. When she was sufficiently mortified, it was his arms, she sought solace in like a small child. You'd have to know Jeanette to understand the scene. Usually, she is a ball-breaker extraordinaire. I guess Gunny raised these girls while Charles went about dealing with his horrific grief over his wife's death. It's not that she doesn't love her father that strikes you. It's these two men who are the only people she cares about.

"This is a different kind of family, not a bad family, actually. In this house, everyone gets to speak his or her mind. It's all done with deference and respect. Even when Alexander didn't want Levi to go with me, it was only out of concern about his safety. There are tremendous love and care here, and you can feel it in everything they do and say."

Duke asked, "So, is he coming with you or what?"

I said, "In all good conscience, I can't keep him out of this. Levi was left out of this in the beginning. Now that we've found this lead to follow up on, he's hauling around a lot of guilt. So, yeah, he comes with me."

Duke spoke, "Well. I'd better express something else, so we can get our reservations correct. When we find out about their location, I'm going with you as well. Sitting here waiting has driven me to the edge of a completely new set of phobias. Now, you go and eat your Wheaties like a good American superhero. I'm heading to the airport, and I'll call you when I get to Washington."

I took my shower and shaved. Since I was not going to leave the apartment, I dressed in jeans with a sweatshirt.

I found the kitchen, and Levi was sitting at a large table,

eating what looked like oatmeal.

He said, "Jake, good morning. Can I interest you in some of this oatmeal with white raisins?"

I said, "Yes, that looks good, and by the way, I just got, off the phone, with my office. I had Duke get on his way to DC. I told him to call Mr. Alexander's office and speak to Rhonda about accommodations. Perhaps, Rhonda can find out who he's supposed to meet and get him a reservation tonight. I would normally have Brett do that, but she's making some headway on her search. I want to leave her alone to find out if she can get more information on outgoing private flights."

He asked, "Did she find out anything about the boat or plane charters?"

I said, "First, there were two charters that match our criteria. One was in Toronto, and the other is in a small place called Mt. Hope. They were both charters returning at about the same time as our schedule. One was a large boat, but the other was a Beaver floatplane. That's a very popular plane in Canada for landing and taking off on remote rivers and lakes."

At that point, I looked up as Charles walked into the room. He wiggled his fingers at me to continue.

"The bad news is, if it's Toronto, there is a considerable seaport there. Furthermore, it's a colossal port for seaborne shipping. Too many ships left there during the time we're talking about in our simulated schedule. If this was a planned grab, then Mt. Hope, because of its size and remoteness, would be the better choice for our perps, especially if we believe this guy Peter Osterhaus about the Arabic word he overheard for a plane.

"Brett had verified that the Mt. Hope Beaver charter returned late at night when no one was on duty to check it in. That in itself is suspicious. I'll need to speak to Patty and her boyfriend today. Duke will collect photos of any suspects who the bureau might know to be implicated in human trafficking.

"I plan on having Tony go to Toronto with someone. Mr. Chapman and I will head up to Mt. Hope."

Charles was the first to speak. "That sounds like a first-rate plan. By the way, where is your friend Tony now?"

I said, "I don't know. Regina was supposed to drop him off at a hotel and let me know his whereabouts. I'll allow her to sleep for another half-hour before calling her. In the meantime, I'll book the plane tickets for us."

Charles said, "Nonsense, you're going to take your entire team, and that means our corporate jet."

I replied, "Charles, you are ruining me for all future commercial flights."

He went on to explain, "They simply don't have seats large enough for Levi. Since he's determined to play cowboy, he might as well be comfortable. Son, I'm holding you personally accountable for his well-being."

I replied, "As I said last night, Charles, I think it will be Mr. Chapman, who will take care of me. In fact, I'm sure he will. This oatmeal is great with raisins, but there's something else in this."

"Yes, it's a secret: cinnamon and something else. I can't quite figure out," alleged Mr. Chapman.

Charles said, "Marisa's the second-best cook here."

"Oh," I said quizzically, "who is the first cook in this house?"

Levi spoke up, "Why; I'd think a young boot like you would have figured that out already?"

Charles joined in, "Jake; Levi's hobby for years has been French and Italian cooking. He's been successful in wheedling himself into some of the finest kitchens in New York. He uses my personal wine cellar as a bribe to the best chefs and their recipes."

I said, "I'll have to obtain your expert opinion on my coco-au-van Osso Buco or bouillabaisse."

The Gunny looked over and said, "I assume we share a common love of cooking as well?"

I said, "Yes, we certainly do, and even though I live aboard a boat and lack your fancy equipment. I can, if properly inspired, make some interesting dishes using a minimal cooking platform."

They both began asking questions about the *Switchel* and what it was like to live on a sailboat. How far can she sail? What equipment does she have? What does her name mean?

I explained as best as I can the sense of freedom and fantastic quiet one experiences sailing off the wind. As to the name, *Switchel*, it means "a hot cup of tea" in Nova Scotia. Her expression was quantified by the Irishman from whom I bought her. He was pretty adamant about my retaining her title. Naturally, I consented to his wishes.

I said, "I began sailing with my dad at an unusually young age."

Charles said, "I guess you don't have much need for a suit and formal attire living aboard a boat?"

I said, "No, Charles, I don't, and believe it or not, there are days; I don't even put on my pants. However, I admit dressing for dinner last night was a treat. The suits felt great, and I want to thank you for them. It made me feel quite human and a bit urbane. I just wouldn't care to do it every day."

Charles looked me in the eye and smiled. "Son, there are plenty of days, especially lately; I would love to not have to put on my pants in the morning. I'm off to the office for lack of something better. You two keep me in the loop, as I feel rather useless in this entire pursuit. I hope someday when this is resolved to experience something like what you feel when you sail, Jake, something totally tranquil."

I said, "You have a standing invitation, Charles, you and Mr. Chapman. In the meantime, we are going to keep you very busy. Duke is going to join us in Canada tomorrow, and if possible, we are going to keep requiring fresh material as it becomes available from your people in DC."

He rejoined, "Good. Then I guess we can go our separate ways. Levi, please show Jake to my study and call Rhonda with a heads-up on my arrival. Tell her, my E.T.A. will be about twenty minutes."

Levi asked, "Who's going to drive you to the office?"

Charles said, "Don't you think I can drive a car by myself?"

Levi said, "Charles, you haven't driven a car in fifteen years. I don't believe you're even insured. I know; for a fact, your driver's license is not valid."

Charles said, "Then tell Rhonda to have that Pratt kid come over here to get me. I'll be downstairs if that's all right with you, boss?"

Gunny looked at him and said, "Yeah, you're right. Like Pratt is even going to understand how to get here."

Jeanette walked in at that moment, and Levi turned to her. "Jeanette, drink your coffee and be on rapid standby to drive your father to his office in ten minutes. Then be where he can reach you later to pick him up. He's taking you out to dinner tonight, and he wants you to pick the restaurant."

Jeanette said, "Oh, Daddy, we haven't eaten out together in such a long time. What about you, Levi? Aren't you and Jake coming with us?"

Levi said, "I'm going on a little trip with Jake for several days. You give me a kiss and get going to your father's office."

Like that, she came over, hugged, and kissed Levi on the cheek.

As she left the room, I remarked, "You're going to have to tell me how you achieve that someday."

Charles chimed in, "Yes, and explain it to me while you're at it."

Levi spoke, "It's charm, gentlemen; a natural charisma administered with a strong hand. You deal with love when you deal with children."

We went on our separate ways, and I obtained Regina's phone number. I dialed her, and she answered on the second ring.

She answered, "Hello; this is Regina. Who's there?"

I said, "Regina, this is Jake. May I have the phone number of the hotel where Tony is staying?"

She said, "Jake, Tony's here with me. We went out to get something to eat last night, and it got extremely late, so I put him up on my couch. Let me see if he's out of the shower yet."

I waited for a few moments. This is not what I needed, a romance in the making during our search.

Tony came to the phone. "Hi, Jake. I'm over here at Regina's apartment."

I returned, "No, kidding. I didn't think Regina had a Shriners' convention going on there. What are you doing? No, never mind; I don't need to know but get yourself over here with your bags packed. We're flying to Toronto today."

He asked me, "How about taking Regina along with me? We could play the married couple. It's a perfect cover, you remember, Hart to Hart. They were always doing undercover cases."

I thought about it, and it might be a good cover. I needed everyone with me except George. The truth was if I asked the wrong person a question, I'd rather have Regina or Tony backing me up than George.

I said, "All right, ask her." He made a feeble attempt to cover the phone. Then he said in a voice loud enough to be heard without the phone, "Hey, honey, do you want to go to Toronto with me today?"

I heard her reply, "Sure, babe, that sounds like great fun."

He said, "Yeah, Jake, it's cool with her."

I remarked harshly, "Tony, this is not a honeymoon, and this girl is not one of your Chicago bimbos."

Tony came back with, "Jake, I love you, man, but sometimes you climb up the wrong trees. This girl is exceptional. You don't understand how much she digs me, and I've never spent time with such a smart girl. Regina doesn't make me feel like trash. She makes me feel like I want to do everything right. That means starting from the beginning. Do you understand?"

I said, "I guess so, but I want you to remember that every waking moment, Julia, if she is still breathing, is living a life of humiliation and abuse. I won't let anything or anyone get in my way of finding her. Are we completely clear about that?"

Tony said, "Yes, Jake, you're right, and we're with you all the way on this entire search. We'll pack our clothes and be over there ASAP."

A moment later, Gunny knocked on the door and walked in.

He said, "I have everyone assembled and ready to go. We should be wheels up at Teterboro by twelve-thirty. By the time we get into the car, Charles will have made the additional requests you asked for at breakfast."

I said, "Good. I'll pack, so by the time Tony and Regina get here, we should be ready to go."

He asked, "Regina is coming with us on this mission?"

I replied, "Yes, it was her idea to team up with Tony. It does make for an excellent cover."

He asked, "What hotel did your friend Tony sleep in last night?"

I said, "Please don't ask me that question."

He said, "I didn't assume; I would have to ask that question. Regina has been trying to get involved in this since the very beginning. She even kept company with one of those FBI guys for a time."

I said, "Well, don't worry about her. I'm going to have a talk with Tony."

He began to laugh. "It's not Regina that I'm worried about. That girl is a world shaker and a heartbreaker. Her daddy taught her way too much about men. It's why she and Julia came together like gravy and biscuits."

I said, "I've always thought of Julia as the delicate type."

He replied, "Really? Let's see. She was New York State amateur tennis champion, captain of her college baseball team, and first alternate in the last Olympics in archery. She was a silver medal winner in the biathlon at that same Olympics. You look at that picture and say, 'Oh, look at this sweet, helpless female.' She's soft as butter to the people she loves, but she can outshoot, ski, and out-tough the best in the world, and in unarmed combat, only Regina surpasses her abilities.

"The problem is, I taught her every bullshit line ever used by man. I believe, until this day, she's never truly loved anyone outside of this family except Patty and Regina. It's not from lack of suitors, and besides me, she's the only one who can manage Jeanette. No, whoever made the mistake of grabbing her has a real problem on their hands. She's not going to fold up and die without one hell of a battle."

I sat, listening to him, and his words gave me great comfort. This entire search for Julia has made me lose my sense of separation. That wasn't good for a mission or me.

Gunny looked at me and said, "The search is really getting to you, isn't it, Jake?"

I said, "I know I should be more detached if I'm to do my job properly. I don't want to disappoint Charles. He hasn't once treated me like a hired hand except for his constant money discussion. Even so, I understand his grief, and I respect him for sharing it with me."

Then, I thought it the right moment, and I said, "You know, when I got out of the Corps, I swore I'd never take another life because the weight of all that killing had embittered me. That's why I went into Missing Persons with NYPD. I wanted to save lives without taking others. At war, it's always a soldier against a soldier, and the other fellow doesn't want to be there any more than you do. It's about following orders and fighting for the guy standing next to you. Always it's that guy next to you. You see immoral things, but for the most part, soldiers aren't corrupt within themselves. They're ordinary people who have to do evil things to survive. I found out working in Missing Persons that there are genuinely bad people in this world. They have to be eliminated, or we as a society won't survive. Nevertheless, in the end, I couldn't do the work on their terms, so I left the police department to take on this job my way.

"I got involved in this to do a favor for a friend of Duke's. In that process, I found I'm very skilled at this job. We saved a few lives because we had no one to answer to but our own principles. This case is different because I knew Julia, and it's very personal. Surprisingly, it's more honest, and I know I'm going to have to kill whoever's responsible for this, and knowing Charles, you, and Julia is going to make that a lot easier for me to accept."

Levi said, "Yes, I know. Charles truly admires your sense of independence and honesty. He called me that first night. When he met you in Florida, you could have sworn Charles found his own long-lost son. He knew about you, Julia, and even last night; he bemoaned you're not pursuing her at that time. She told us all about you. That's partly why Jeannette is so hostile towards you. She thinks you hurt her sister."

I replied, "That couldn't be further from the truth. What would I have had to offer someone like Julia? It was damn hard to ignore her phone calls because I liked her so much. That's it. He does remind me of my father. He never questioned my decisions. He let me blunder along and always spoke to me as an equal."

Levi said, "Your father sounds like he was a knowledgeable man."

I said, "He was, and I wish he's here this moment to advise me. You see, I'm roaming around with only this one theory. Partially because it's all I could come up with. The other alternatives are too gruesome for me to accept. This is not like me. I always work with several theories at the same time."

Levi said, "Listen, Jake, you're the only person who has come up with an idea. I, of all people, want to believe in the possibility that she's still alive. Don't forget, that's my little girl. I've sat up through enough colds and flues and school plays to earn the right to say and feel this way. By God, don't second-guess yourself now. I've had to travel a long distance to believe in you. I do, wholeheartedly, so enough of this bullshit. Let's go and find her."

He turned on his heel and left the room as he required no further answers. Somehow, his confidence provided me with a great feeling in my heart. I stopped dwelling on my uncertainty and packed my bags.

At ten, Tony and Regina came bounding into the apartment. After dutifully kissing Mr. Chapman on the cheek, Regina introduced Tony to Levi.

The first words uttered by Tony were, "Are you related to Gunnery Sergeant Levi Chapman, USMC?

I interrupted him, "Yes, this is former Gunnery Sergeant Levi Chapman, but he is Mr. Chapman to you. You are not to quiz him about his days in the Corps. Do you understand me?"

Tony said, "But Jake, my dad used to tell me stories about him."

I interrupted him, "Tony, I said no, and damn it, I mean no. Both of you need to keep your eye on the ball. I have plenty of mission information for everyone, so let's head out to Teterboro Airport."

He wouldn't stop. "Anyway, Mr. Chapman, my father served with the Second Corp, Third Engineers, in Vietnam."

Levi took the situation in hand. "Yes, Tony, I know. They were a very distinguished group of Marines."

Downstairs, at the street level, we were met by a Rolls limousine with a different driver. Levi said, "Good morning, Craig."

The driver said, "Good morning, Mr. Chapman. Please let me store your bags, and there's fresh orange juice in the refrigerator, sir."

As we crawled into the backseat, I asked what happened to the other Mercedes.

The Gunny replied, "That's an antique, and I won't let anyone drive her but me."

All this time, Tony and Regina were sitting as silent as two mice.

I looked at them both. "You two will be dropped off in Toronto. Before we get there, there'll be a driver and hotel room reserved for you. The room will have twin beds as it's necessary to maintain your married-couple cover. We have acquired only one room. You can get an adjoining room in different names if you desire."

Regina popped in, "No, Jake, Tony and I, are becoming adept at sharing a bathroom. I even packed my pajamas."

Tony joined in, "You know, Jake; I'm a gentleman, and you're giving Mr. Chapman a truly misleading impression of my character."

I said, "If I did that, I apologize profusely."

All this time, the Gunny was sitting there pouring orange juice for all of us, smiling like a Cheshire cat.

He said, "You people should know how lucky we were to acquire Craig. He comes all the way down from Spanish Harlem to get this orange juice fresh squeezed for us. Try this. It's made from pure Valencia's oranges."

I soon realized he was correct. It was sweet, and it made me wonder why I ever stopped squeezing my own oranges at home. At that moment, the phone rang. The Gunny picked it up and handed it to me, mouthing it was Duke.

Duke said, "You'll never believe where I'm calling you from."

I asked, "Duke, where are you calling me from?"

He answered, "I'm in a suite overlooking the White House at the Hay-Adams Hotel. I swear to God; Charles Alexander never does anything, second class."

I said, "Don't get too comfortable, because as soon as you get those sat. Photos and any suspected trafficker pictures; I may need you to get on a plane for Toronto. When I give you the word, you're to rent a car and make a short drive to a town called Mt. Hope. Check with Rhonda, and she'll give you directions as to where we are staying. Don't leave Washington until you speak with me first. We have to stay completely fluid from this day forwards. Do you have your appointment?"

Duke said, "Yes, in an hour. I'm meeting with. . . Can you guess of all people?"

I said, "I can't imagine who you're meeting with down there."

He said, "The heads of the C.I.A., F.B.I., N.S.A. and deputy chief of staff will be at the meeting. No one can hide anything from us. The meeting is in the West Wing."

I said, "That's excellent, Duke, but you know these people, so don't let them manage you. They have no hold on our clients or us. In fact, it's quite the contrary. You make these people understand that every day she's alive, she's being tortured and abused. They should think of their own children in this kind of situation. Play hardball, and tell them if there's any positive outcome to this, they will all share in the credit. On the other hand, if we find her dead without their assistance, then I will make sure that every newspaper in America writes the story of how the FBI dropped the ball in their search—who did that and how it caused her death. We will make sure every goddamned newspaper in the U.S. and Europe writes the story!"

The rest of our people nodded in agreement.

I turned back to the phone. "Duke, I'm sorry for my tone of voice."

He said, "That's all right, but I'm worried about you. You're right; I will have to play hardball with these people. They think I don't understand that they picked the West Wing to intimidate me. Someone didn't do his homework. If they did, they'd have realized I've been in that dwelling, including the

Oval Office, more than a few times on briefings. I'll let them start their bullshit about needing to know, and then I'll jump on the table. Can I speak to the Gunny?"

I said, "Yeah, he's sitting right next to me."

Levi said, "Major McGarrity, how are you, sir? What, oh yes, I remember that. So you were that shave tail lieutenant. Who was your NCOIC in Nam? Oh, First Sergeant Sinclair, I knew him well. We did a tour together at ROTA Spain. Yes, I know the assistant commandant Lieutenant General Wingate. He was my commanding officer in Vietnam. I know he has friends as the head of Navy Intelligence. I overheard your conversation with Jake, but you and I know you'll be lucky to get one-third of what we need there. It will be mostly background material.

"You'll have to go through our old-boy network to get anything from an operational point of view. The general owes me big-time, so don't be afraid to mention me, but please only if you have to use that. The very same and the NCOIC of the White House Detachment, a first sergeant named Collins, have dinner with him tonight. He drinks Jack Daniels. If the general stalls you, which I doubt he will, then you can speak to the sergeant major at eighth and I, barracks. Oh, you'll recognize him. He's the only twenty-five-year Sergeant major with four rows of ribbons. His name is Bill Moran. When you see the stitch marks from the previous ranks he held, it will crack you up. Yes, it's good to serve in this with you as well. We will see you tomorrow at some point and fly first-class. Please, that is a direct order from Charles Alexander himself."

At twelve-thirty on the dot, we taxied down the runway, and I began to feel better. We were finally on our way. Under my breath, I prayed, "Please, God, help support Julia to hold on until I can locate her."

Chapter Nine
Canada

Two hours later, we landed at Brampton Airport, outside Toronto.

I said, "Tony and Regina, with any success, we'll be rejoining you tomorrow. You have the names of the charter companies. If you get any word about a boat, then try Markham Airport. It's on the eastern side of town, and I doubt the international airport would be a good choice to get a sleeping girl out of the country with no passport."

Ten minutes later, we were in flight again. We made the short hop to John Monroe Hamilton Airport in Mount Hope, Canada, after flying not very far.

The Gunny rang off the phone and chuckled, "Would you believe this? The only accommodation in this burg is a Super

Eight Motel."

At that moment, Mike stepped out of the cockpit and said, "Mr. Chapman, it's always a pleasure to have you flying with us, sir."

Mr. Chapman said, "Thank you, Mike, but I need you to stow this in your hide-hole." He handed him a service issue.45 automatic.

Mike held forth. "I haven't seen one of these for a while. It must be an antique."

The Gunny said, "This particular piece is a matched pistol put together for me from the special arm's master at Quantico. It shoots outstanding and hits what it's aimed at every time. If it hits you, you don't get up again."

In what seemed like no time at all, we received clearance to land. When we taxied to the end of the runway, two Royal Canadian, Mounted policemen stepped aboard our aircraft. Grinning, the tall one queried, "Are you gentlemen bringing any contraband into Canada?"

We spoke a collective "No." I said, "We're here to arrange

a fishing trip, and we heard the salmon run in this town is somewhat respectable."

They both smiled and said, "Yes, it is," at the same time.

The taller of the two asked, "Are you staying with friends or at the Super Eight?"

I told them we would be staying at the Super Eight Motel.

The shorter one said, "Well, Joe Flynn, the owner down there, can give you the right information on charters and good places to drop, your hooks, heh. You men have a nice stay in Canada, and please spend some of your American money. We can always use more US dollars."

I couldn't help myself. "Don't you Officers wish to see our passports?"

They spoke as one, "No, Joe will check them at the motel. Besides, you're not up to any mischief, are you?"

I gave them one of my warm smiles of avid submission.

As they stepped down on the tarmac, Gunny and I both looked at each other at the same time with a parallel grin.

Mike came back to the main cabin. I inquired, "Is there a way to lock this plane down before we disembark to town?"

"Of course," he said. "We do it with an electronic device. It's similar to what new cars use but more sophisticated. The problem is, the maintenance people can't get on board, and it begins to look suspicious. If you're worried about the weapons, don't be. They couldn't get that unlocked if they tried. There's a lock underneath this, devise you've never even seen, but they could never discover it."

I asked, "What if they discover it by mistake?"

Mike answered, "When we first had this put in, we took the factory guys on a maiden voyage to L.A... We asked the Gulfstream people to find the box. In other words, we told them it existed, and after three hours of searching for it, their people gave up. Insofar as something else is supposed to be where those guns are, if they were to find the lock and break it open, it would create a very nasty fecal aroma because it has a double bottom to the tank itself."

I said, "Okay, you've convinced me. We can leave our guns on the plane."

Again, as we disembarked, two town cars were waiting to take us to the local Super Eight Motel.

When we checked in, I asked to speak with Mr. Flynn, the proprietor. A balding gentleman of about fifty came out from behind a curtained area in the back area of the office. I told the others to check-in, and we'd get together at the diner across the street that I observed on the drive-in here.

I said, "Mr. Flynn, my name is Jake Reynard. I would like a moment of your time in private, sir."

He said, "Sure, son, come back in my parlor. I guess that was your girl, Brett, who called me?"

I replied, "Yes, sir; it was, and she said you were willing to help us with our problem."

I walked through the curtains, and there was a lovely, warm, comfortable room. There was a fireplace with a log blazing in it. As my mother would say, lying about were all kinds of Katcha's, lining the shelves and tables. There was little doubt. These premises were occupied by people from the Emerald Isle or were of Irish descent.

I took a seat by the fire, where he motioned at me to sit, and began, "Mr. Flynn, about six months ago, you had some guests who might have appeared different from the usual American or Canadian guests you get here. They would either be Japanese or Middle Eastern types of fellows. Do you recollect anyone like that? There would have been two or more."

He looked at me carefully as I strained to put on my best Boy Scout's face.

Then he asked, "Why would you be looking for these gentlemen, and who are you really?"

I thought about that for a moment and decided to tell him the truth. I said, "My companions and I represent a private individual whose daughter was kidnapped about that time in Burlington, Vermont. The police and FBI never thought to think in terms of a water escape to Canada. Now we have ascertained that at least two middle-eastern men were in Burlington during her abduction. One would have had a scar on the right side of his face. This trail has led us here. It is not a kidnapping for ransom, but we believe it's kidnapping for sexual exploitation."

Now it was his turn to contemplate, then he shouted toward the front desk. In a thick brogue, he yelled, "Ralph, get Harry Michaels on the phone, and tell him to get his ass over here as fast as he can, and I mean double-quick. I sent three men like you described over to Harry's last September to see about a floatplane charter. I remember them because it's not the right time of year for a salmon run. The fish are too high in the rivers by then. The guy with that scar looked exactly like a villain out of an old movie."

I said, "Yes, that sounds like our suspects. How long do you think it will take for Harry to get here?"

He replied, "Oh, I figure in about five or six minutes."

I said, "Okay, I'll need another of my companions, present."

He said, "Here, use the telephone. Which one did you want?"

I said, "I want the tall black gentleman who accompanied me."

He said, "That's easy. He has the only king-size bed that I have in the motel. Let me dial his room for you. What's his name, by the way?"

I said, "Mr. Chapman," and he dialed a room number.

He spoke, "Hello, Mr. Chapman, could you please come to the front office? Thank you, sir."

Harry Michaels and Levi arrived within two minutes of each other, and we all sat down in Mr. Flynn's parlor.

Mr. Flynn asked, "Harry, challenge that feeble memory of yours and try to recall those two Arabs I sent to you back in September. Do you recall them?"

Harry said, "Sure, I remember the two because they hardly spoke a word. I rented them my De Havilland Beaver for a week. They paid in cash, which was strange, and when I asked for passports as identification, they hummed and hawed a lot, but I insisted."

I jumped in, "Did you get to see those passports?"

Harry responded, "Are you crazy, son? Do you think I'd rent out my Beaver without correct identification or proper pre-flight check? Why, I'd have to be nuts to do that, heh. I saw their passports and the pilot's license. We normally only check the stamps and don't keep a record of that stuff."

Then old Harry started beaming and said, "Well, I photocopied those passports in case of damage. Those two not only checked in early but in the middle of the night. I found my *Lorelei* sitting by the dock without damage. There were no clients either. No, fish were caught on that trip. The plane was a pigsty; I can tell you that."

Now it was Flynn's turn. "You know, they came in on a private jet like you folks. What bothered me most was what if they caught something, and what were they going to do with a plane full of dead un-refrigerated fish? They didn't strike me as catch-and-release types. Manuel, my friend, at the airport, told me you had a much longer range of travel than their plane did."

I couldn't help myself and asked, "You people remind me of what it's like to live in a small town. Did anyone else notice whether or not one of those guys had any scars across his face?"

Harry said, "Did he ever. It went from below his right ear to his jawline but in a really jagged line. He was the one who did all the communicating in English."

The Gunny jumped in, "Harry, is there any chance. You still have a copy of those passports with their pictures?"

Harry said, "Of course. They wouldn't be of any use without passport photos. I have them back to my office. What is this, and who were those people? Are they terrorists, and who are you guys, FBI or RCMP?"

I said, "Gunny, I've filled Mr. Flynn in about Julia. You should do the same for Harry, but do it on your way to his place. Retrieve the passports with the photos. I'm going to track down Duke and tell him to stay in D.C., so we can fax him the pictures and the names. Maybe, we'll get lucky, and they won't be counterfeits."

I thanked Mr. Flynn for all his help. He looked me in the eye and said, "Who is this girl to you, Mr. Reynard?"

I said, "She's the daughter of a man I happen to be very fond of. At least, that's how this began at first. Now, I guess she's become my mission if you can understand that."

He said, "Yes, I think; I do, son. Go with God's speed with your hunting. I'll pray you'll find her alive."

I returned to my room and called Duke on his cell phone. He picked up my call on the third ring.

He said, "I've got my meeting in ten minutes. Tell Gunny I've already met with his people. They're all willing to help, especially the big fellow. He was angry. He said, and I quote, 'Levi gets whatever he needs, even if it's an assault on a sovereign nation.'"

I responded, "We won't need that, but I do need you to stay in place. Give Brett a fax number where we can send you photos of our perpetrators."

He said, "You were that lucky up in Canada?"

I said, "Yes, we were, and thank God for small towns. If they'd gone out of Toronto, we'd be here for six months trying to recreate an escape method.

If this chase leads us abroad, either I will pick you up in DC, or I'll have you take a plane to Marseille. We can meet up there. I have a feeling this is going to move extremely fast from here on out. Please have Brett pack all my field gear and send it air express to D.C."

He said, "That's not necessary. I brought all your field gear with me. I have camouflage utilities and night-vision gear as well."

I said, "Duke, you're always thinking. Since Levi's friend is so eager, why not ask him for a point man from Recon or Special Forces? We'll need some Intel from them when we get into Indian territory."

He responded. "That's a great idea. I have his home phone number. He remembered me and said they're very few Mustanger's left, and we can't afford to forget the ones we have left. I have to say his remembering me touched a warm spot. He probably knows I'm worth more money than he is. I'll see you later, Jake."

I laid across the top of my bed, and twenty minutes later, there was a knock on the door. I opened it to see two grinning faces scrutinizing me. It was Gunny and Mike.

I asked, "Well, you both look like you just ate a canary. What did you get from our friend?"

Levi said, "We have two passports with complete likenesses of the subjects herein described."

I glared at the two photos, one Azza Mazin Hanna of Oman and one Fahd Ghayth Mahmoud of the United Arab Emirates that lay before me. Our friend Fahd had a long scar bisecting his face from his right ear down to his jawline.

I said, "I'm sure these must be our guys. We have to fax these photos to Duke immediately. Gunny, can you call my office and speak to Brett. She'll have the fax and phone number for Duke. Mike and I are going to the airport to see about the flight plans these people filed and acquire the registration numbers. On second thought, we might as well; all go to the airport. They probably have a better fax machine there than we can find around here. Mike, how difficult is it going to be to get that plane's information?"

Mike said, "It's all information in the public domain. The thing is to have someone take the time to look it up. I don't imagine they get that many international private flights landing here. We should try to find someone who remembers this particular bird. Let's call George and ask him to try to get it underway."

I asked, "Where is George now, anyway?"

Mike said, "He's at the airport overseeing refueling. I sent him out there over an hour ago."

I said, "Then let's call him and see if he can get those numbers and their flight plan. In the meantime, let's saddle up, get out of here, and bring all your bags while I settle the bill. If need be, we can stay tonight in Toronto or DC, but I'd like to get to DC by tonight if it's practicable."

I went to the office and told Mr. Flynn that we were all checking out, and above his protests, I paid him the two-day guarantee that we'd reserved in advance.

Forty minutes later, we entered the coffee shop at the airport where George was sitting, in a booth, sipping coffee.

George spoke first, "No luck on the numbers. This guy responsible is really hard-nosed about us not being properly credentialed officers of the law or Royal Canadian Mounted Police. When I mentioned the public domain issue, he laughed at me."

I said, "Okay, first, we attempt to do it in a nonviolent way. If that doesn't work, we go at it the hard way."

I tapped some numbers into my cell phone and waited for a moment.

I finally spoke, "Duke, where are you right now? Great. I'm having a problem with a priggish little airport manager. He says he won't give us the flight information and registration numbers on that plane our perps came in on. We are nearby, and I want to take off as soon as possible to pick up Tony and Regina and move on to join you in DC. We're going to need five rooms with a late arrival. I'm going to wait here. If you can't raise up the state department, I'm going to do something life-threatening to this little prick, and we'll all need some bail money."

As I closed down my phone, Mike looked at me and said, "You're kidding, I mean about the violence remark?"

I said with a balanced tone, "Do I sound like I'm fucking kidding?"

He replied, "No, you don't seem like that at all."

I said, "Listen to me, Mike, before this deal is over, it's all going to get extremely violent. For the second time, if either you or George wants out, that's not a problem for me. I have military friends who can fly the last part of this mission, and we are going to need someone who can fly a chopper anyway."

Before I even finished my remark, George chimed in, "I'm fully qualified to fly any helicopter you can get your hands on, and I am in this for the endgame, and I love violence."

Mike said, "I didn't mean that the way it sounded, and I'm in as well."

Those sheiks and emirs pay big bucks for white American girls. I doubt Julia was taken with all that expense and trouble to serve in some kind of whorehouse. No, if she's there, it's because she fit someone's specific desires, and it's somebody extremely powerful. It will be your job to get us to a neighboring country, ending your involvement until we get her out. Then you will take her to a specific doctor in California whose name and address will be made known to you. That's if Tony, Gunny, or I don't make it out with her. I know Mr. Chapman will get her out, but he won't know what to do with her once she's with you. That's where Regina comes into all this.

She can keep her sedated and calm and hand her over to my doctor friend in California. I'll clear all this with Mr. Alexander. Once we go tactical, it will be Tony, Gunny, Duke, I, plus another guy I may get from Special Operations."

Levi interrupted my train of thought, which was moving at a hundred miles an hour. In truth, I spoke all those words because I refused to believe she was dead. My sense of urgency was in high gear and moving quickly into overdrive.

He must have been reading my mind as he said. "What Jake said is correct. As soon as we get her out, Julia will require a lot of help dealing with her experience. He's right in planning for that outcome. If there is a doctor whom Jake has faith in, then whether the guy is in Timbuktu or California, your job will be to get her there with all speed. I'll speak with Charles, and as much as he may want to see her right away, I agree with Jake. It won't do either one of them any good until she's at least partially recovered and approximating someone like the Julia we all know."

That all said, I called Tony on his cell and told him to get their gear packed and head for the tarmac in Toronto.

He said, "Oh, no, Jake, you should see this place. It's sensational."

I answered, "Well, when this is done, I'll send both of you back there to finish whatever you've started, but for now, let's get it together."

We sat, waiting for an hour and a half until my cell phone finally rang again.

It was Duke. "We have the flight plan and registration numbers."

I said, "George, get us that flight plan to Toronto. Then on to D.C., and explain to them, we want a minimum amount of time on the ground in Toronto. We have to touch and go as it's only to pick up two passengers."

We took off, and I began to feel a sense of elation mounting. I've always felt this way before a mission. First, the adrenaline rush, and then before the task itself, composure would set in. I had a gut feeling we were getting close to finding Julia.

We landed ten minutes after we took off, with Tony and Regina awaiting us at the landing area. They boarded the plane, and after they stowed their gear, they took the two seats behind Gunny and me.

Mike came back, and I asked, "How long before we can get clearance to take off?"

He said, "We're third in line, but we'll taxi out now and line up."

In what seemed like moments, we were airborne again. When we leveled off at forty thousand feet, Regina leaped up and started taking orders for drinks and sandwiches. I opted for a Ham and Swiss on rye with a Coke, suddenly realizing I hadn't eaten anything today but that oatmeal early this morning.

When everyone was settled in with his or her food, I turned in my seat and faced Regina and Tony, and said. "Let me fill you two in on where we're at as of this moment. We started with a description of the two suspected perpetrators who chartered a Beaver floatplane. They had more than enough time to go from Port Hope to Burlington and back. The person who owns the charter company calculated the fuel used and said they used more than sufficient for a round trip. They also revealed their passports, which he would have typically held, but they put up a stink. He took them to his office and photocopied them without their knowledge.

"We have those photocopies. We sent them on to Duke, and he came up with two names, one from Oman and the other from the United Arab Emirates. This is what they look like. With help from DC, we are reproducing their flight plan. Those registration numbers of the private jet that took her out of the country are in play. These people are not really smart and are stupid as hell. It seems they handed over actual travel documents.

"We're on our way to Washington, DC, so Duke can fill us in on the balance of the story about the abductors. Tony and I will come up with a plan of engagement when we discover their exact location. Tony, you didn't exactly sign up for any hot stuff, so you can detach in D.C. if you wish. I could sure use your gun on this mission. Regina, we can put you on a shuttle back to New York when we arrive in Washington."

Tony started to speak when Regina turned and shushed him. It was all; I could do to keep from laughing out loud. Tony stopped mid-sentence like a chastened child. Regina began, "Let me understand this. At least one of you speaks Arabic or Farsi? Every one of you has had proper EMT training, and you know how to handle a woman who has been severely traumatized at the hands of a collection of degenerates?"

This was all spoken in a tone I could only describe as incensed and intransigent. I spoke up and said, "No, but we can acquire someone who does all those things."

"Oh," she said, "will they also be able to wear the Hijab?"

I asked, "What in the hell are you talking about, Regina?"

She said, "'O Prophet, tell your wives and daughters, and the believing women to draw their outer garments about them that is better so that they may be known to be Muslims and not suffer annoyance.' That's from the Koran 33:59, Jake. I am conversant in both these languages, and I have more than an acceptable amount of emergency medical training. If you expect to enter a Muslim house dressed in masculine garments, they will know you for a Westerner instantly.

However, a woman of appropriate modesty is allowed anywhere. She isn't viewed as a threat. In fact, it's considered bad manners to gaze upon a woman's face who is not your wife. Besides, this is my best friend we are talking about, and I am going, even if I have to purchase my own ticket."

Tony jumped in at that point. "If she goes, then I'm traveling with her."

I looked at Gunny, and he shrugged his shoulders.

I said, "All right, Regina, you made your point. How and when did you develop these skills?"

Regina said, "I have a lot of time off when Mr. Alexander is not flying. Most people who own these types of planes charter them when they are not being utilized. When we were employed, it was made clear that no one had used this plane except his own family and a few very special people. When we went to him three months later and expressed how much time we all had off, all he said was 'Take up a hobby,' so we did. Mike taught me how to shoot, and I taught George and Mike basic EMT training."

I said, "So we have three qualified medics on board?"

She said, "In truth, yes, you do."

I said, "Then, I agree, but what's up with you and Tony? You're beginning to act like co-conspirators."

She answered, "Tony and I like each other very much. We have a lot in common besides being Italian, and that's our personal state of affairs. It makes for good teammates. Isn't that true, Tony?"

He answered, "Yes, honey, once again, you've said it perfectly." Tony then said, "Jake, remember the little situation we got involved in down in Sierra Leone?"

I replied, "Yes, I remember all of it. Do you think if we go to Marseille, you can find my man Pierre?

Tony answered, "If you mean Pierre, the man, I'm positive we can."

I said. "Good, then I think I have a way; we can all do this with Regina's help."

Tony jumped in, "You overlook something, Jake. I have two

little girls, and no matter how I feel about their mother, I love my girls. I can only imagine what Mr. Alexander is going through now. Besides, if you go in hot, you know you'll need my gun to cover your ass. No disrespect, Gunny, but Jake and I have been on more than a few missions together, and we have a certain rhythm, a cadence, you understand?"

Gunny replied, "Yeah, I can dig that. I'm only along for the ride, but if we get us into some killing, then you just keep out of my way. Okay, little guy?"

Tony looked at Gunny and said, "Yes, sir, Gunny Chapman."

We ate in silence, and for the balance of the two-hour-and-thirty-some-odd-minute flight, we all rested as well as we could. Before disembarking, I said to Gunny, "After we check-into the hotel, please call Charles. Fill him in as to where we are on all of this. If all goes well, we should be airborne in less than twenty-four hours and on our way to Marseille, France."

Levi asked, "Jake, why Marseille, and why not get what we need from the State Department?"

I answered, "Look, I know we're going to need some false

passports and weapons. I know Charles has the president's ear. However, no administration is going to sanction a covert operation by any group of civilians. Hell, they don't even acknowledge the ones they create on their own. If we end up terminating somebody famous, I don't believe for a minute that the agencies involved wouldn't give us up to the oil interests. If it's in what they consider the national interest, we're gone. We are going into the oil country, and every one of these people has money and more than enough money to pull this type of deal off. They also have cousins and uncles, and they're not interested in the wrong or right of any of this. They will only want to know who sanctioned their brethren's death.

I don't want to spend the rest of my life looking over my shoulder. We're going to leave a minimal footprint on this entire matter. Is that okay with you?"

He replied, "Yes, it makes good sense. I told you before, all the tactical issues are yours and yours alone to deal with."

I said, "Also, there's another good reason for Charles not to know about all this."

Levi said, "I think I get your point, Jake."

I said, "We are going to need some cash, and I don't even know how much. What Charles should do is set up a numbered account under a bogus corporation, and if he doesn't know how to do that, I'm sure one of his slick attorneys does."

Levi asked, "How much money do you think we will need?"

I answered, "We'll need enough money to lure these rats out from behind their wall of solitude. I'd guesstimate one or two hundred thousand dollars."

Levi responded, "Don't worry about that or how we do it. By the time we get to Europe, more than enough money is waiting there for us. The thing about Charles that nobody realizes is that he did not set out to make this enormous amount of money. That's a reasonable aspiration for a man of his background and education. Nevertheless, he never set out to make the amount of money he now possesses.

"Before this, all happened with Julia; he set up multigenerational trusts for each of the girls at his wife's request, one hundred million dollars each, and he said to me, 'Levi, we have to figure out a way to spend of some of this money on a huge problem. This money has become an embarrassment. All the people I know besides you and the girls want either my money or the influence that it yields. We need to find a problem in this world, find the right people, and give those people two or three billion dollars to resolve that problem. The girls are taken care of, and if something were to happen to me, the girls would inherit. Every gigolo and con artist in the world would come knocking on their door. I want them to experience the type of love their mother and I shared, the one you get only once in a lifetime."

I asked, "So what did he do? What problem did you, and he decides to go after?"

Levi said, "He put together a very diverse think tank, and in the middle of all their deliberations, this disaster befell Julia. Since then, he has shown little interest in anything else but this search to find Julia. I confess, I was beginning to accept her death, but not him. He's her father, and that is about all there is to that. If you let him down, believe me, there'll be someone else to pick up this quest. He'll hunt for her with his last breath. My friend, if you do find and return her, you will win more than even you can comprehend. You'll acquire more than money from him. He's a man who never forgets a good deed or a friend."

I said, "You must know, Gunny, there's nothing in this world I won't do to find and bring Julia home. While we're on that subject, I want you to tell him what I suggested as our initial course of action. My friend's name is Dr. Bart Milton, and he's currently ensconced in his new clinic in Carmel Valley, California.

I want you to tell Charles to contact Bart, and he needs not worry about discretion. Bart is a brilliant fellow. He plays by the rules, and his honor is beyond reproach. Most important, he knows what this type of abuse can do to a person. Tell him we want to keep her calm for the trip home, so a woman named Regina will call him about what medications to employ for this trip."

He asked, "Where will we get those medications? Do we get them in Marseille?"

I said, "We can get anything and everything in Marseille;

believe me, Gunny."

I turned to the others and said, "After we've checked in, I know Duke has a suite. We'll catch up on some sleep and meet in the morning around six-thirty for breakfast.

George, can you get us an indirect flight plan beginning the day-after-tomorrow, and the same for the day after that, so we can arrive in Marseille, France, on Sunday. George, we need to make two or three stops, as if someone were trying to pursue us. It will be difficult, but remember, we are on a high-speed track. Can you get this accomplished?"

George said, "Yes, and before we get to where we're going, I think we might want to change the plane's registration numbers."

I asked, "Are you sure that you can achieve those specific items, George?"

He responded, "Not only that because I've been giving this some thought. I think we should change them more than once with similar existing off-line aircraft for service or repair."

Mike piped up, "I'm going to stay here and grease some

palms to have all the maintenance done swiftly and get us ready for an over-ocean flight."

I said, "Gentlemen and Regina, we have a car waiting, so let's go get some shut-eye."

We arrived at the hotel at about eight o'clock, and I found Duke's suite after I stowed my gear in the room he'd booked for me. When he answered the door, I saw Levi sitting, in an armchair, sipping what looked like a single-malt scotch.

I remarked, "I should have known you'd beat me up here."

Levi said, "I wanted to see what Duke had gotten from these Washington people. He insisted we wait for you, and when I mentioned you were going to sleep, he laughed and poured me a rather decent scotch."

Duke handed me a beer, and I sat down while he began speaking. "No satellite stuff, but we know where they flew first: Shannon Airport in Ireland. What's more, we know these guys have come up before as possible traffickers, although usually for small-time stuff."

I asked, "Small-time, and now they have a private jet at

their disposal?"

Duke went on, "That is the weird part of this entire abduction. Their plane is a Lear 45 registered to an Arabian company called United Emirates Oil and Maintenance. When they find out the individual ownership, the Intel people will send it to us via radio."

I said, "Crap, that's precisely what I did not want to be done. Now the spooks will know where we're flying too and how to track us. You, of all people, should know we use those people to verify only what we already know.

"You should have had them believe we are still in Canada chasing polar bears. If some cowboy gets it into his head to grandstand or tries diplomacy, we're screwed as well as Julia. The only chance that we have is to go in quiet, with false papers, and find out where they have her. Then we kill every one of those bastards. We can't leave witnesses alive."

Duke said. "You're right, Jake. I just wasn't thinking."

I answered, "Too late now. What's done is done?"

"You know," said Levi, "I never have had any use for this

medal they gave me. However, I do have an inkling. Let's say, for the moment, I was to let it leak what I'm doing to retrieve Julia and why. I have an idea that leads me to believe she's in Russia. I might need some help along the line getting in and out. I have this ill-earned reputation as a crazy bastard, and if I were to say the Russian Mafia has her. They'd figure out who she is, then these people in the Pentagon and the state department are going to reason that Charles is going to pay up a ransom. We go to Zurich and make a large cash withdrawal. I guarantee they'll have someone watching us as soon as we file a flight plan."

Mike, who had just joined us, jumped in and said, "Next, we could file a flight plan for Croatia. There we can change the registration numbers one final time. Then it's on to Marseille."

"Gunny," I replied, "that's a brilliant plan. By now, they all know that you work for Charles, and you would be the natural person to handle a ransom request. One thing, you will have to use a payphone to call Charles. Tell him on no account should he speaks any further with the deputy or, for that matter, to anyone in government. Explain our plan, but make him understand. He mustn't trust these people anymore. Any attempt by them to solve this problem would only be at the expense of Julia. They would have no concern for her or her safety in this situation."

Levi said, "I'll make him understand. Then, I'll make a few innocent phone calls to begin the leak."

"Now, I really feel like a moron," Duke said.

I said, "Don't. Neither one of you ever was a field operative. Nor have you worked with these types of people. That's why you have friends at all these departments, and I don't. What I mean is, we all have our own talents, but we all have two things in common."

"What is that?" Duke asked.

"Jake, you're a cold-hearted bastard, but I love your attitude," said Levi. "Let's drink up and get some chow. I'm hungry as hell."

Chapter Ten
Moving On

We all met up for breakfast the following day in Duke's suite, as I requested, and everyone seemed in good spirits.

I asked, "Why does everyone look so happy?"

Tony jumped in, "The Gunny was just telling us how he spread all these rumors about Mr. Alexander being contacted by the Russian mob. I said that no matter what movie you watched, it's always the Russians who get blamed, so everyone will buy into it."

"You're right," I said. "Maybe the next time around, we should blame the Albanians. They never seem to be answerable for anything."

That declaration brought about a soft chuckle.

I said, "Down to business. Is everyone ready to travel?"

They all shook their heads affirmatively.

I declared, "I don't see any reason to stay here another day. We do need to get those new plane numbers. George, can you get that done today? And yes, we will want two sets of registration numbers."

George replied, "It's already in the works. I have two different people putting together two sets that Mike and I came up with last night. They're real numbers, but we know the other two planes are out for major services. They won't be in service for a minimum of two weeks. One is in Africa, and the other in California. We know that, but the FAA doesn't. We spoke to some of our friends at Gulfstream. We should be able to pick them up at about twelve or one today."

I said, "That's terrific. You people know your stuff. Gunny, did you talk with Charles and fill him in on where we are at and how to handle those other matters?"

Levi said. "He was a little naive until I reminded him how the FBI had dropped his case without even telling him about it in the first place. Then he said an amazing thing, or at least, it was unparalleled for him, "Levi, let's do whatever Jake tells us to do, and I quote him, "He's all we have, and we have to do it exactly the way he requires it to get done. That includes the California doctor. I know within my heart, Jake's going to get our girl back safe and sound."

Jake, when he said that, he was crying."

My throat tightened, and for what seemed an eternity, I couldn't speak. Finally, I said, "Well, everyone knows where we are, and time has now become our enemy, so let's eat up. Regina, you're in on this, and I need you to call Bart and get a list of any medications you may need for Julia. We can get whatever you require in Marseille."

Regina said, "It's done, Jake, as soon as we reach a decent hour on the West Coast. I don't want to wake the poor guy up at this hour."

I said, "Damn it, you're right. I forget it's four hours earlier out there. We should be airborne at about two o'clock?"

Mike said, "We will be able to take off by then, but we have to call airline catering and order food. Does anyone want anything special? No, then, I'll have Regina order the best that they have. There's no use starving during this overseas flight. We are going to have a lot of ups and downs in Europe, first Ireland, and then Croatia."

Tony jumped in, "What, no, Italy?"

Regina shot him a look, and he went back to eating. I grabbed some eggs and bacon off the sideboard and began to create my own breakfast.

The Gunny spoke, "The other thing Charles said is to make it look like a legitimate payoff. We should withdraw the money out of the Zurich account, and he gave me all those numbers."

I asked, "How much are we talking about in dollars?"

He replied, "He transferred five million, net of fees."

I said, "If we get caught with that amount of cash onboard, it will all be confiscated."

Levi said, "Jake, I told him that, and he alleged, "So what?' Charles has lost any sense of money as a quantifiable value.

I'm proud of him for this way of thinking."

Tony looked at me, and I said, "By the way, have you given any further thought to the offer I made you last night about working with us?"

Regina popped in, "What type of offer was that?"

That's when I knew they had slept together. Tony looked at her and said, "Can't we talk about this later?"

I said, "Oh, I see you; two have other things to discuss, so I'll put that on hold for now."

Regina said, "All right, everyone listens up, as I don't want to repeat myself. I may have made the biggest mistake of my life, but I have shared my bed with this skinny Italian from Chicago, this street character that comes with two kids in the package, and no visible means of support, and trusts me; that's not the entire story.

"Before anyone judges him or me, remember I can probably kick everyone's ass here except Mr. Chapman. Now, how did this all come about? Let's say under his coarse exterior is someone who reminds me of my own dad. You all know how much I love my father. So I'm invested in him, and it's going to continue until he attempts to hurt me. Then I'll kick his ass to the curb."

George was the first one to speak. "It's about time, Regina. Mike and I were afraid you were going to assume the veil and take the vows. We give our blessing and welcome you to the world of wonderful crackpot love affairs."

"Here, here!" spoke up Mike.

I had to put my two cents in, so I remarked. "At least, you have all the rules straight, but let me tell you something about my friend Antonio. Besides Duke, I've never known a better or more loyal friend. He's a faithful fellow and true to his word. Since leaving the service, he's had to pass up some outstanding jobs with the police force. He stands on his head to keep his little girls in food, who, by the way, are both totally adorable. He has been offered an excellent job by the Lost Children Group with an inordinate salary and lots of time off between assignments. Duke, I made this offer without consulting you, but it goes without saying, you have the last word."

Duke replied, "Jake, you know I always back you in these

decisions, and I think Tony would make a great addition to our family. I've already been talking in depth to the Gunny, and I'd love to hire him and Regina."

I said, "Well, Charles Alexander might have something to say about that. Regina, as I told Tony, this would entail a move to the West Coast of Florida. From what I see on his puppy-dog face, I think perhaps; he might rather live in New York."

Before Tony could get a word out, she said, "Now, listen up, boys, no one is going to bust his balls but me. Are we all clear on that point upfront?"

We all chimed in together, "Yes, Regina."

She said, "That's better, and by the way, as these guys will tell you, I can, damn live anywhere; I desire and keep my job. However, we are getting way ahead of ourselves. I've owned up because these two guys are like my brothers, and I could never lie to Mr. Chapman. So that's it, and if this all ends tomorrow, it's not going to impair our mission to find Julia in any way."

Finally, Tony spoke up in a meek voice, "Do you mean; I could be used sexually and abandoned just like that? How easy do you think I am?"

That was it. Everyone, including Regina, bent over and began laughing hysterically. I thought Gunny was going to fall off his chair. It was what we needed, and there it was. That same roguish smile he used when that soldier pissed all over his back.

Regina recovered enough to say, "My stud," leaned over and kissed him while we all applauded.

Killjoy, that I am, I told everyone to meet downstairs at noon, except Mike and George.

They began to file out, and Tony turned to Regina and told her, "I'll meet up with you in our room."

I said, "You mean on top of everything else; we paid for two rooms, and you only used one?"

Tony said, "Take it out of my pay."

I saw Duke motion to me from behind Tony's back, not to go on any further with my taunting. Tony started to apologize with that elfin grin on his face, so I ceased my comments.

I said, "It's okay, Tony. I'm only pulling your leg."

He replied, "I had no clue; she was going to do that, Jake. I swear to God."

I said, "Well, that's because I'm not used to seeing you with someone like her. Let me tell you something, my friend. That girl is the real deal. If you screw this up, you're going to regret it forever. I mean, do you get the total picture here? She's fighting to place herself in harm's way to help her friend out of a horrible place where all the normal rules apply. You and I know all about that from our jaunts to Africa and Afghanistan. Jesus, this girl is a first-class trooper."

Tony replied, "I know Jake and believe me, I'm not going to do anything to mess this up. Not only do I believe she's the real deal, and this may sound crazy, but I feel like I've been waiting for her all my life."

I said, "Well, I wouldn't know anything about that. I've never been that lucky."

Now, it was time for Duke to chime in. "Tony, my friend, your heart always tells you when it's your turn. When it is, you have no choice but to go in with both feet. We have to depend on you to watch over her when we get to where we're going. On a brighter note, whatever Jake told you about our little enterprise is true. We don't turn away people in need, and I mean good people who could really use our assistance. You could do a lot worse than to throw in with us. When you do have your girls, you'll have two built-in babysitters with Brett and me. Jake wouldn't know it, but our girl Brett is champing at the bit to get married and have kids."

"Really?" I said, "I didn't know that. I always thought Brett was the ultimate career woman?"

Duke said, "Jake, what you know about women could be written on a Q-tip. Take Ann, for example. An amiable enough woman, but she didn't want an adult. She wanted a child she could save from himself. Brett and I saw it coming a mile before you caught on to her act. More pointedly, she will be back scratching on your front door the first moment she finds Bartley with another woman because Bartley is a child, and he's incapable of staying loyal to her or anyone else. It's simply not in him to remain faithful. She wants a child, and he wants a mother. Too bad she has this whole thing about fidelity."

I said, "You're probably right, Duke, but right now, she's the last person on my mind.

Chapter Eleven
The Flight

We were all assembled at the airport by twelve, everyone, except Mike and George, who were still absent, looking for those new tail numbers.

I said, "Has anyone heard from either Mike or George?"

Regina said, "I heard from them both. They said they would be delayed as they are still waiting for those new registration numbers."

I replied, "We might as well go to the lounge until we hear from them."

Mike walked in about ten minutes later and said, "George will be along soon. They made a mistake on one set of numbers. I'll need to preflight the plane to be ready for takeoff when he arrives."

We drank our coffee and, after that, drank a few more. One hour became two and then at three. George finally walked through the door.

He said, "Sorry, everyone, we're ready to go, and we should take off now. We have good weather, and I think we made amazing time getting to Shannon, Ireland. I would say about six and a half seven hours of flight time. Maybe less, but after that, we begin the ups and downs."

We boarded and took seats like a pack of tourists on holiday. I sat next to Duke, with Levi behind us. Tony and Regina occupied the two seats in front. The chairs could all be released from their stationary position after takeoff, and we could form a rough semicircle. There were three additional seats as the Gulfstream 550 seats, eight singles with two divines for two, and a rear bed in this particular configuration. The two rear-opposing divines could be folded down, pushed, and locked together to form two more beds. In ten minutes, we were airborne, and in twenty more at cruising altitude, Mike came back and spoke to Regina. He asked that we all kept our seatbelts on but loose. Duke and I unlocked our seats and turned them toward Levi.

I asked, "Is this going to give you enough legroom, Gunny?"

He responded, "Yes. For a moment there, I thought you fellows were placing me in the back of the bus!"

I said, "Ha-ha, I believe things are a little different today. I also think we should eat and get a little sleep. However, if you people want to talk about strategy, then I'll stay awake for that."

He asked, "Does that include you, Jake?"

I said, "Mr. Chapman, my family raised my brother and me to be color blind. In my instance, that came in very handy, as Tony can attest. We had one man of color and another Hispanic member of our team. Both of these guys were terrific team members."

Duke chimed in, "I've been thinking about something, and I want to run it by everybody. I once had input and contacts with Afghans when we were supporting them against the Russians. There is one individual, in particular, that I befriended.

Although he fought against the Russians when they left, he was no longer comfortable being mujahedeen. Being a Sunni Moslem, he did not desire to live among the Taliban, mostly Shiites.

"The last time I heard from him, he was living in Saudi Arabia. If he could be enticed to help us, I know we could find her if she's anywhere in the Middle East or those countries of origin among the people who made the initial kidnapping."

I asked, "What makes you consider; he would help us?"

Duke said, "Well, the last time I heard, he was making a good living selling arms and smuggling goods under sponsorship from the CIA in Saudi Arabia."

"I see, so we could actually have allies in the enemy's camp, so to speak," Levi said.

Duke continued, "When we get to Marseille and retrieve the papers we need, I'll take the first commercial flight to Riyadh. I'll see if I can get his assistance with the resources we require. It would be a great jumping-off point for either Oman or the U.A.E. I know it's a little risky, but this fellow Aamir Mahmoud

Latif owes me big-time."

I asked, "How does he happen to owe you, Duke?"

Duke said, "When the Taliban moved in and took over, he knew if he returned, he could be arrested. His wife and two daughters were still in Kabul. When he came to me for help, I made an arrangement. Our boys were still operating out of the other side of the river in Jalalabad, and I had them go in and pick up his family. We flew them all to Islamabad in Pakistan by chopper, and then everyone was sent on to Riyadh in one of our C-130 cargo planes."

I said, "You broke a few hundred Marine Corps rules using military transport for civilian passage. You took a giant gamble."

Duke said, "I did, but you know, I never have forgotten the faces of all the people who helped us in Vietnam. When we were trying to get out, they were all left behind at the mercy of the very people they attempted to assist us in defeating. At the embassy, we turned our backs on them as we flew out. Besides, a little insubordination once in a while is good for the soul, right, Gunny?"

Levi said, "There's no use in being a gyrene if we can't improvise to suit the occasion. Hell, every good Marine knows that."

I joined in, "I believe, gentlemen, what we have here is the beginning of a plan. I know I'd rather start with weapons in Arabia than try to smuggle them in on this plane. This way, we keep the old man; out of whatever happens to us over there. If we get busted, we're going to need all the juice he has with the state department."

I said, "Duke, we agree, and when we get to our first port of call, book that flight to Riyadh. Go on ahead of us and see if you can get this rolling at the other end. First, fax him the photos and see if he can locate the two kidnappers. If he has any friends who can help us locate our suspects, tell them we are paying very substantial reward money for information."

Duke said, "You got it, Jake. I'll try to find out where the best locations for crossing the borders to these other localities."

I said, "Excellent, and we have twenty grand onboard, so take it all with you. Make sure you're generous with it because we'll be bringing a hell of a lot more funds."

We sat back and enjoyed the airline fare, a genuinely decent meal: Roman-style lasagna and a rather lovely Chianti Classico. I commented on the quality of Regina. She told me they got all their food prepared by a unique catering company with offices in Paris, DC, and New York.

I settled in for the long flight in the rear bunk and fell asleep rapidly. It was an uneasy sleep, and so much so that Levi came back and gently shook me. Then I heard him say, "Easy, son. Relax. You're wound up tighter than a clock spring."

I looked up and saw everyone else was asleep.

I said, "I had a terrible dream, Gunny. I dreamt; I found her, but she kept slipping away from me."

He said, "My granny would have had a field day with this dream of yours. She swore that every dream has a symbol attached. They never represent what you think they do at first glance."

"Really?" I said. "What do you think my dream meant?"

He answered, "I'm not my granny, but I believed from the first moment we met that you were sent to us to get our Julia back. What's more, Charles does as well. That's why he tried to throw all that money at you. You see, Charles doesn't believe in the nobility of people as a rule. That's what happens when you surround yourself with nothing but greedy people. Why, if it weren't for the girls and our personal relationship, he wouldn't have anyone of value in his life, someone he could truly trust.

"I believe for the first time in a long time, he's begun to put his fate in God's hands. He and I spoke about that before we left. I told him that God would send us one of his soldiers to settle our hearts on this matter once and for all."

I said, "You're putting a hell of a lot of weight on me, Gunny."

He said, "Don't worry about that, Jake. As one of God's messengers, you'd never be aware of his plan, but the outcome would remain the same. There's no use in even thinking about it because it's completely out of your hands. You keep doing what you're doing, and this will turn out exactly the way it's preordained."

I thought about what he said as he leaned back into his seat. I admit; it gave me a sense of serenity. He didn't understand how wrapped up in God I was or how I'd prayed for forgiveness for breaking his commandments about taking a life. Here I was about to break them again, and I dreaded the effect on me down the road.

Chapter Twelve
Ireland and Beyond

We arrived at Shannon Airport within twenty minutes of the time George had predicted, and as we were refueling, Mike came over and asked, "How do you want to do the next leg of our journey?"

I spoke quietly, "I want Duke to disembark somewhere where he can get a direct flight to Riyadh tomorrow morning. We also need a place; he can get a visa with as few difficulties as possible."

Mike thought about that a few moments and said, "I'll get, on the radio, and plan this out." He came back fifteen minutes later, and when he spoke, he had all our attention. He began, "We have two choices, and both options solve different problems. The first is Zurich, so we won't have to wait in anticipation of the money to transfer again. The second choice is Frankfurt, which benefits from being closer to both Croatia and Marseille."

Duke jumped in, "This requires no thought. Frankfurt, I have tons of military contacts there, and it won't compromise our cover at all. Besides, I know the CIA station chief in Frankfurt, and I can contact him there. He's an old and very dear friend of mine."

I looked at Levi, and he shook his head in the affirmative.

Mike interrupted my thoughts. "Jake, we can continue to Frankfurt and be there in one and a half hours, depending on air traffic. It's a busy airport, and we can have the money transferred to a Frankfurt bank. Then George and I need a little downtime for sleep."

I said, "Yes, I can see that in your eyes, but that brings me to another point. When we get to our final objective, we need to get the hell out fast and get Julia to California as soon as possible. How do we accomplish that part of this deal?"

Mike said, "This plane, under normal flying conditions,

can fly about 6,750 nautical miles or 7,767.9 air miles. At our cruising speed of 600 miles per hour, we would need one refueling stop for the thirteen hours of flight time to our California terminus."

I said, "I guess you've given this a lot of thought."

He said, "Whenever you fly, it's always best to prepare in advance."

I said, "Then give this some thought. Find an inconspicuous place to refuel. Pick a small airport and have Julia's passport waiting so all of you can clear incoming customs quickly and get her to Dr. Bradley Milton."

He said, "Jake, you seem so sure she's still alive and that you can get her out."

I said. "Mike, I'll get her out, or you'll be flying coffin's home. Now, get us fixed up with some rooms in Frankfurt. Make sure the plane is ready for a long flight, and as far as the rest of this is concerned, she's alive until I see otherwise with my own eyes. Believe me, I'm going to get her out of that hellhole if it's the last thing I do on earth."

Mike turned, and Duke grabbed me by my shoulder. "Jake, I've never seen you wound up like this. Easy, son, we are all uptight, but yelling at this guy won't help."

I said firmly, "I won't allow any negative people around me. You know that, Duke. As to the rest of it, I'm in a mission mode now, and I need to stay this way. I have to be pissed off and ready to go. If someone gets their feelings hurt, then screw them. We can always straighten that out later."

Chapter Thirteen
Germany

We all settled into a grand old hotel called the Steinberger Frankfurter Hof. We acquired the suite of rooms this time, and it was beautiful in the great tradition of the turn of the century before Germany got involved in all her wars. It was rebuilt, of course, but like most things in Germany, it was done to keep the original architecture and furnishings. In the bathroom was the most gigantic claw-foot tub I'd ever seen. I couldn't resist, so I drew a bath and jumped in and soaked for thirty minutes.

After a shave and some fresh deodorant, I began to feel somewhat human again. I dressed in the other suit Charles had made for me with a blue shirt and a pinkish-colored tie, as is now the style. I had to admit, I cut quite a sophisticated figure in the mirror.

That accomplished, I went in search of the bar downstairs. I no sooner got off the elevator and turned to my left, and there was George. Before I saw the bar, I said, "George, you wouldn't know where the bar is located, in this place?"

He looked at me and said, "I would have thought a Marine would know that by instinct. Come on, I'm going there myself."

We walked a short distance and turned right into one of the most beautiful barrooms I'd ever seen. There sat Mike, Tony, and Regina around a large table, in the corner. I walked over and took the seat next to Mike and said, "Mike, I'm sorry for jumping down your throat that way on the plane. I hope you can see your way clear to pardon my bad manners."

Mike said, "Jake, I believe we need someone with your passion. It's just strange that we all knew Julia so well, but it took you, a relative outsider, to believe in her still being alive and keep us motivated to this idea."

I said, "In my own defense, I don't know what has me driven about this idea of mine, but I've really come to believe it in my mind and my heart. Julia's out there waiting for us. I don't know how or when it began, but it's a feeling I have in my gut, and it's been driving me forward in my search."

Anyway, trying to change the subject, I said, "Wait until you see the bathtubs in this place. I just sat in mine for a half-hour, and I highly recommend it to everyone."

I saw Tony giving a sideways look to Regina, and somehow I knew they'd be taking their leave of us soon. With that thought in mind, the waiter came over and asked, "*Herr Oberst*, may I offer you something to drink?"

I said, "Yes, you can. I think I'd like a superior Rheinhessen Spatlese and four glasses, *Bitte.*"

He left, and I said, "If you've never tried this wine, believe me, it's extremely worthwhile. By the way, where are Mr. Chapman and Duke?"

Regina spoke up, "Duke went to pick up his ticket and then went to see somebody from Military Intelligence. Gunny is at the bank trying to get the funds transferred. At least, he's attempting, as it's rather late."

Well, I thought; everyone *was thinking and doing their assignments.*

I asked, "Did Duke say when he intended to take off for Riyadh?"

Mike spoke up, "Yes, he said he would be leaving in the morning and be there in five and a half to six hours. There's only one flight a day. It's Lufthansa, and it's either that, or he must wait another day. Since it's so late, if Gunny can't get the money until tomorrow, then he will wire it to Duke in Riyadh, which I told him was a much better idea than traveling around with such a huge amount of cash. It opens us up to currency violations, which is an unnecessary risk if we maintain a small footprint. If you want confidentiality and someone to keep his or her mouth shut, there is no one better than a Swiss banker. They couldn't care less where the money comes from or where it going as long as they get their fee."

I said, "I agree with you, and as a matter of fact, if Gunny does get the money today, we'll have him wire transfer it to Duke after he calls us."

Those words were hardly out of my mouth when the waiter and Levi showed up at the same time. As he sat down, I told the waiter, after sampling the wine, to bring two more glasses and another bottle.

Levi began, "No luck. We have to wait until tomorrow morning to get our hands on the money."

I said, "That's all right." I told him we had decided that wire transferring the money to Duke was the safer way to go. I also told him to recoup ten thousand of the twenty we had already given to Duke.

Then I asked Mike, "How much cash do you think we can stow in that hide-hole of yours?"

Mike said, "I think we could get at least forty or fifty thousand in there in hundred-dollar bills. Don't forget, we can all legally carry ten thousand each in cash."

I thought about that a moment. Then I turned to Gunny and said, "Let's transfer two hundred fifty thousand to a correspondent bank in Riyadh and make sure Duke calls us in France for the wire transfer numbers. Withdraw eighty thousand in cash, and we can divvy it up among the hide-hole and ourselves."

Levi said, "I'll do that first thing in the morning."

I said, "Yes, and I think if we can get clearance for Croatia early enough, we should be ready and onboard by eleven o'clock if that's okay with everyone else?"

They all agreed and set off for separate dinners and rooms except for Levi and myself.

I asked, "Are you going to babysit me, Gunny?"

He said, "That depends. Do you need babysitting, son?"

I answered, "No, but I think I could use a good meal with a decent company."

He replied, "Well, I don't know how suitable my company is, but I'll accept an invitation to eat anytime. Do you have any suggestions?"

I said, "I was reading a German gourmet magazine in the bathtub, and one of their suggestions is a place called Größenwahn for a wild game dinner if you're up for that. However, this hotel is also noted for its cuisine."

Levi said, "I get tired of hotel food no matter how fine it is. I hear they have venison here. I think they call it *Reh* or something like that. It's supposed to be exceptional."

I said, "Then let's get a taxi and go to the restaurant I mentioned."

We settled the tab and hailed a taxi. We had a substantial wild game dinner and drank another great German wine, this time a Moselle. Throughout dinner, Gunny talked more about the family and his lengthy ties to them. He also spoke about Julia with the most enormous affection and his concerns about her future mental health.

I strained to reassure him that Bart had tremendous skills in helping people overcome being prisoners and experiencing all types of torture. I told him when we get to Marseille, everything will speed up.

He told me, laughing as he said it, that he thought everyone was in awe of how far and how fast we'd already come.

Then he said. "If we find Julia alive, will you cut and run again, Jake?"

I replied, "Not on your life, not until I know she's that Julia, I met so long ago. I've come to realize that I'm not ready for a world without Julia Alexander."

Later as we were saying good-bye in the elevator after dinner, I said, "Get a good rest because you're the only one here she's going to feel safe with. Your face is what she'll need to see when we get her out. If there's any killing to be done, let Tony and me handle it. Please think about that aspect of this mission."

I opened the door to my suite of rooms, and Duke was sitting in a comfortable chair with a scotch in hand.

He said, "I had to tell you in person. We had some great luck today."

"Well, what kind of luck exactly?" I asked.

Duke said, "Do you remember my friend Aamir and what I told you about him?"

I said, "Of course, course, I remember but wait, let me get Levi."

Levi had walked halfway down the hall when I called him to come back. He returned and took a seat. Then I asked Duke to speak to us both.

Duke continued, "Well, I went to see an old friend of mine at the embassy. We jawed about things in general, and I started to inquire about Aamir. It seems Aamir is still an asset for our boys at the CIA. My friend could put me in touch with him on a secure line. I filled him to the point that I felt comfortable and made him aware this was strictly a private thing, but any help he could render would be much appreciated. He went on to tell me that as his friend, he was insulted at any mere mention of money and that all his resources were open to us. He asked for fax copies of the passports to be sent and gave me a secure line to call him on arrival.

"I came back, retrieved the passport photos, and faxed them to him. He is looking for those two rag heads as we sit here. Believe me, Jake, he's our best hope. As to the other matters, whether its vehicles or arms, we can get it all in Saudi Arabia."

I asked, "Duke, are you all booked and ready to leave early tomorrow morning?"

He said, "Not only am I leaving tomorrow, but take a look at this new passport."

He thrust his passport toward me, and I opened it. It stated the carrier, "One, I. Mc Garrity is in the embassy service of the United States government and, as such, be awarded all such privileges afforded by this diplomatic status." It also had the special paper and jacket of a consular passport.

"How in the hell did you pull that feat of magic off?" I asked.

He went on, "Friends. I still have connections in high places. Enough said. I thought if we get in trouble, this could help us down the line. I still want you to pick up a dummy for me in Marseille if you can find your friend, Pierre."

I said, "I'll still need your photos," and with that, he handed me four passport pictures. "Well, you have had a busy day. You know Duke, the hairy part is yet to come, but I can see the obstacles toppling. I think we're going to pull this off. If she's alive out there, we're going to find her."

He said, "If we don't, it won't be for your lack of trying; that's for sure."

The following day, dawn came early. I was up and packed by eight. I called Duke and asked if he was ready for breakfast.

He said, "Yes, and I have to depart for the airport within the hour."

We met downstairs in the main dining room. Levi was there already eating a huge German breakfast of soft-boiled eggs with all their different sausages, loaves of bread, and cheeses. I ordered the same, as did Duke.

"Listen a second," said the Gunny. "I'm going to call the general today and fill him in on our true destination because we may need some Recon support. I've been thinking about this all night."

I jumped in, "I thought we agreed to go clandestine at this point in this mission."

Levi said, "We did, but if you don't already know this, then I'll tell you. Lieutenant General Wingate is the same young sorry-ass captain whom I dragged out of Vietnam. He's responsible for getting me that damn medal. We have what you might call strong ties. If I tell him to keep this private and low-key, he'll do that for me. That's a guarantee you can believe. We're going into a strange country where there are already US extraction teams, weapons, and some very well-informed Special Forces people operating throughout the area. If we have needs, we can get them handled through our network, just like Duke got that passport. Jake, we have to use all of our assets."

I said, "Gunny, I only hope this doesn't turn into a cluster fuck. Okay, I'll trust your judgment on this because you know the guy. I don't know him at all."

Our breakfast was completed. We packed up and went on our separate ways. Levi, Regina, with Tony in tow, and I headed out toward the airport. It was eleven-thirty local time when we arrived, and we all went straight to the plane and boarded. Mike was already on board, and he came back to speak with us. "Okay, boys and girls, this is where we're at. George should be here in five minutes, and then we can take off. We will arrive at Zagreb, Croatia, fast, and we have arranged in advance for a private hanger where we can make our mischief with the plane's numbers. Since we have no corporate logos to deal with, this should go rapidly, and we already have a flight plan for Marseille written up with our new numbers. There will be no disembarking in Zagreb. That's one of the conditions for getting this hanger, so you will all have to sit tight while

George and I will make the appropriate changes."

"Don't you need help with refueling?" I asked.

He said, "No. As a matter of fact, what I want is to have the least amount of people know of our existence there as possible."

I stated, "Well, you're the boss on the flying, Mike, but how long will it take before we reach Marseille?"

Mike said, "With any luck, we will have dinner there this evening."

Gunny turned to me and said, "So, Jake, is it Bouillabaisse du Ravi tonight with a Cassis Blanc de Blancs?"

Tony asked, "What in the hell is that?"

I replied, "If you're a good boy, you'll see it for yourself. Believe me, you won't want to miss out on this particular meal."

George came on board, and we began to taxi down the runway as the door was being closed.

Chapter Fourteen
Marseille

It was dark out when we arrived in Marseille, and once more, the ground transportation was awaiting us when we arrived. The rooms were arranged in advance at the Parc Borély Hotel, another five-star hotel located at the harbor.

Today, if you want to move from city to city without drawing attention to yourself, you stay out of the neighborhoods where the criminals frequent. You visit among the wealthy. All police organizations monitor poor communities for terrorists and criminals. They pretty much accept the idea that terrorists don't usually stay in five-star hotels, which, of course, is a very foolish mistake.

Those were the plans we'd made, and thus far, they'd worked out. I told Mike and George, "We need the same setup as Zagreb: private hanger, new numbers, and we would pay for our rooms two weeks in advance. We will make it known we're scouting movie locations and would be here for at least two weeks. We would be going in and out to the surrounding areas, so tell them to take notice that we would get all of our messages by cell phone."

We put our stuff in the rooms and met in the lobby. My turn to choose the restaurant this time, and I took them all to Le Wagon. It's not only one of the best of six great bouillabaisse restaurants in Marseille, but it's also set up in a train car, so the dining experience is unique. The Bouillabaisse du Ravi with six types of fish was excellent, and everyone ate and drank the local Cassis Blanc de Blancs wine.

After an outstanding meal, we sat sipping the last of the wine when I spoke. "Tomorrow, we will begin. We have to be ready and available in our rooms while Tony locates our friend, Pierre. We all need to go to an address he will give us separately. Don't take taxis from the hotel. Remember, above all else, we must look like we are here to scout out movie locations. As long as we are, we will never really leave

Marseille or the surrounding area. That means we leave only when it's time to fly. We fly with the clothes on our backs. Regina, I know you're not going to like this, but you have an important role to play. You must stay in Marseille for the duration. It will help us maintain our sense of residence here."

She began to speak, and I cut her off, "Regina, we are going to an Arab country where, under the best of circumstances, any Western woman stands out. However, that was worth the risk of your language skills. We now have a native speaker in Duke's friend Aamir, so you'll be needed here to look after Julia when we locate her, and she's out of danger.

"The entire problem of familial recognition will be handled by Mr. Chapman. After all, he raised her, and she will feel safer with him more than anyone else. We may not all get back here at the same time. If anyone has to take a different route out, say overland, then Tony and me, because of our training and experience, are the best ones to achieve that."

Tony turned to her and said, "He's dead-on, honey, and I won't be able to do my job and look after you at the same time. Besides, it gives me something to look forward to when

I return. I've never had anyone waiting for me at the end of an operation."

She looked at all of us and said, "I'll need all your room keys so I can jumble up your beds each day."

I shook my head in approval. "That's using your bean, Regina. I knew you wouldn't be a pain in the ass about this crap."

That settled, we sent George to pay for our hotel bills in advance. We returned to our rooms for a last good night's sleep before embarking on the trail of the two bastards who abducted Julia.

The following morning, I was having breakfast in my room when Levi strode in.

I asked, "How did you ever get a key to my room?"

He replied, "Regina has duplicates for all of our rooms, and I thought I would surprise you, but not if you're going to bite my head off. Your disposition in the morning is dreadful."

I asked, "Do you really think we have any concerns here about my state of mind?"

He said, "No, I'm messing with your head. Do you know how firm your tone was last night with Regina?"

I answered, "Yes, I do, and I knew if I didn't take use that tone, we would have had a two-hour discourse. I don't need that from anyone at this point. Not only would Regina's ongoing safety keep Tony's mind otherwise occupied, but mine and yours as well."

He said, "You're right, Jake. I only wanted you to know I agree with you. I, for one, will never question any of your orders."

I said, "Well, while we are on that topic, I also meant what I said about your role in this affair as well. I know you'd love to punish these people for what they did, but your first duty in this entire operation is Julia. If she's alive, get her out of there safely. Are we clear, on that point, Gunny?"

He said, "Yes, we are; besides you, people are the covert experts. I guess when the killing needs to be done, you know what you're doing."

I said, "Gunny, Tony, and I learned from the best. I'm sad

to say that we have done our share of wet work in the past under orders. I'll gladly dispose of these two pieces of shit and the bastard who sent them here. These people are walking around over there in some made-up world of their own. They don't realize, for a moment, the horror and hailstorm they are about to face. However, once this over, I never want to talk about it again, all right?"

He said, "Yes, Jake, I know exactly what you mean, and as to the other, I'll protect my little girl with my life."

I responded, "Good, Gunny, because you're the last person on earth I want to have a dispute with."

Levi said, "I've grown very fond of you also, son. When this is over, you, I, and Duke are going to spend some quality time together."

I said, "Amen, and bless you for that, brother."

Then at twelve-thirty, Tony came through the door. "I met with Pierre, and his direct quote was, 'If Jake doesn't materialize at my house and dine with me tonight, tell him I will never forgive him.' He also asked that we all meet at this address around three o'clock. He said to arrive separately. I have to call him now with the nationalities we want on the passports."

I was tempted to have us all become French or British, but I remembered something from the training I received at Langley. They said, "When you're traveling in a foreign country, pretend that if you run into a native speaker from the government on your passport, you can pass their examination. If you pick a nationality you don't have, down cold, you put yourself at risk of discovery.

So with that in mind, I told Tony to have Pierre make up five passports, French Canadian for me, and American or Canadian for all the others, with unoriginal names, of course. My mother taught me French at her knee. "Have him make the name on mine, Jean-Louis Joubert?"

I said, "Tell him that we will be three joining him for dinner. Get the address if he's not going to be at the old one. He often has his people do these jobs with little or no liaison with him."

"But with you, he wants to socialize, correct?" Levi asked me.

I responded, "We have a history not only from my activities in the Corps, but I worked an NYPD kidnapping case over here once. He not only helped me but put himself in harm's way in the process. We have a bond, Gunny, and I want him to meet you. I know you'll love this gentleman. It's difficult not to treasure him. He's about the most captivating rogue you'll ever have the opportunity to meet."

Gunny looked at Tony, who was shaking his head in agreement, and said, "Well, I guess I'll have to meet him after all that buildup."

We accomplished our business with the passport forger at a small warehouse on the other side of the harbor. When I asked the price and the amount of time for completion, he directed all queries to Pierre.

At seven, the Gunny, Tony, and I knocked on the door of what appeared to be a small charming house within the Pannier district of Marseille. A lovely blonde woman opened the door and said, "Messieurs; I am Madame Tress, and my husband is awaiting you in his study through that door. Please come forward and make our home your own."

I thanked her in French, and she replied in English. I complimented her on her English, and she blushed for me.

Pierre was standing at the doorway, observing all this, and said, "Jake, you must not compliment Claudette. It makes her always with the red on her face."

Then he came over and gave me a great bear hug. When I freed myself from his grasp, I made introductions all around, and he just stood and stared up at Levi and said in French, "Claudette, Vous mieux met qué deuxième rôtit nous avons discuté." (Claudette, you'd better put on that second roast as we discussed.)

I laughed, and my two friends just looked at me as I said, "It's a private joke, fellows."

We followed Pierre into a large study, where he'd already had a bottle of Graves opened and a Les Baux de Provence Domaine des Terres Blanches Rouge that was obtained from a small chateau winery nearby.

I said, "Pierre, you remembered my fondness for Graves."

He began, "How any self-respecting person with a French

family name such as yours can drink a white wine when you are not eating fish, cheese, or fruit is beyond my understanding."

I said, "I'm not sophisticated like you, Pierre. Of course, it is understood, nor as successful with women either. By the way, is this not a new Madame Tress?"

He said, "You know, Jake, there is nothing more superior than love. However, it is always somewhat constrained by the contract of marriage. That is why we have mistresses in France. It makes us better husbands, *Oui*? Anyway, my previous wife did not understand this concept, so I promoted my mistress to this not-so-exalted wife's position. Therefore, with all this expense of changing wives and mistresses, it keeps me working harder. I swear, if I didn't have this penis, I would be a wealthy man. On the other hand, if I didn't have one, what would be the use of having any possessions at all?"

We all laughed at his statement, as there was a cynical truth in that for some people—at least the concept. For myself, if you can call them that, my affairs had always been handled one at a time. I guess that was why I remained friends with all these women I'd shared my bed with over the years. I not only maintained their self-esteem but also tried to add a little to it as well.

As we sipped our wine, Pierre said we had time before dinner to get our little business out of the way.

I asked him about the price of the passports, and he quoted me twenty-five hundred apiece. I knew he was making little or nothing on the deal at that price, and I said so.

I could never take money from me for something personal to you. Our mutual friend Tony has told me this action is very intimate with you."

I told him it was and decided to fill him in on the overall circumstances without mentioning Julia's name or father's. When I concluded, he looked at me for a moment then spoke, "Jake, what you are about to attempt is extremely dangerous, but I think I can help you in two ways. I have contacts, some very close connections in Arabia, and some of the surrounding areas. You will need a satellite phone, so wherever you are, we can maintain contact. I have the very latest, and I will loan it to you. If you can return it at the end of your mission, then it's free. You need to know that the damn thing costs with the coding devices are about five thousand Americans if it is not retrievable. Your partner, it would seem, is working with someone in Riyadh. Actually, he sounds like a friendly competitor of mine.

No matter, we will get you, the phone and the passports by seven tomorrow morning. I take it; you don't want to arm yourself here, which I agree with in principle. If your friend is who I think he is, then he can provide everything you will need at its point of use there. Let me excuse myself for a moment to tell my man. He must work on your papers all night."

With that said, he left the room, and Levi turned to me and said, "You're right. He is one hell of a charming guy."

When Pierre returned, we sat for another twenty minutes before his wife came in to announce dinner. Pierre told us we were in for a great treat as Claudette had attended the Academy Gastronome in Marseille. At about fifty, I could see he was at least twenty years older than his wife, and I asked how long they had known each other.

Pierre said, "You know, we met about eight years ago when Claudette was eighteen. I decided to take a course at the culinary school where she was studying. There we discerned this chemistry between us, and if that is present, it cannot be denied. We began as lovers, and now we have been married, about a year. Claudette is about to bear our first child in under six months. Anyway, we are delighted, *Oui, Cherie?*"She rejoined. "Yes, we are, Pierre, and as long as there are no new chemistries, we will continue to be very happy." She said all this with a smile on her face, which tempted me to say, "You know, of course, Claudette, that besides your beauty and charm, there is a far more important reason you are precious to Pierre."

She looked at me. "What exactly is that, Jake?"

I said, "Where else could he possibly find someone who looks as beautiful as you and can cook this well ?"

Pierre said, "Jake, don't encourage her. Believe me, French women are difficult enough without putting too much tribute in their heads. Look at her; you have made her blush again. Jake, you have used up your entire quota of compliments. Now, there will be no living tomorrow with *Mon petit amour.*"

The rest of that evening was spent in that same frame of

light banter, and everyone seemed to enjoy one another's company immensely. Pierre made me promise to come back to attend the christening of his first child. I promised I would, and after many kisses and hugs, we departed at twelve to our respective sets of rooms.

Six came early, and I dressed in jeans and running shoes for the trip to Arabia. We gathered downstairs and boarded a Peugeot station wagon Regina rented at the airport.

We arrived at the hanger a little after seven-thirty. Pierre, Mike, and George were already standing there.

"You sleepyheads finally made it." That was, spoken by George.

"Take off is in twenty minutes, so let's get banging." I motioned at Pierre to step aboard this plane, where he handed me the phone with the passports and visas.

I asked him, "How did you get these visas to appear so authentic?

He answered, "That's because they are genuine. I have a friend at the Saudi Embassy. These are registered under the names on your passports. Jake, you have never been there, and I warn you, there is no such thing as being too cautious. I don't know if you used this French identity on purpose, but it will work out well for you as we French do a lot of business in these countries."

I said, "Yes, I'd thought of that, which brings me to another point. Do you have a landline, and can you have it manned by someone answers as 'Something Oil and Equipment?'"

He said, "Yes, I can, and this is the number with a business card. It will be staffed by someone around the clock. Be careful, my good friend. These adventures are for much younger men. I want to see you again when this is all over in my child's christening. You will be the godfather according to and in accord with my wife's desires. I believe she is quite smitten by you."

I waived Levi over and whispered against his ear to retrieve all our money. He returned after a moment, and I laid twenty-five thousand dollars in Pierre's lap.

Pierre said, "Jake, this is too much. The dinner wasn't that good?"

I said, "Pierre, I probably won't come back here on the way out. It's what you asked for and the price of the phone. I can always use the newest technology. The rest is a gift on behalf of us here for your baby. If I get clear from all this, I'll see you at your baby's christening."

He looked at me with seriousness in his eyes, then he said, "That will be wonderful, and I'll look forward to your visit with great anticipation. There is an instruction book in English and French, and you will have a very long flight. I'll let you take your leave. Please call me when you arrive as I may have some more news. When you call that number, ask for Mess. Carter and the girl will patch you through to my cell. Jake, I could not help but notice that both you and Monsieur Chapman are deeply involved in this girl's destiny. Is she this special and so highly valued by you, *Mon Ami*?"

I replied, "She's someone very close to Mr. Chapman, and finding her is of utmost importance to me. Any help you can give me through your contacts would be appreciated more than you can possibly understand."

Pierre said, "I realize that, and I will leave here and begin to phone my friends. I will see if these names you gave me mean anything to them. I will not express what your interest is, but I will attempt to secure their current whereabouts."

I said, "Yes, it would be great if you can accomplish this, my dearest friend."

Pierre said in a lower tone, "Please, speak nothing about it, and have a pleasant flight, my good friends. Monsieur Chapman, I know if this young lady is still alive, you will find her and the people who abducted her. I am elated it is not I who will engage either of your wraths in this matter."

That said, the doors were closed, with Pierre waving at us from outside of the hanger. Two minutes later, we were airborne. For where I expected, we could find the answers to Julia's whereabouts.

CHAPTER FIFTEEN

RIYADH

The flight to Riyadh was long and fatiguing, but I became familiar with the secure satellite phone that Pierre had given us. I also showed Gunny and Tony how to use it. We landed in Riyadh at about 7:30 p.m. and went through customs with our new passports and visas without a hitch. I saw Duke waiting on the other side against the glass in the customs area.

As I approached him, I held forth in a hushed tone, "I can't believe customs went that easy. Did you set us up with a hotel?"

He replied, "Did I ever. Wait until you get a look at your new accommodations."

We waited outside for the others, and in ten minutes, we were all sitting together in a massive limousine. Tony began to speak, and I hushed him. I said, "We are all tactical now," and he shook his head and said nothing until we arrived outside our hotel.

Duke grabbed me aside and said he had already checked me in. He and I proceeded straight to my room. I told the others my room number, and they agreed to meet me up there in an hour.

We walked into the elevator, and once inside, Duke told me he had a surprise waiting for me.

He used an electronic key provided by the Al-Faisalabad Hotel and led me into even a more extensive suite of rooms than the one in Vermont. I looked at him quizzically as he nodded toward the couch, where a tall Muslim man sat, drinking what seemed to be a sparkling wine.

He said, "Jake, let me introduce you to my dear friend Aamir Latif. Aamir, this is Jake Reynard, my partner."

I said, "*A Salomé Aleichem*, Mr. Latif."

He replied, "You are a friend as any friend of Major Garrity's is a friend to the entire Latif family."

Duke intervened, "Jake, before I left to retrieve you, Aamir was telling me he had some information on those guys, which will be confirmed by tomorrow morning."

Aamir said, "Yes, Mr. Jake, I have it on good authority that the two you are seeking are in a small village within Al-Hofuf. That is in the extreme eastern part of this country. It is located on the largest oasis in the world, Al-Hofuf."

"How far is that from here, Aamir?" I blurted out.

He replied, "By car, it's four hours to Al-Hofuf, but then to where they are, I really don't know. This oasis is enormous."

I asked Duke, "Have you filled Aamir in on what our mission will entail?"

Aamir interjected, "Yes, Mr. Jake, and if you want, I will hold their arms while you slit their unholy throats. I also have two daughters. Allah himself would never protect the doers of evil that would bring any harm to either of them."

I said, "Well, I'm glad you feel that way as we will need your communication skills and general knowledge of this area. We need to isolate these two and take them somewhere. We can hold them until we verify all the information they give us. Only after that will I personally introduce them to Allah. What time do you feel we can get the exact whereabouts of their current location? We also need someone on-site to watch over them until we get there."

Duke said, "We're way ahead of you on that. Aamir has some goodies and transportation for us."

I said, "That brings me to a point, Duke. On this leg of our journey, I need you to stay in Riyadh. I'll require you here in case there's a hitch. I'll need logistics and support, and your being at the embassy will help me with any secure communications wherever we end up."

Duke asked, "Why don't you leave Levi instead?"

I replied, "Simple. Levi doesn't have a diplomatic passport or the clout with the embassy that you have. Furthermore, this is your bag; it's what you do best. Julia needs to see a familiar face. He's the one to keep her calm if she's still alive. It's going to be tough enough to prevent Levi from killing all these people outright. I wish; I didn't need him there either.

"Aamir, do you have any people we can use to safeguard these people once we secure them? There will be plenty of money in this operation for everyone. You make the deals with reliable people, and we will pay them all very well."

He replied. "Jake, I think you need an isolated or abandoned house and supplies for a week or two."

I said, "That sounds about right, and small arms that are concealable for three and combat knives. Maybe you can arrange for some flashbangs and one or two phosphorus grenades. If you can get your hands on at least two small-caliber handguns with silencers, it would be even better."

Aamir said, "No problem, Mr. Jake, and I will arm myself accordingly."

I said, "Aamir, we deeply appreciate all you are doing for us. You will be paid handsomely, but I want you to return to your family when this is all over. I want no repercussions laid upon your door."

He replied, "Major McGarrity has told me you are a caring man. I can see this is true, Mr. Jake."

I thanked Aamir and set a time to be adjusted if necessary for the early hours of the next day. Aamir replied, "That meets with my approval, and I will acquire adequate transportation tomorrow. We will speak sometime in the morning. Good night, gentlemen. I want to be at home to eat dinner with my wife and daughters."

I said, "*Salomé Aleichem*, Aamir."

He returned, "*Va Salomé Aleichem*, Jake."

When he left, Duke started in on me about coming along on this mission. Finally, I had to get harsh with him about his role in this entire foray.

I said, "Listen, because I'm only going to say this one time. The entire purpose of us being here is to get Julia Alexander away from these people who stole her. No single person's thirst for action or own motives is going to jeopardize that mission. If we are hung up, arrested, or killed, you need to go through the embassy and act as if you don't even know us. However, you get Marines or Delta Forces to get her out and screw everything else. If we're alive, Charles can always buy us out of a jam with his money. Okay, partner, are we together as ordered on this or not?"

Duke said, "Okay, Jake, I'm with you. I'll do what you ask. Hell, I'm used to having sergeants telling me what to do. Remember, I was a private once."

With that, we both began laughing. I asked if I was allowed to drink in this hotel. Duke poured me a beer. The rest of my crew walked into my room with Levi leading the way.

I stood and said, "Listen up, just ask the bartender and our roving diplomat at large what your poison is, and he'll fix you up."

When they all had a drink, I bought them up to speed. The first thing Mike brought up was, "Why don't we use the plane to go to Al-Hofuf? They have a first-rate airport there."

I explained that the plane must remain here for the duration. We needed a helicopter for the next phase of this operation. Anyway, we need the flight to be ready for a rapid exodus from Arabia.

They agreed, and I looked at Mike and reminded him the aircrew was to stay very close to Duke. He would handle everything here while we were away on this operation.

They all took their leave after only one drink, and I asked Tony to stay.

I said, "Listen, we're okay so far, but in the next phase, we're going to need some serious support. I'm going to ask Levi to call General Wingate and see if he can muster us some with an assault chopper with two combat vets to fly it. If we need to start going over national borders, we're not going to benefit from visas. It's extremely risky, so we'd be better off going in with stealth and getting out rapidly."

Levi spoke up first, "I agree with you, Jake. The only thing we have is the element of surprise. We have to make the best application of that as possible."

"You know me, Think Tank. I'm wherever you need me," replied Tony.

Duke jumped in, "Think Tank? Was that your call sign in Recon?"

"Yes," I said. "Now ask this wise-ass what was Tony's handle?"

He then said, "All right, I'm game. Tony, what was your handle?"

Tony answered with a grin and said. "Street Trash, all right, we're even, but don't ever mention that to Regina, okay?"

I replied, "Not unless you really piss me off, I won't."

The morning gave me my first look at Riyadh. Its enormous buildings are located in the city center. It possessed a contemporary look, clean with many sizeable taller designer boxes standing like sentries against the light-blue sky with the sun shining down over the desert.

No sooner had my breakfast arrived when I heard a knock on the door, and in walked the entire crew.

I said before the group, "Gentlemen, we are now operational, and for future deniability. I want you pilots to do what the pilots of a business jet would do on a business trip. Please spread the story that you fly for a French oil equipment company with Canadian partners opening business negotiations with the Saudi government. Please don't get drunk, and for God's sake, stay celibate while you're here. When we leave, if we all leave together, it's going to be in one hell of a hurry. I want your ideas for a destination where we can get medical assistance rapidly."

They all went about thinking about this. I asked Levi to prepare to go to our embassy with Duke this morning and use their secure phone to call General Wingate. I would call Pierre and wait here for a word from Aamir.

Mike finally said, "Jake, I think if the old man can arrange it, we should fly straight to Landstuhl Medical Center outside Ramstein Airbase in Germany. We could avoid German customs with Duke's papers, and with the right landing clearances, we'd be in excellent shape. They handle all these boys from Iraq, Afghanistan and have the world's best equipment. However, we'd have to have those clearances in advance. We'd need to get Regina for her medical skills."

Levi spoke up, "You'll have all the clearances you need. All we'll have to do is radio ahead with our E.T.A."

I said, "Arrange to get Regina here as you said, but make it fast."

As Mike and George filed out of the room, Duke began to speak, but I hushed him until they were through the door. "Okay, Duke, fire away."

Duke said, "You'll need a master plan in place for when we locate these people."

I said, "I agree. That's why I want you to get Levi into the embassy with a secure line. It's time for him to make that call to General Wingate and get us some covert assistance. Gunny, we need the use of a Cayuse 500 or 600 MD helicopter with long-range capacity. I know they have them here with the Tenth Special Forces Group out of Eskan Village flying from Prince Sultan Military Air Base here in Riyadh. We need one well-informed pilot who can avoid radar and knows how to bullshit these people. We will also need three M4 Carbines with ammo and silencers and the grenades we spoke about before. I want to travel across light and move fast, so let's try to get this going by tomorrow morning. We need that chopper, and if they don't want to give us the weapons, that's tolerable. We can get them through Aamir. We can't get a chopper with that kind of range. It gives us multiple escape routes, and I want all the exits I can obtain."

Levi said, "I understand you, Jake. You'll get your helicopter no matter. As for the rest, I'll make sure we get everything you need."

Somehow, I knew we were running out of time. I wanted to call Charles, but I knew the Saudis monitored all phone calls, land, and cell, so I used the satellite phone, and he picked it up at home on the second ring. I told him where we were, and I hoped that in two or three days, we could deliver that call he'd been waiting for seven months.

He said, "Please be careful, son, and watch over Levi."

I then made my call to Pierre, and he was on the job already. In an improvised code we'd put together before in Marseille, he said he had the same information as Aamir. If we wanted to do business with our two friends from UAE, we would have to move east to Al-Hofuf. That's where we would have the best chance to deliberate with them about locations and shipping points for all our new product lines.

After that phone call, I felt genuine relief as we had two

completely independent sources confirming those two's whereabouts. I was waiting to hear from Aamir. I wasn't disappointed when at twelve o'clock he came walking through my hotel door.

I asked, "Aamir, I thought you would call first?"

Aamir answered, "No, Jake; I don't enjoy the prospect of a three-way conversation with the Saudi government. That's what we would have in this hotel. The good news, we have located those two in a border town called Salwa in the far eastern part of this country. It is many hours from here."

I replied, "Don't worry about that. We have people working on some air transportation as we speak."

We ordered lunch and began to wait. Duke and Levi had been gone for quite a while, but it was very early back home, so that could have been the holdup. At two, Tony finally came in and sat down bitching about waiting. I sympathized with him as I sat there, caught up in my own embittered mood.

I wondered how Julia's day was going. Did she have a premonition that help was on the way? Then for the first time in a long time, I began to pray. I prayed not for God to protect me but to allow her to be alive and help me defend my companions in the coming days. I said these prayers with a fervor I hadn't expressed since childhood. No sooner was I finished than the two people I wanted to see most in the world came through the doors with huge grins on their faces.

I blurted out, "Don't keep me in suspense. What the hell happened?"

Duke said, "Levi, I'll tell them as I'm the ranking officer in the room. You won't believe this. First, we were doing great with the general. We thought we were okay, but we needed one more clearance from the chief of staff at the White House. His first thought was to send in an A-team and let it be done with full military sanction for legal purposes. He was reminded that in that situation, the Saudis would have to be included. That means time, and it's time we don't have. I told them this was strictly a covert operation and had to be masked as a training mission so that Saudi air command wouldn't go nuts about us flying all over the place.

"Then they had us wait for about an hour while they went

back and forth. I guess the president got involved at some point and told Wingate to do whatever he must, to get Julia out, but to protect their collective asses legally.

Now comes the good part. I mentioned in going over our respective bios that we were all still members of the inactive reserve. He's just signed four orders, and we are all back on active duty for the duration of Operation Lost Child. You, my friend, have been recalled and commissioned as a first lieutenant in our Corps with complete tactical control over this entire operation.

We will have those orders delivered here within the hour with desert utilities and boots. We have two Special Forces individuals assigned to us with our weapons. I will have logistical command as the ranking officer.

I will act as a liaison to General Wingate on this operation. It's now Staff Sergeant Camorato, Tony! There will be a chopper in at first light. The Special Forces people will bring all the gear we need. There will also be an entire A-team on standby if we need them."

I replied, "You guys have certainly had an interesting day.

I have mixed feelings about becoming an officer and being placed on active duty. Nevertheless, you have to take the good with the bad. Gunny, did you get a promotion out of this deal?"

Levi said, "Hell no. I told the general it would screw up all my retirement checks, and I've had enough problems with that crap. Those damn office pages haven't a clue about what they're doing in payroll."

Tony said, "So, Lieutenant, what's our next move besides moving on to Al-Hofuf?"

I said, "We're not going to Al-Hofuf, but to a border town named Salwa on the extreme eastern edge of Arabia. It makes sense that they would live there. It shares a border with Qatar and is close to the United Arab Emirates. After we pick out a landing zone, Aamir and I will go to this village and find those people. I intend to lure them into the desert with the promise of being able to deliver Stinger missiles at a reasonable price. Otherwise, we'll just snatch them depending on what their security is like."

"That sounds excellent, LT," said Tony.

I didn't correct him because I felt that the general had this in mind, so we would all operate better if we acted within a military mindset. I would run this team that way so everyone would respond to me as Marines.

I said, "I spoke to Pierre, and he confirmed that first location Aamir has given us, but this is new Intel, and I think we should respect it. Gunny, I believe you have the money, and I'd like you to give our friend Aamir ten thousand dollars. And, Aamir, you will have to explain a two- or three-day absence from your family. If we are successful, another forty thousand dollars is coming to you. We will try not to put you in harm's way. Your services will be strict of an intelligent nature, helping us locate our targets and interpret them. I hope that compensation is adequate. As to your people, we'll compensate them on-site."

Aamir said, "Jake, the money is more than enough by tenfold. I have a family to support, which is not easy here. I want you to know I am absolutely ready to fight by your side if required."

I replied, "I appreciate that, my friend, but as you said, you have a family, and the men in this room have no one. We are better suited to the risks involved. We would like to meet you at a designated area that Gunny will give you at five a.m. if that's all right with you."

Aamir said, "I will be there on time, my friends." He then proceeded to the dining room with the Gunny, where a map was arranged.

After they got through and Aamir left, the rest of us got down to business. We still had the problem of where to stash these two after finding them and extracting the information we need.

I said, "I think we're going to have to improvise some of this along the way, and I think Duke; you should move to the embassy for the duration. We need to have you in a place where we can reach you that has secure communications. We trained these Saudi Special Ops people. They're pretty good, especially on their own turf, so we don't want them chasing us."

Duke agreed and said he wanted to eat a final meal with us, then he'd close out his room and make his move to the embassy. Levi had a number where he could be reached, and we made plans to meet for what might be our last dinner in one of the more elegant restaurants downtown.

At dinner, we were all subdued, and unusually, we all ordered the same thing. We all had large steaks with baked potatoes and salads and many dressings. We ate battle food with no local fare, only proper old American combat nourishment.

I remember eating this type of food before every mission. I ever went on in the Corps when it was available. There was a foreboding sense of being under orders again. On the one hand, it made it feel legal and correct, but I wasn't too keen on having the very same people in D.C. who botched this giving me orders. I made up my mind there and then. We would go to radio silence when the operation began. I knew we would kill some people before this was over, and being back in the Corps, even though it was only on paper, made it feel proper and correct. However, I wasn't about to be second-guessed by some idiot behind a desk in D.C...

I know to an ordinary citizen. It seems like twisted logic, but to me, the ingrained esprit that every Marine feels is always there. That's why whenever two of us meet, the first thing we say is "Semper Fi." There is a brotherhood felt by everyone who's served in our Corps. Maybe, it's because we're the oldest service or the most minor service or that common tearing down and rebuilding we endured from the beginning. However, it is there, nonetheless. It's a brotherhood and a unique one at that.

That was why Duke was suffering in his non-combatant role. He had to send us off while staying behind with us on the evening of this mission.

Duke spoke. "I know; all of you men are sober and upright Marines, but in this dry country, I have secured a bottle of scotch, which is extremely hard to come by. It's installed in Jake's room as we sit here. I know; all hard-chargers need some sack time, but in the evening before a battle, it's the prerogative of the officer in charge to buy a drink for his men. So, let us adjourn to our designated joint NCO-Officers Club and toast to your success tomorrow."

That spoken, we all went up to my room, where Duke poured us each a stiff shot. We drank to the Corps and to General Wingate and to finding Julia for Levi and Charles. It was the first hard liquor; I'd imbibed in three years.

They all filed out of my room at No one was high except for the anticipation of the morning and our mission.

I sat there for a time worrying about getting these guys back alive. Say what you want, but it was my responsibility, and I was feeling insecure for the first time in a long time. I knew how to breach a secure position, but not without casualties. It weighed upon my mind until I drifted into a restless sleep.

Chapter Sixteen
Jumping Off

We were standing on the tarmac at Prince Sultan Military Air Base at a remote section of the field. We were only given a cursory look at the front gate, and our papers were barely glanced at. Someone with a lot of authority greased the skids for us.

The helicopter came in from the north at about 5:35 a.m., an MD 600, currently the choice of Special Forces and Seals. When it landed, a lanky, personable captain came over to us and asked for the officer in charge. I stood forward and informed him I was that man, and for this mission, he was to address me as Jake, and I introduced him to Levi, Tony, and Mohamed.

He grinned at me and said, "Yes, sir, and my name, is Mick,

and that's Clem on the guns. I told my guys to put their civvies in the small gripsacks provided. The captain came in with his gunner and handed us weapons, and I told everyone to do a weapon's check. I asked about the special ordinance I'd requested and was told it was all aboard. I began to explain what I thought they should know when the captain halted me mid-sentence.

Mick said, "Sir, with all due respect, we know this is a snatch and grab. We have to go to God knows where, and you're the boss on this mission. We will command the aircraft. Sir, we are Tenth Special Forces, First Battalion, and we aren't even here.

"We were told you might have casualties, and we have a stretcher, capacity for two, and room for six-plus ourselves in the bird. This operation never happened, and we are on a routine training mission in the eastern desert of this country. It's a joint operation between the Army and Marine Corps. Those are our orders, and I expect they meet with your approval. There's gossip at headquarters is that you guys are Force Recon Marines, and Clem and I want you to know despite that, if it gets hot, you'll see two Army guys kicking ass and taking names beside you."

I said, "All right, now that we have the dance card straight. Let's attempt to find a quiet place to put this bird down near the village of Salwa."

Mick said, "Already ahead of you on that one, sir. We have a route and a landing zone."

As we jumped aboard the chopper, I spoke a silent prayer for Julia to hold on as we'd be there soon.

We lifted off. The Gunny gave me the biggest smile I'd ever seen on his face and turned his enormous thumb up.

After seeing the Gunny, Tony lifted his arm up and shouted, "Ooo-Rah!" I quickly returned. Aamir looked at us all like we were all crazy, and from his point of view, I guess we were. The anticipation of taking action after waiting and being patient was eating at us. It was the third week of March, and a little more than a month ago, I had begun my search, but it had seemed like a lifetime ago. I thought to myself if I would see the face in that photo, which started me on this long journey. I had a premonition of impending danger for all of us. Two and a half hours later, we landed in an isolated spot outside the village of Salwa. We had set down a little south of town, at the edge of the high Arabian Desert, and Mick shut down the engines before noon. The temperature was blistering, and I reminded everyone not to get dehydrated. I said. "Take your salt pills and drink plenty of water."

We were there ten minutes when an old Land Rover came driving up the dirt road next to where we stood. A short, heavyset Arab got out and walked up to Aamir, and they embraced. When the ritual hellos were completed, Aamir came to me and introduced his friend.

Aamir said, "Jake, this is my dearest friend Hassan, and we will go with him to his home. Tonight we will take these two who have plagued your life as we already have their house under surveillance by another colleague of ours. I think the captain should take his machine and put it three miles directly east of here, near the great inland sea. He and his helicopter can claim a mechanical problem if someone comes to discover them. There is an oasis and spring, but few people visit it as sometimes the spring brings forth salt. They can bathe there, as it is common to view American soldiers swimming in the strangest places. Saudis do not go swimming, especially in wadi's or springs."

I turned to Mick as he had overheard the entire conversation, and he said. "We need time within twenty minutes to pick you up."

I looked at Aamir, and he informed us that we should think in terms of two or three in the morning, or we could drive to the spring. That would be more silent during those late hours when we intended to make the snatch. The sound of a helicopter would wake up everyone in the village where these events would take place.

I told Mick I agreed and asked for his two handguns and three combat knives. He cocked his head for me to follow him to the bird and said to Clem, "Give Jake the two silenced Ruger, .22 L.R.s, and the three combat knives we've been transporting."

He handed me the suppressed pistols and said, "Do you need help with these?"

I smiled. "No, I don't think so."

He said, "Force Recon, I knew it. Either that or you guys are Seals. Anyway, if you've handled these before, you've just reduced our anxiety level. We get real nervous dealing with amateurs, if you know what I mean."

I said, "Let's just leave it at the fact that we've been on this particular dance floor before. I think you'll both survive this operation."

I waved them off the desert floor as they fired up the bird and gave us a salute.

I said, "All right, let's get this show on the road."

We spent the balance of the day drinking cooled tea and trying not to get sick from the desert heat. We weren't acclimatized, and I was fearful that it might hurt us if we weren't careful. We had polled a shade screen that Mick left us, and it provided some cover from the relentless desert sun.

As the sun went down, it began to cool dramatically. I remembered that about the desert. Aamir received a call about eleven o'clock and was on and off the cell phone in a moment.

He said, "Your kidnappers of this woman are sleeping, and may; Allah's revenge be upon them."

That was all said with zeal, I hadn't anticipated.

I replied; I hope they hadn't felt they had sold out of the actual teachings of Allah."

When we were done, I'll be damned if we didn't look like something that had swept out from the desert night. Of course, the Gunny still looked like a small mountain, but somehow they had found a black Abaya that fit him.

At 1:00 a.m., we moved outside the shade tent and began walking in a gang-like manner. We were tightly bound close together the way the Arabs do. We walked for about ten minutes and came upon an intersection where the houses were still made of the dried mud, which typified these smaller villages. Aamir whispered for us to wait, and he would return in a moment. In a matter of minutes, he returned with another man who spoke with him in Arabic.

Aamir said, "My friend does not speak English, but he gave me the layout of the house as he entered it yesterday when our enemies were out doing whatever they do. He thought it important to know the exact whereabouts of everything in the household."

As his companion drew me a rough diagram in the dirt, it became apparent that the house was composed of three rooms with sleeping quarters located in the rear of the house. I told Aamir that someone could retrieve the Range Rover as it was too far to carry these guys after an abduction. He agreed and told his friend in Arabic to get the truck and pull it up to the house's front door in precisely five minutes.

We waited five minutes, and I said to Tony, "You go in the front, and the Gunny and Aamir will stand watch on the corners while I move in on through the rear. We have to move at the exact same time. We don't know if they have arms at this house, so, Aamir, your station is at the front corner, and Gunny will take the rear. When I give the signal, Tony, you do it like we've done it a hundred times before, quick, hard, and put them to sleep without killing them. Don't take any chances as we only need one of them breathing."

We moved out to our point of entry. I listened outside

the door, and I could hear snoring. I tested the handle and couldn't believe my luck when it began to open. These guys were asleep with no security. I guess they thought, in their country and their own village, who would dare break into their house? I went and whispered to Gunny, "Tell Tony to try the door as it might be unlocked."

He went around the house and came back a few moments later.

Levi said, "Jake, it is unlocked. Do you believe these dumb sons of bitches?"

I said, "When I lower my arm, give Tony the sign, and we will enter together. Give us a moment and then follow us inside."

I lowered my arm, and instead of smashing in, I moved slowly through the door, and these people didn't stir. They both lay there side by side as Tony came through the other door. I motioned with my hands towards the one closest to me, withdrew my Kabar, and used the heavy side of the handle to bop scarface in the head. He stopped snoring and folded up like a tent. Tony followed my lead and more comfortable than getting a tick off a dog; we had our two kidnappers sound asleep and manageable.

About three minutes later, the truck pulled up to the front door coasting the last half block. We lifted the two inert bodies and put them in the rear of the car. Tony sat close to them as the guard, and I sat alongside Aamir in the driver's seat. We were about to pull away when Gunny jumped out and put some money into the hands of our lookout.

He got back in, and we drove slowly away from the scene of our capture. My heart was racing as I had expected it to be more difficult than it had. I'd rest a lot easier when we were on the chopper and headed deeper into the desert.

We arrived at our rendezvous at two-twenty, and Mick and Clem were waiting for us as promised.

I jumped out of the truck and walked over to them. Mick asked, "How'd it go? Did you secure the two rag heads?""

I said, "Yes, we did. Those two both asleep in the truck as we speak."

Mick said, "I think we should get these bastards on board, restrain them, and get the hell out of here."

Mick grabbed some plastic ties and went to the truck, where he bound their hands behind their back, and he and Gunny took the first guy on board the aircraft. Tony brought the second one, Fahd, and put him in as well. Aamir told me that arrangements had been made to pick up the truck in the next hour, but if we needed it, we could always call.

I told him I thought we would be better off getting out of this area entirely as we don't know if these two have friends who might miss them. He agreed and told me of a small Wadi with little or no water that was very unfrequented but accessible by air not more than ten or fifteen minutes away.

I let him tell Mickey where we were going. I went back and wiped down the truck for any signs of our presence. As we were taking off, my guy with the scar began to come out of his state of unconsciousness.

Thank God, I thought. When you tap someone on the head, you can be easily overdue for it, and I was out of practice. Actually, I should have brought a sap and tapped him with it.

He began to yell, but it was impossible to hear him above the engines. Besides, it was better to let him remain anxious about his fate. Tony began motioning to throw him out, and I made it as if it was not the proper time. This was a game; we often played it with prisoners. I knew it hadn't lost its effect. Tony grabbed the guy as if to toss him, and I unbuckled and stood over him to remove his hands from the man.

The guy began kissing my hands.

He had no idea, what was in store for him, but Tony made it clear he wanted to kill him? We glided down next to the Wadi, and it was a pitch-black landing.

I grabbed him, and we all disembarked into the moonlit desert night. I could see many miles in each direction, and I agreed with Aamir. This was a perfect spot for an interrogation.

Clem; shut down the bird, and suddenly, it was eerily quiet on the desert floor. I removed a flashlight from my belt and took out the picture of Julia I carried under my shirt. I pulled off the Arab clothing and stood in US Marine Corps camouflage gear. By now, they both recovered enough to tremble, as I did my little unmasking.

I spoke to both. "Listen carefully because I know you both

understand English quite well, and we have flown a long distance to meet with you. You have made a terrible mistake, but we don't think you knew any better in your defense. You took a woman from Burlington, Vermont, and the first thing you must tell us is, to your knowledge, is she still alive, and do you know the current whereabouts of her or her body?"

The one called Fahd spoke first. "Sir, as of two days ago, she was very much alive."

I shined the light on the photo and asked, "Is this the woman you are speaking about?"

"Yes, that is her, but she is not with us, Mr. Soldier. She is in Qatar."

With the statement that she was still alive, I heard Gunny breathe in deeply, and I felt a sense of overwhelming relief pour over me as well.

I yelled, "Where in Qatar is she? Who has her, and what is their purpose with her?"

He said, "She is the property of a wealthy man named Abayyah Umm Said; who has a huge house filled with many women from throughout the world? He has unique tastes in women and pays dearly for his pleasures. He is very wealthy from his oil business. However, his tastes in women turn more into these western types. His house is very isolated on the other side of the inland sea. It is guarded by a much larger force; than you have here. Perhaps, you will let us make amends by negotiating with this man for her release. I think he would do that for a price, as she has already tried and failed to kill herself once. For a mere woman, she is having the most difficult time adapting to her circumstances."

I put my trembling hands down by my side and said, "Yes, I know what you mean. Our American women are difficult, but her father wants her back anyway. You could be of great service to me if you lead us to an area where we can land and gain access to this man's house."

He said, "How will we all get across the border? I am certain he will kill us if we betray him!"

I said, "It is not him you must worry about. Be sure of one thing: we think you made a simple error in judgment, but if you lead us into a trap or try in any way to betray us. We will kill you first, and it will be with the maximum amount of pain possible."

He asked, "What is to ensure that you will not kill us anyway?"

I said, "I am going to leave your friend behind with a fellow countryman of yours, and if you guide us and assist us with the layout of the rooms, we will have no reason to kill either one of you. The man who has her must die. So, at worst, you have lost a customer. You need not worry about his wraith as he will be with Allah in paradise."

He said, "Why must he die? He has done nothing to you. It was that American who betrayed her."

I asked, "The American? Which American is that?"

He said, "He was the professor, and he said she required a true lesson in humility. In all fairness, he did think we would return her after a suitable time had passed. He came up with the idea to grab her on this running thing your women do in the mornings. We, like you, had a mission from our Sultan, and we misled him somewhat in our plans."

I said, "Because it's his fate, and the father of this woman is a significant man. His honor demands this abuser of his daughter must die. Who is this American that you speak of, and how did he assist you? This agreement we have is for a restoration of honor to her family. This Sultan must pay with his life."

He chewed on that a moment, and I went to Mick and started to show him something on the map as I looked over at them both talking.

I asked, "Mick, do you think we can avoid radar and get over this sea without being seen?"

He said, "No problem. We can fly this baby fifty feet off the water for about ninety percent of the trip. We fly parallel to the border on training missions over this inland sea all the time."

Mick said, "There's a large village called Umm Said that's east of our destination, according to this guy. If you want my advice, I think we should cut the other cock sucker a little, so this guy will have something to hang on to more than your word. I mean, then he'll know you're genuine. These guys usually need a demonstration of force. If the tables were turned, they would have removed your head by now."

I thought about that for a moment and knew he was correct.

I shouted, "Aamir, you are going to stay with our friend Azza Mazin Hanna? When I call you, have your friends pick that one up and take him to a hospital."

I made sure they both heard me. I went over quickly and slowly stuck my Kabar in Azza's gut, very close to the liver on the right side. He looked at the blood flowing out between his fingers and fainted, dead away. It was dark red, so I knew right away that I'd cut him too close to the liver itself.

"Why did you do that?" the other one shrieked.

I explained, "Put on a pressure bandage, Tony. Now, you know that if we are not back in ten hours, your friend will die."

He asked, "How do you know he will last that long?"

I explained, "Because I did not penetrate his liver, and he can only bleed out, which will take him, at the least, half of an entire day. I answered your question now, or would you like me to demonstrate this ability of mine on you as well?"

The Gunny motioned me to one side and said, "I guess the fact that we are activated makes this seem correct and proper. I just hope you're going to kill both of these bastards before we leave this country?

"Yes, Gunny, that's precisely what I intend to do. You know, I think it's a risk, but we should use the satellite phone and tell Charles we are sure she's alive.

"Hey, Mick, do you have any other secure type of communication gear on this rig? This satellite phone of ours isn't the best, and I want to call my mom. I forgot to tell her I wouldn't be home for dinner."

He just looked at me and began to laugh. "Sure, Jake. We got everything you want, including some pretty civilized field chow."

I said, "All kidding aside, the Gunny needs to make a secure call to the States."

"You just give me the number, and I'll fix him up."

Levi traipsed over to the chopper, and Tony came walking towards me. He knew what I was thinking before; I said it. "He'll be all right. Where is he going to run? Besides, I think he may have crapped his pants."

I said, "If he continues to stink, take him to the Wadi and make him clean up. I don't want to smell him all the way over the inland sea. By the way, this is a one-way trip for him, no matter what I said. I'll do the deed when the time comes, but he might fall out of the Hilo after opening up. Did you hear him speak about this Peter guy and how he betrayed Julia?"

Tony said, "Yeah, I did, but what are you going to do about him with no witnesses?"

I said, "I don't know, but he'll pay for his treachery in this."

Tony said, "You know, Regina would never forgive me if I didn't kill one of these bastards. The last thing she said was, 'If you love me even a little, and you find the two mother fuckers that did this, "You better come back with their blood on your hands." I'm telling you, Jake, that girl is hardcore."

I asked, "She really said that to you?"

Tony said, "I kid you not, but don't tell her I told you."

I said, "That's a deal, and you must never share this knowledge regarding Peter with Julia."

Scarface looked after his friend, unconscious on the desert floor, when Gunny came over. He said, "I just talked to a real happy man. Lord, you'd think somebody handed him the keys to heaven. Of course, he wanted to call the Pentagon and have the entire second Marine division move in, but I got him to calm down. I told him you had the situation well in hand. I did give him the grids and told him if he didn't hear from us in forty-eight hours, he's to call these Army boys in Arabia and send in two A-teams to get us out."

"He was choked up, and he said to tell you to be careful. He couldn't stand the loss of three people. He cared so much about it. Jake, I never heard that old man speaks this way about anyone, and it was straight from his heart."

I said, "That view goes both ways. I feel strongly about Charles. I could never let him down in any way."

Levi asked, "What are we waiting for?"

I whispered, "Mick, can you come here a moment?"

Mick replied, "What can I do for you, partner?"

I asked, "How long do you figure for this flight, and what about our fuel situation? I mean, can we get back to Riyadh on the fuel you have left?"

Mick replied, "The answer to your first question is about two hours, depending on their radar. Our radar tells us about their stuff along the border. Their guys don't fly at night, especially where we are going, so we shouldn't have a problem. As far as the fuel goes, we have enough fuel to spare, and we will arrive on target at those bewitching hours before daybreak. That makes perfect timing in my book."

I said, "Good. Now here's the plan. Before we take off, we call Duke at the embassy and tell him where we are and our flight plan. He's to have our plane with Mike and George aboard ready to go between six and eight tomorrow morning at Prince Sultan. They can give us the exact coordinates so you can put us down right next to the hanger. Mick, we're going to need some of those backup choppers to free all the daughters. I don't care where they're from or who they are. Everyone in this place dies, and all those women get their freedom back. If your boss has a problem with that, you can have him call the chief of staff in DC. Our guy will pick up the tab on all of those women.

"Now, we have to time this deal, so we get within one or two clicks of that house. Then Tony and I will do a two-man recon of the house. When we're done scoping it out, we will take the outside sentries. We will return to you guys and begin our penetration before dawn when we hope they'll all be asleep. First, we take out their communications, and then we take as many of the outside guards as are left before we go to guns. Make no mistake, they all have to die, but we have to be careful as there are women, and I don't want any of them to be hurt. Are there any questions from you guys?"

Everyone looked at me, and no one said a word. "Good, how about we get something to eat? Tony, my friend, you're the guy who's the chef in the field."

I waived Aamir over. "Aamir, when we leave, we won't be back, and this guy is going to be in a lot of pain when he wakes up."

Aamir said, "Say, no more, my friend. When you leave and are out of sight, I will send him on to Allah."

I said, "Believe me, Aamir, you'll be doing him a great favor as that belly cut is the worst kind of pain. Arrangements will be made to compensate you for all your help after we get out of here."

We all ate what chow we could, which wasn't much, and waited for further darkness. The desert winds started to kick up a little, and aside from the sand, it gave us relief from the relentless heat during the day. I sensed a feeling of déjà-vu like the time Tony and I were in the mountains of Afghanistan, and we knew we were in a place where the enemy had all the advantages. It's hard to find cover and concealment in a desert or on the side of a bare mountain.

That particular feeling of vulnerability had proceeded with my taking a round from a sniper, and had I not moved, it wouldn't have just been my leg but my head. I had that same feeling now, but I knew when night came, I'd be more in my element, and it would level the playing field. I always felt safe at night; it's a Recon Marine's most significant friend.

Chapter Seventeen
Into the Night

After 12:00 a.m., we took off. The first part of this was the pilot's job, and these guys were the best. I sat next to Gunny and said, "Gunny, I want you on the outside, and I'll do the penetration with Tony. We go back a long way with this kind of stuff. I almost sense in advance in a building which way he will go, where, and when he does. It goes back to when we discovered he's right-handed, and I'm lefty. Once I locate Julia and secure her safe exit, I'll hand her off to you to take in the helicopter."

Levi said, "All right, Jake, I know what I'm here for, and I know my age and its limitations."

We'd been flying in a circular pattern, working our very slightly south now for over an hour. We were over the inland sea, skimming across the top of the water. It was disconcerting to being this close to all that water as one slip of wind or drop in power, and we'd hit that water hard.

We were moving further south now and going faster when Mick came over the headphones and said. "We will be at our initial LZ in ten minutes; everybody, get locked, loaded, and put them on safe."

Ten minutes later, we landed on a moonlit desert night next to a large dune. As I jumped off, they shut down the engines. I was talking to Fahd and Tony, and we all got the same impression. We were less than one click from the house. Mick joined us as Fahd was drawing us a picture in the sand. The layout of the house and compound was built around a central courtyard with a natural spring at its center. The harem was located at the right rear on the lower floor inside the house. The outside walls were scalable, but I didn't know if our Special Forces guys had bought any grappling hooks or ropes.

Mick said, "We have the lines and grappling hooks, but we first have to work out a plan of penetration after we get a closer look-see. I'd like to go with Tony, so you, Gunny, and

Clem can stay with the bird, if that's all right with you, Jake?"

I said, "Yes, I guess your eyes are as good as mine for a small recon like this. Listen, try to find something we can use as a diversion, and see if we can penetrate the women's quarters directly. I really don't want to go through that front door. Tony, manacle our chum here to the Hilo skid. I don't want him wandering off while you're out playing."

"You got it, LT," Tony replied.

I said, "Guys, on the chance we are discovered, fire two rounds and the cavalry will come running. Which reminds me, in the extreme, do we have any high-power weapons onboard?"

Clem said, "Jay, we have an electric mini-gun that will tear apart a concrete house like a power hammer with a chisel."

I said. "Let's hope we don't need it, but it's nice to know you have it if things get dangerous. The most crucial thing is to try to get a headcount of the personnel on the inside and exterior of this house. When we move out, no one gets is left behind alive, or we have failed in this mission."

Within moments, they gathered up the gear; they needed and were on their way. Now came the hard part: the wait. I looked at Gunny and could see he was feeling the same way I was.

"I hate this part of the operation when you have to wait for intelligence."

The Gunny looked down at me. "I hate it too. That's why we did all that hurry-up-and-wait crap in basic training, remember?"

I replied, "Now that you mention it, all we did, was hurry up and wait. Do you think that was a dress rehearsal for this kind of mission?"

Levi said, "Son, I was in the infantry, and not some fancy boy who jumps out of airplanes. All we ever did was some walking, wait, and do some shooting."

I said, "We fancy Recon operators went out, and grabbed the finest intelligence available, so you guys would know what the hell you were walking into. We were more like thieves than soldiers because we did our job with the objective of not being seen or caught."

Levi said, "I just hope and pray my little girl is okay. Jake, are you a religious man?"

I replied, "Yes; in my own way, I am, Gunny. Do you want to pray together?"

Levi spoke, "Yes. Dear, Heavenly Father, please protect us as we prepare for battle. Grant your blessings in this hour of need. Let us perform to your standards on this mission." At that point, Clem came over and bowed his head while putting his hand on mine.

The Gunny went on, "Protect those we have come to liberate, and grant us your divine intervention for their safety. For evil has been done in your name, and if you allow us, we will act as your hammers of justice. We know how you expect your soldiers to act. We will send these evildoers on to you, and you shall mete out the justice that is yours and yours alone to deliver. We implore you to protect us from this wickedness and allow us victory in Jesus Christ's name. Amen."

Clem was the first to speak. "Gunny, I think that's the best battle prayer I've ever heard. It makes this ole Tennessee's boy's heart feels good to know you're all God-fearing men."

Levi said, "Son, I'm a deacon of my church, and I know we will all return safely. God, in His infinite wisdom, has sent this young David to lead us into battle and bring all our people home."

I said, "Thanks for your faith in us, Gunny, and I am reminded; you expressed *people*. Clem, how many extra people can we get in this bird? We may have two or three American girls, and who knows what else, but everyone gets to go home from this evil place."

Clem spoke, "Well, we already kind of thought of that and have birds standing by in Prince Sultan Air Base, but Mick had them move two other birds to Salwa Air Base, so we can get those birds here inside of ten minutes. There'll be no need for going covert with them. They'll come in and go on back to Sultan."

I said, "I hate to say it, but you guys think of everything. I guess my mission planning is a little rusty."

Clem said, "Well, our outfit, the First Battalion, Tenth Special Force Group, is on permanent station at Panzer Kaserne in Stuttgart, Germany. When you want to come on over, we'll catch you up as we have some of the best people for this particular line of work. Under this new program in place, all services that are Special Ops can train together. We've already had some Force Recon guys come through our program, and they were some pretty good old boys."

I added, "That's really good to hear because, in times of peace, Marines get the short straw in training and equipment. I always held the idea that was because they thought we were expendable."

In all this time, two hours passed, and finally, Tony and Mick came back over a dune. We all huddled. While Tony drank some water, Mick began to fill us in. "These guys are standing guard in the middle of nowhere on posts outside, and all of them were sound asleep. Do you believe that I got within a meter of the two-front guards, and I actually heard them snoring? Here's the layout. We only saw those two on the outside and no roof guard, one master line for electricity coming in, and no phone lines. They must all use cell phones, but I can't see a tower anywhere, but they may have a satellite dish on the roof. We should assign one person to locate and destroy the phone lines. I think we should run our assault from the roof after taking out these two-front guards and all go in together. It's too dark to synchronize a climb from different directions. We're always taught to keep our firepower balanced. It's an easy twenty minutes there and back. Since we will be wired as we clean out the house, we can tell Clem to bring up the other birds. Does that meet with your approval, Jake?"

I said, "Yes. Clem was telling me you have two birds ready to go in Salwa. I think you should tell them to begin to move up. I don't care where these other women are from. We're taking everyone's home with us."

Mick looked at his partner and said, "He's the head man, so get a third and fourth bird going direct to this target out of Salwa. There's a window at the rear where you can view the women in their quarters. It's barred, but I count at least thirty women there."

I asked, "Do either one of you; guys speak this lingo?"

Mick answered, "We both do."

I said, "Well, who wants to be the third man? I want gunny outside to retrieve our special package since he's the only one she'll recognize."

"Well," Mick jumped in, "do I get to say, 'US Marines in the house?"

Tony said, "Yup, that's exactly how we announce ourselves. Is there a problem with that? I mean, we do want to strike fear into their black hearts while giving the hostages peace of mind, right?"

Mick asked, "I've always wanted to be a Marine for a day. Does it mean I get to go to your fancy birthday party?"

The Gunny spoke up, "Son, you two not only get to go to the big party in DC, but if you're still over here, I'll have a private jet pick you up, and it will be stacked with more champagnes than there is in the entire city of Reims, France."

Mick said, "Sounds like a good deal. I want you, rag-head bastards down on the floor. US Marines are in the house! How's that?"

"Good enough," I said. "Now, let's saddle up and move on down the road."

I was putting on my communication gear when Tony said. "This guy is good. You should have seen the way he snooped these two-front guards. I mean, he got balls."

I said. "These boys are both pretty tough, and I'm glad we have them with us. They thought this out better than we did. I think when this is over, you and Duke and I should get some up-to-date training. Even their gear is distinctive."

"Well," Tony said, "at least we're going to make a pile of money out of this whole deal. I heard from Regina; the old man offered a million just for information?"

I said, "Tony, I'm sorry, but I thought you realized when we were inducted back into the Corps. We can't take any payment from civilians for a sanctioned rescue. It's a matter of military law. You're still on our payroll as promised, but there'll be no bonuses on this one."

Tony said, "You mean; we are getting nothing, nada, for being in this sand-hole."

I said, "You know; you're right. You didn't sign up for any of this. You stay with the chopper, and we can do all this with two people."

Tony said, "Fuck you, Lieutenant, sir. Where you go, I go. I didn't think of the official part of this and being reinstated back into the Corps."

I said, "Listen if it's any consolation, Duke, and I intend to give you some big relocation money for joining us in this company. It will cover your support until you're on your feet and a nice apartment, and it's a wonderful place to live. That's it for now, so let's move out."

I took the point with Mick, and we moved out at a brisk pace toward our objective. I knew they all wanted this over, but I cautioned myself internally to take it slow and easy. No mistakes, I want to get this entire group of women back to their loved ones in one piece.

We came to the slight rise that looked down upon the house, and I called Tony forward. "Tony," I said, in a whisper through our headgear, and that was disconcerting because it sounded so loud in my ear.

Mick was smiling at me and pointing at the earpiece volume control on the side.

I said, "Tony, as Mick and I move down to take out the front two, you circle the perimeter and make sure no one else is on the other side that might have been overlooked."

He raised his thumb, and we all began a slow crawl down the slope. I told Gunny to remain in place as support until we took out these two guards and then move on down to the front door.

Mick and I were now within two meters when one of the guards suddenly turned. Instinct set in, and we both flattened out on the desert floor. A moment later, we looked up and saw he was still sleeping and had only adjusted his body. Mick stood up on the left, and I took a position on the right. He motioned at his pistol than his knife. I answered by removing my knife and made the sign for a throat cut.

I grabbed my man and covered his mouth as I started that razor-like blade on its trajectory across his throat. I cut in deep so I'd get no gurgle or movement. He was at my feet dead, in a moment from no blood entering his brain. Nothing new there, and I cringed at the thought of how easily I could go about this business of killing after all these years.

Tony came around the other side of the building at that exact moment. We were dragging these two guys to the side with him saying, "Good idea. I did a walk around, and there was one in the back. I missed him the first time out."

I asked, "Did you take care of him? Is he sleeping with Allah?"

Tony, ever the clown, said, "He sleeps with the sand fishes now!"

That was all I needed to start laughing. Then Mickey put it best, "Tony, I have to say it. You are one crazy son of a bitch."

I said, "Let's try the grappling line directly over the women's quarters."

Their agreement came by moving off in that direction, and I said into the mouthpiece, "Gunny, can you read me?"

He answered in the affirmative, and I said. "Move on down and try to put on one of these guy's sets of clothes and act like you're standing guard in case someone comes to relieve any of these three."

He said, "You got it, Jake. If they do, I'll send them on to Allah?'

I said, "That's it, big guy, show no mercy."

Mick got a secure purchase with the grappling hook after the second try, and he ascended first. He was out of sight for a minute and then came back to the side and motioned us upward. I went next, with Tony following. At the top, I looked in all directions and could see only one road, a coarse dirt one coming, to the house and going out. Mick led the way to a small raised door in the roof. He took out a burglar's pick and began to work on the lock.

I whispered, "My lord, 'Be prepared' must be your motto as well."

He said, "Not as classic as Semper Fi, but we like it well enough."

I said, "All right, you two, listen up. I'm going down first after Tony cut's those lines to the satellite dish, and as soon as I get my bearings, Tony follows, with you taking up as a rearguard,

Mick."

They nodded, sensing I was no longer in the mood for banter. Suddenly, Mick had it open, and there was a narrow set of stairs leading down to a moonlit landing below. I made my way down, which was difficult with all the gear I was hauling along with the carbine. At the foot of the stairs, I found myself on a full gallery that went around the entire second floor. No visible guards, but we all knew there would be more that would have to be dispatched. I pointed in two directions and motioned Mick to stay in place here.

I whispered, "Tony, you know what to do. Let's clear them out one by one as quietly as possible."

I took out the silenced Ruger .22, moved to the first room, and tried the door. It opened without as much as a squeak. I was in what looked like a sitting room. This gave way to a set of open arches and a large bedroom situated above the women's quarters if my instincts were correct.

Sure enough, there was a short, fat bejeweled shape sleeping with a beautiful brown-skinned girl who was as tiny as he was large and obese.

I moved towards the bed. Then I pinched that Sultan's nose and rapidly slit his throat while covering the little one's mouth with my other hand.

I said, "We are United States Marines brought here to bring you home. Do you understand me? And if I remove my hand, you must not cry out, or I'll have to kill you. Do you understand English? Do you understand exactly what I have said? Nod, yes, if you understand me."

She shook her head up and down, and I slowly released my hand. She took in some air and whispered, "I'm Darlene Pratt, University of Michigan."

I asked, "Darlene, is there a way to get directly to the other women from up here?"

She said, "Yes, over there in that corner are stairs, and he would use them to come down to us and . . ."

 She began to whimper softly.

"Darlene, I know there must be other guards. We must be quiet a little while longer. Can you gut it out a little?"

She said, "Yes, I can. I should wake up the girls quietly and tell them you're here."

I said, "Yes, but before that, I need you to tell my partners where all the bad guys are situated."

I had no sooner said that when in walked Tony and Mick. I asked what happened. "Did you two clear the entire floor of guards?"

They both said, "No, but in case you forgot, we are all microphoned together."

"That's correct," said Levi from out of nowhere.

I stood there a moment, and Tony said, "Is this the head pervert?"

I said, "Yes, and he has already been tried and convicted."

Darlene said, "I'll show you where the guards are quartered. If you can, you should let the girls see this bastard dead. There's a huge man downstairs in the harem itself. I'd be cautious of him. He's mean and super strong. One time he picked me up with one hand and threw me across the entire room."

I said, "Do you know a girl named Julia down there?"

She kept us together and gave us all hope. Finally, she gave up herself and tried to commit suicide after she'd experienced a ruthless night with this piece of garbage. They stopped her in time. That's why Hassan is allowed in the Harem to prevent any of us from attempting that again."

I asked, "Is she healthy enough to travel?"

She said, "We're all prepared to crawl out of here on our bellies if you're ready to show us the way."

I asked, "How many of you are still down there?"

She answered, "There are eight of us from America and thirty kidnapped women from other countries."

I said, "Let's do this by the numbers. I'll go down the stairs with Darlene. She can help keep the girls calm, and I'll make them aware of our need for silence. Darlene, are there any more guards on this floor?"

She said, "Yes, in the next room to the left are two guys, one is a valet type, and the other is a guard with a gun."

I motioned for Tony to take the Ruger from Mickey and finish them off. I proceeded to the other steep dark stairwell and began my descent. At the foot of the stairs, someone in the room shouted, "Watch out!" I moved, but not quickly enough as a large knife entered my right shoulder to the hilt.

It's times like this that I thank God; I'm left-handed as the colossal guy standing in front of me took two headshots from my Ruger before collapsing.

Mick came bouncing down the stairs, looked at my wound without a word, and gave me a quick shot. Then he started taking out a combat wound package.

I said, "Leave it in. If you remove it, I'll bleed out."

I whispered through the darkness, "United States Marines, ladies. Please be as quiet as you can. We are here to return you to your homes. Is Julia Alexander nearby?"

She rose from the far corner and walked towards me with a defiant look on her face. It was as if she would dictate what happened next.

As she approached me, I saw how gaunt she looked. Even in

her extreme condition, she was still as exquisite as her picture. I'd know those eyes anywhere.

"Yes," she said. "I am Julia Alexander."

"Well, I'm Lieutenant Jake Reynard. I have been sent by your father, Charles. Levi Chapman is outside waiting to take you home."

She began to weep as it all hit her all at once. "Levi is here."

I said, "Don't you run away. We have a few more people to take care of, but I want you safe, so stay beside me. Take my hand here, and we'll go upstairs together. Don't worry, there's no one alive up there to hurt you, okay?

I then said, "Mick, you and Tony move the others out while I take Julia upstairs. In case one of those guards get this far, I can protect her better from the upper staircase."

Tony said, "Good thinking, LT, and I'll let the Gunny help us mop up. Are you sure you can make it upstairs, okay?"

"You bet your ass; I can," I said, and I began walking up the stairs. When we reached the top of the stairs, two people were standing across the other side across the room with what looked like old M1 rifles, with which they proposed to shoot us. First, I stepped in front of Julia, and she went down two treads behind me as I covered her and felt the concussion of that initial bullet hit my left thigh. It was a stinging sensation, but I knew right away; it was a through-and-through wound. As that was going on, I heard the distinct sound of carbine's firing, and I heard Tony downstairs yelling, "All clear!"

Two carbines were chattering away upstairs, and a few minutes later, the firing became increasingly intense. I reached for the wall as the person to my left was screwing around with a jammed extractor, and I shot him twice. Once was enough. The second person fired and hit me on the side of my armpit. While I was falling, he began to rush us. That's when Julia grabbed my pistol, rolled over me, and put one right between his forehead and nose.

The firing continued for a few minutes more and stopped, as suddenly there was a grenade explosion. I could hear through my earpiece Mick's voice saying, "Guardroom resistance cleared," from two different people, one of whom was Levi.

I turned to Julia and said. "Can you help me get up into this room?"

Tony walked over, looked at my wounds, and proclaimed the leg shot had missed my femoral artery. The chest wound was a glancing shot, which spun around my ribcage and out of my back. He started to wrap them both to stop the bleeding.

Next, Levi came through the door and lifted Julia up in the air as if she were a small child. She began to weep openly as she dropped the Ruger. Mickey slipped in next to her and gave her a shot in the upper thigh.

She turned toward Mick and asked, "What was that you did to me?"

"That was only something to make sure you don't go into a shock, baby girl," Levi said.

She looked up at him and said. "I knew you would come, but I did a dreadful thing, Levi. I committed a mortal sin against God."

"Now, now, don't you worry about that, little girl. I'm going to take you home, but first, we have to look after our friend,

Jake."

It finally dawned on me. "Son of a bitch. I'm wounded, and you; you wop; you're unscathed. I can't believe it."

"Levi," she said, "Is this is the cop, who doesn't return phone calls, and who's he calling a Wop?"

Levi said, "No, your friend Jake. That other one is Regina's fiancé, Tony. I wouldn't worry about all that cussing and stuff as these are two good ole American boys. The boy with the knife in his shoulder is someone; you're going to get to know a lot more about because he's the reason we're all here today."

"But, I thought that you, Levi, I thought."

"No, little girl, that fine-looking Lieutenant is the reason we're all here. However, we'll talk more about that later. Now, you just relax. You're going to get a little sleepy soon."

I looked at her and said, "You're still the loveliest Colleen in the room, and this time, I'm going to hold you to that corned beef sandwich."

She looked up and uttered, "It really is you, Jake."

I saw the injection working on her as she began to slip away. Levi walked downstairs with her. Then we heard the chopper blades rotating outside.

I said, "Mick, please get them all out of here. Take as many as you can get in your chopper. Are you sure the entire house is empty? Tony and I will wait for the last bird."

"That order sounds incredibly courageous, Lieutenant. Now, here's a news bulletin for you. First of all, my name is Captain John, Michael McAlister. The tactical side of our mission is completed. Since I outrank you, you will sleep, and you're going out on the bird with her. We can't separate you two now that you've found each other again. The Sergeant and I will stay and guard the other young women while we wait for more of my people. There's no sense in you hogging all this hero-worship, and that, Lieutenant, is a direct order.

"Now, since you got what you came for, gentlemen. . . Tony, on second thought, I hear that second bird coming in, so you can leave too. I believe you, fellows have a plane to catch."

He slipped me another shot as he said all this, and Clem came across the room with a stretcher. I tried to tell him it wasn't necessary, but all that came out was gibberish as I felt myself slipping down that dark, slippery slope.

The last thing I remember was Mick's whispering in my ear, "Clem and I will see you in DC on November tenth," and then everything turned black.

Chapter Eighteen
The Long Ride Home

I awoke with the sounds of the blades still whooshing in my head, and as I looked to my left, I saw I was in a green-colored room. A tall nurse entered the room, and I yelled, "We have to get her out of here, out of Qatar!"

The tall nurse said, "You're a little disorientated, Lieutenant. You'll be in and out for a while longer."

"Where the hell am I, anyway?"

"You're at Landstuhl Army Hospital. You've just had two surgeries on your right shoulder and your back."

Then I saw him sitting in the corner, beaming at me.

I said, "Charles, what are you doing here?"

He replied, "Son, let the nurse finish her summary first."

The nurse went on, "You had a bullet wound in your thigh, but that's coming along nicely, no permanent damage that we can find. As to your chest wound, it's just a scratch, and we removed that bullet as well. Your thigh wound was a through and through with no arterial damage."

I said, "Is anyone else I came in with still here?"

"There's a Major and a Sergeant. I believe they are getting something to eat and thank God for that. That Sergeant, I thought he was your mother the way he complains about everything. He's going to drive me crazy. Thank God. Your father was here to keep him from doing that."

I said, "You'll have to forgive him, Captain. We've been together for a long time, and I think he feels guilty. I said something should have never said to him. It seems every time we get in action together, I'm wounded, and he walks away. I said something stupid that I will have to square away with him. How long will I be here, anyway?"

She said, "That part is up to your father there. He has full control over this part of your situation."

Charles spoke, "We have the jet coming for us, and we have to have you ready for travel by tomorrow morning if the doctors clear you for travel."

I said, "I am going to be gracious for once and accept your gesture with humility."

Then Duke and Tony came walking into the room.

Duke was the one to speak first with the nurse. "Did you see the story on the front page of *Stars and Stripes* about those five guys who rescued thirty hostages? They were all subjected to human trafficking. Well, this was the man in command of that mission."

I said, "Oh crap, they didn't print our names, did they? I mean, that could ruin our business."

Duke replied, "No, they didn't, but General Wingate and Charles here want you to know the Corps will do anything that you desire to have done."

Charles said, "You people must have things to catch up on, but don't overtax his strength. I'm going back to the hotel for a nap." He walked over to my bed and held my hand, and said,

"Son, you've put your body through a lot, so don't attempt too much at one time. Tomorrow, if the doctors clear you, we'll be on our way home. I'll see you for dinner back here tonight."

As he walked away, I noticed a tired shuffle. I'd never seen before in him.

Duke muttered, "My God; he acts exactly like a father to you. This will be interesting when we all get to California."

I asked, "California? Why in the hell am I going to California?"

Duke spoke up, "Charles told us you were going to take your own advice. He and Dr. Brent want to make sure you're entirely up to speed after this mission. Charles needs to be reassured that you didn't suffer any adverse effects from all these wounds.

He knows that you took out most of those bad guys. What he didn't know, nor did anyone else, is that you told Brent you made a pact with God that you would never kill again."

I said, "Well, the way it all worked out was something different. With us being returned to the Corps, I didn't break any deal that I can see. I mean, God is God, and the Corps is the

Corps. I think they have an agreement as to who does what to who and when it gets done. God is the ultimate judge. We can only ensure the evildoers show up for their appointments. Did everyone get out all right? Those two Special Forces people were great guys, aren't they?"

Duke spoke, "Yes, everyone got out okay, and you've been sleeping for four days. Those stab wounds ripped into your shoulder ligaments. You're going to need a lot of painful rehabilitation on these injuries.

Thank God. You called Regina, as she knew you were bleeding out inside and got some blood to you. That's the other reason for California. It seems your doctor friend has a great gym, and you won't be fooling around on your boat for a long time. Besides, for a guy who was so hell-bent on finding this girl, you haven't even asked about her."

I said. "Well, of course, how is Julia doing out there?"

Duke said, "Hmm, should we tell him or what?"

Tony asked, "Well, shall we begin here at Landstuhl? Do you remember talking to her on the plane?

I said, "No, I don't remember anything."

He said, "Well, that might be a good thing. You kept telling Julia, her eyes were always in front of you. You also said that you knew she was waiting for you. It was all incredibly romantic."

I said, "Oh, god, no, please don't give me that crap. You've got to be kidding me, right?"

He went on, "Well, is there anything familiar with these thoughts?"

I responded, "Are you sure? She was so far out of it. She may not even remember any of that."

Duke went on, "Anyway, she was checked out physically, and everything is satisfactory. The good news is, and this is strange; she saw that Sultan guy dead. She saw them deceased. That was something Regina told Tony to do. You let Julia see him dead. I don't know if that was a good idea or not, but her doctor seems to think it was the correct thing to do."

I said, "Listen, I remember everything in that house and that look in her eyes. She is strong. I mean, really tough. She saved my ass with a headshot at the last shooter. That shot's not even in our book. When I took that last round in my back, she grabbed my Ruger and put one right between this guy's eyes while moving forward out of a rolling position."

Tony finally spoke, "That's what Regina said. She got closure. Julia would have enough to deal with because of the rape and abuse of her. I, of course, said something stupid like she should get over it. That it wasn't as if Julia asked to be treated that way. Holy crap did Regina blow up at me because I talked about a sensitive subject, which she says is beyond my understanding or feeling. I didn't know anything about it at all.

" Julia is in California with Levi, who is talking about renting a house or apartment to be near her. Charles has been out there once and then here with you for the last three days. I don't know who's running Wall Street."

Duke stepped into the conversation at that moment and asked. "Are you clearheaded enough to discuss business for a moment?"

I replied, "Yeah, I believe so. What's up?"

Duke went on, "Tony told me about what you said about our fee. I have a six-million-dollar check sitting on my desk, or so Brett said after I got her down off the ceiling. Tell me why you want to give it back, Jake. That's all I ask of you. The girl's safe when everyone else thought she was dead. The old fellow really wants to show his appreciation to us. Besides, Jake, you weren't out there alone."

I said, "Okay, Duke, I understand your reasoning. Please, take ten thousand from our side of the deal and give it to Tony for his relocation. Then I want you to give back the entire check."

Duke replied, "Jake, all I asked is. Why, and you owe me an explanation. We are partners, aren't we? Ah, the hell with partners. You're my closest friend."

I spoke. "I'll say it once. It's like I told Tony; we were all put back on active duty. I have to tell you, if it weren't for those two Special Forces guys, we would have been undone from the outset. They thought of everything, and when I went through that door and said US Marines, well, you'd just have to have been there. Those women listened to every word.

They did exactly what we told them to them. I found all those years had slipped away, and I was representing something bigger than myself or anything else I'll ever do in my life. I can't take money for that. That's my honor, and it's our honor as Marines. We couldn't have done this without that support, and for all I know, I may still be on active duty."

Duke said, "I've got news for you. We're all still on active duty. We will be until the General gets to debrief us, personally. You know, he was here, and the scuttlebutt has it that our current commandant is retiring in September before the birthday bash, and General Wingate is going to become the new top Marine.

" I mentioned your dilemma to him, and he said we should handle it within the tradition of our Corps in mind. I told him you would say what you did. I only needed to hear it from you. I can tell you one thing, Charles's is going to go crazy over your refusal. However, from you, I suppose he'll accept anything.

I believe men like Charles don't like to be indebted to anyone. When it comes to you, it's different. He's been here for three days, and he sat with you after each surgery. You don't remember anything because of those drugs they gave you, but he sat with you in ICU all night twice as if you were his own kid. He refused to leave even when he was told by the nurses to get some sleep. He said, 'If you want me to go, you better understand and get the President on the line. I have his phone number if you don't have it nearby.

He was really something else. I think you have something exceptional with that older gentleman. Nobody understands it, but the two of you. I've gotten a chance to talk to him, and he's quite a man. You know that he's going to throw a bang-up wedding for Tony and Regina at his home in Palm Beach?"

Stunned, I asked, "A wedding for Tony and Regina? What's that all about?"

Tony spoke up, "Oh, yes, I didn't tell you all of it. When Regina and I were here in Germany last week, we began to talk about living together, or at least, she did. I put my foot down and told her that living with each other never proves anything. If we really love each other, we should be married in the church. You know, I was never wed in the church, and my mom says that's why that marriage fell apart. Nobody knew his or her duty, and our roles got discombobulated.

So, I'm telling her this over dinner, and she says. 'Do you really want to marry me?' and I said, 'Are you kidding? I'd marry you here and now and feel like I've just won the lottery. Don't you know how much I love you?' And she says, "Will you meet with my dad and ask him for permission?' I said, 'Of course, that's the only way to do these things. It's the proper way.'

"I fly up there next weekend, but it's only a formality because she already said yes. We won't have the wedding until you, as my best man, and Julia, as her maid of honor, can stand with us. By the way, you'll have to get an officer's mess uniform as we are having a military wedding. She wants to see me in my dress blues, and I told her to stand ready to be stunned. Now you are all caught up, and I hope you don't hold it against me that you were shot and stabbed by those people. I think I'm just a little luckier than you are when it comes to that stuff. Besides, I think you're going to get another Purple Heart out of this."

I said, "Listen, I remember what I said at that house, and

I'm sorry. I was out of line. I was pissed, and I had to blame my stupidity on someone. I had to yell because it really hurt like hell where that son of a bitch stuck me. I got overly anxious and made a stupid mistake. Then I almost got Julia shot by this little sand flea in the bedroom. All I was trying to do was what you told me. I thought she would recover quicker if she saw the head bastard dead."

Duke piped in, "That's the exciting slant on this deal. Julia said you were protecting her from that person by pulling her down the stairs. You shielded her with your own body. It saved her life, and you know, what? I believe her side to this story more than I do yours. You were both in shock at the time. You acted on instinct, and that entry wound is in the back of your thigh.

That's the official story as it has been reported. I think you may end up with more than a Purple Heart before this whole event is finished. As to her, she came in twice while she was here. She sat right there next to your bed in this chair and whispered to you. We don't have a clue as to what was said, but I imagine 'you big handsome bastard' was in there somewhere."

I reacted. "All right, I knew you guys would start this crap if I asked about her. Listen, I'm only somebody who happened to help her when she required it. When I get to California, I'll try to be a friend to her for the old man's sake, if for nothing else."

Tony intervened, "Jake, you get some rest, and we'll be back here with Charles in the morning to pick you up for the flight home. Remember, we were miked-up together, and we all heard that corned-beef-sandwich remark. That's something you'll have to share with us someday."

They walked down the corridor when the Duke turned to Tony and said, "You know, the old man is smart. He said if we get these two together in California, nature will take its own course. We have to keep this a secret for Jake's sake. If he knew that Charles Alexander was determined to have him for a son-in-law, he'd revolt because of his own obstinate nature.

"I met and spoke with her. I believe she's just what Jake needs. I think he's what she needs as well. You know, it's like you and Regina. I knew the first time I saw you two together that you guys would be outstanding for each other."

Tony said, "Duke, I don't feel right taking Jake's money for this move."

Duke said, "Son, you'll get all your relocation money. It comes from the company's funds, and that's all of our money. Learn to separate the bullshit from the reality in this whole deal. I only wanted Jake to have something to chew on. I knew upfront he wouldn't change his mind about the money.

He will never change when it comes to his ethics, his word, or betraying his honor.

That is why, and don't you ever tell him this, he's my sole heir. If these two get together, I'm going to buy them a house in Sarasota. Charles and I have plans to be grandfathers, and those plans include Levi. I want you to know we're becoming attached to you as well. Son, don't screw this up with Regina. She's the girl you want in your corner forever."

Chapter Nineteen

California

The flight was a reunion of sorts as, one by one, Mike and George came back to chat with me. Charles seemed pleased to be with me, and I was touched by his gesture. As Mike explained to me doing the Arctic route, we were going nonstop, which is a much more direct route to California from Europe, going as it does over the polar cap.

I explained to Charles last night during dinner what we had to do about the money sent to our firm. We were all drawing government pay and, as such, couldn't accept remuneration from any private source. For a while last night, he was silent, and I think a little annoyed about my non-acceptance of the money. Then he began to smile, and I knew he had come up with some alternative scheme.

The next day when we were airborne, I told Regina, I felt a little hungry. He stood up and followed her to the galley. That was senseless. He wouldn't even allow Regina to serve me a sandwich. He insisted on doing it himself. I couldn't help but wonder when the last time Charles Alexander had served anyone coffee or handed someone lunch. I was about to say something when from behind him, Regina shushed me with a gesture. It implored me to let it go. He wanted to take care of me.

After we ate lunch, he sat down next to me and began to unravel his newest scheme.

He began, "Jake, I believe Levi or I told you before all this happened with Julia that we were working on putting together a Foundation to dispose of some of this money. I've accumulated a lot from my efforts with my firm."

I said, "Yes, Charles, I think that was a noble idea, and it's something that you two should begin to work on again."

Charles continued. "Well, you know, with us both getting older and no grandchildren in the immediate future, I only have the two girls. That friend of yours, Dr. Bartholomew, says

Julia may take some time to deal with what's happened to her. I don't know too much about this P.T.S.D... I know what it means, but I feel a little powerless when I'm out there. It was easy the first time we saw each other because she wanted to know everything that was done to affect her rescue, and of course, she felt guilty about attempting suicide. Julia's a stringent Catholic."

His tears had begun to fill, and I reached over and put my right arm around him.

He said, "I mean, I felt mortified. I should have sought your help long before I did."

I said, "Listen, Charles, this is something; you're going to have to come to grips with over time. You did what any reasonable man would have done in your shoes. In the end, the government that let you down came through in ways you wouldn't believe. Those two Special Forces fellows are out there in harm's way as we speak. They had the equipment and the training and stood beside us when we went through that door.

They were the ones who worked this mission out. That's how

we affected the release of all those women. You started all that in motion, and Levi, because he dragged a young captain, who was by all accounts, almost dead, out of a pitched battle thirty-five years ago, got us everything we required."

He said, "Jake, this is just the type of modesty; I've come to expect from you."

I said, "Charles, it's not modesty. The last thing I remember was Levi carrying Julia out of that hellhole. The next moment, I woke up in that hospital room in Germany with you standing vigil beside my bed."

He said, "Okay, Jake, there are a few people who remember things a little differently, including those two Special Force soldiers. They both said they 'would serve with that lieutenant anywhere, anytime.' However, let's get back to what I was talking about."

I said, "Charles, I'm sorry to keep interrupting you, but there are things about Julia, you should know. It's why I had you bring her out here to my friend Brad in California. First, when you see her, never say, 'How are you feeling?' She doesn't know how she's feeling. She may think she does as she battles for control but believes me, she can't and won't until she's done some dancing in the shadows."

He asked, "What do you mean by dancing in the shadows?"

I replied, "That's how I used to think about it. All your life, you exercise what you have come to believe is control over your own life. You walk and think in the light. Things happen to you, but you deal with them, and the illusion of control remains strong, and in her case, it gets stronger because of the way she's dedicated her life to the downtrodden and other people with greater problems. She's always been a person who has always been in service to others. Look what happened in New York when that homeless person became aggressive with her and Regina. She just spoke to this unreasonable person rationally, and next thing you know, she's running his life. He had no choice but to follow her. It all reinforced her self-esteem. She felt as good about herself as she should have."

During the conversation, Regina was hanging over the chair, listening in rapt attention. She said to Charles, "Do you mind? I want to hear this too."

Charles said, "No, it's alright, go on, Jake."

I said, "Now, she's in a kind of shadow world, where she's come to realize after a while that she had no control of her own life. By the way, that's why she made that suicide attempt. She was trying to reassert her choices and take back control of her destiny. If she could do that, she believed at that moment, her life would be her own again. It would even if it meant her death in the temporal sense. This doesn't mean she wasn't courageous beyond measure in all those prior months. It only means a sense of futility set in. I heard from one of the girls that she was the leader of them all. She will probably have good days, also some very dark ones. The black ones usually accompany some session with Bart, where they've done some pushing around in those shadows. Have you seen that, or has Levi, for that matter?"

He replied, "Yes, Jake, and by the way, you've explained this whole thing to better than that doctor."

"I understand it better myself," said Regina. "So, what can be done to support her now when we see her?"

I said. "Well, don't hover over Julia. Don't agree with everything she says. Most of all, you're allowed to become upset and express your feelings. If she displays any symptoms of self-pity, or if she acts overly emotional when you're with her, tell her to calm down.

She didn't go through anything that these other women didn't experience. Only soldiers can help soldiers in the end. I believe Bart's going to want as many of those women to share together. They shared this mutual ordeal. Some will come to cleanse themselves in their commonality, and some won't be up to the task.

"Those will be the women who are afraid to try, and it will be their own undoing. I don't claim to know Julia except for a few moments in that house, and that day we shared together once. I saw a defiant cast in her eyes in that house, and a willingness to do what she knew at the moment was correct. She followed orders with no questions asked, and that showed courage, deep down, at the core. Charles, she's not only going to get well, but she's going to be a more robust, better Julia when this is all over. I believe that with all my heart.

I never answered your question. Take her to dinner, and make sure you tell her every time you see her that you love her. When you go out, let it be with only the people she knows and with whom she feels comfortable. Above all, if she is contented, let her be where she wants. She needs to feel safe. Stay away from the things that remind her of what it was like before all this happened. Because it did happen, and she has to face up to that."

Charles spoke, "I've spoken to all these girls' families at the request of General Wingate. I reminded them of the need for secrecy. Some wanted to go public, but we quelled that we are willing to pay for all their bills from the doctors by telling the parents and one husband. When they are ready, we will pay for the girls' continuing education at any college of their choice. That's what I started to tell you before.

"Levi and I have activated this Foundation. I realized that a lot of this positive outcome was because I had the right people and resources to perform this miracle. We know there are many more missing people out there. Nothing is genuinely being done on their behalf. I have the money and the connections, or my little girl would still be in the hands of those bastards. Jake, I realize that I have a responsibility to these people who don't have the resources. To that end, we have created this Foundation, and I am endowing it with one billion dollars as a beginning. Levi and I know that the only person who can head up such an endeavor like this is you. Like it or not, you have that infective sense of leadership and the passion required for this kind of job. Besides, we could never trust anyone else but you to do this job.

The two of us compose the entire board of directors. That's not only flawed logic, but it's irresponsible. We're old men, and this foundation needs permanency. We had a meeting in California and voted you in as the third director of our board.

Before you say anything, we know you bear a genuine aversion to money, but you can't argue with me about giving it away. Especially for something you care so deeply about. All we ask is that you give some thought to this for all of us. It's most of all, for the victims and their families enduring this pain of not knowing is their loved one still out there."

I said. "Charles, I don't know the first thing about Trusts or Foundations. I'm quite sure you can find a lawyer or financial person to do this for you. Understand me, Charles, I'm touched that you both thought of me, but—"

He interrupted, "We already contemplated that, and that's why we need to do this now while we are still able to teach you what you need to know. Besides Jake, the task puts someone in a position to access two or three billion dollars, and that's only a beginning. You can appoint anyone; you want to assist you, whom either Levi or I trust for the financial part of this responsibility. Remember, this is our foundation, and your name is already on the papers. I'm not trying to bully you, but who else has the sense of mission and the skills to take on this horrendous task, son?"

I said, "You did all that without even speaking to me. That reminds me of another bone I have to pick with Levi. He not only put me back in the Marine Corps, but he got them to commission me in the process. He's having one hell of a laugh over that tidbit. Believe me, you have no idea how enlisted men feel about officers. I have become that which I held most in contempt with some exception. He gave me some bullshit about this tactical command, but I figured it out in the hospital. Either he or Wingate wanted to suck me back in. I'm still on active duty and won't be released until I meet with the General. Can you believe that?"

Charles said, "In Levi's defense, he confided to me that it was the General's idea, but Levi is extremely proud of you. Hell, we're both honored for you, so you better get used to it and go easy on him. He has the greatest respect and love for you, as do we all, son."

I said, "If Levi cares anymore for me, I'm going to end up in Iraq as a platoon leader."

Charles said, "Is that what a captain does in the Marine Corps?"

I asked, "A captain? What in the hell is that all about?"

He went on, "Well, I overheard a phone call about credit for time served and jumping the reserve list. I can't tell you about that right now. However, I do know one thing, and that is, you're not supposed to know about any of this. Please, Jake, keep this between us."

I said, "Charles, you keep attempting to do these incredible things for me. I always have to say no. Why not ask me something simple that I can agree with you? Let me take you and Levi sailing, or let's go to a Yankee baseball game together?""

He said quickly, "You've got it. Consider both those requests accomplished, and we will hold you to both."

I asked, "Charles, there is another request I have. It's a favor, actually."

He said, "Regina, could you please open up that bottle of Bollinger Grande Année 1990. It always puts me in a favor-making mood. Bring us five glasses, please. In fact, I forgot with whom I will be drinking. Open two bottles, and we will toast to your engagement as well, so make it six champagne flutes."

Duke jumped in, "Jake, you are about to drink one of the finest champagnes in the world."

Charles continued to speak, "While Regina fills up these glasses, son, what is this favor you need from me?"

I asked, "Charles, Levi, and I promised those two Special Forces soldiers that we would take them to the Marine Corps birthday party in Washington, DC, and the hook is Levi promised them a ride on a private jet stocked with champagne."

He replied, "I see, so you and Levi are in a bit of a tight spot. I'll be using this particular plane that day myself, but don't worry; we'll have the most luxurious jet made pick them up no matter where they are. I'll ensure their attendance through the secretary of Defense.

He went on, "I'll let you in on another secret. If our President is reelected this fall, you're looking at the next Secretary of the Treasury. The President asked me to join his cabinet, and I told him as long as my girls are safe, I will accept the position."

I said, "Charles, I think that's quite an honor. I believe we should all toast you. Cheers! God, this is a great wine. Here's to having someone in Washington that we can all be proud of."

Regina said, "Jake, wait until you see what's for dinner. We picked it up in Paris on the way out."

Charles said, "Jake, I hope while you're in California, you can spend some time with Julia. She has a million questions for this fellow Jake everyone has been discussing."

I said, "Did she say anything about a conversation I had on that helicopter?"

He asked, "No, was it essential, son?"

I said, "No. I think I feel a little tired. So, if none of you mind, I could use a little sleep."

Charles said, "We thought you might, so I had a rear bed replace all those additional seats we didn't require. Go and lie down. I'll wake you for dinner."

I could never sleep on planes, but whether it was the wine, drugs, or being able to lie down, I was out in two minutes.

The rest of them waited until they knew Jake was asleep before they began discussing his present situation. It was clear to all of them that he understood more about Julia's condition than anyone. He knew what she was going through in its entirety.

Charles said, "It amazes me that he has so much faith in her ability to recover from all that abuse. It's like he knows a secret that even I'm not privy to."

Regina was the first person to attempt an answer. "People in love always know and see things in the person they love that no one else can even consider.

Charles replied, "Do you really believe he's in love with her?"

Regina spoke, "I don't know if he perceives it consciously. Nevertheless, I'll tell you one thing. That boy is flat-out crazy in love with your daughter, Mr. Alexander. You weren't privy to that conversation on the plane to Germany. Anyway, can't you observe it in his eyes when he talks about her?"

Charles said, "Levi and I would go to our graves, happy men, if that part of this works out. Sometimes, the people involved can't see what outsiders do and how well-matched they are. I never thought I would ever meet any man special enough for Julia. Jake is that truly distinct man. He's the son; I've always wanted. Now, I have that son, and I won't lose him no matter what."

Tony jumped in, "For what it's worth, I can tell you what he's thinking. He doesn't want her to feel obligated to him.

Remember Patty Hearst and how she married her bodyguard?"

They all nodded in agreement.

Tony went on, "Things seem to have worked out for them. However, I know Jake, and if he thought for a moment, this could happen to Julia out of her fear, he'd jump out of her life like a frightened rabbit. Jake believes in people healing themselves. That's what he's experienced in his own life. I'm not going to tell you some of the things he's gone through, but I know how he came to meet Dr. Bartholomew Milton and how tough it was for him to reach out for his help in the first place.

You see, he did it, and now he believes with all his heart that she'll have to do the same thing. I think that's why he didn't put up a fuss about going out there. Usually, he would want to be on his boat. He knows he'd find his peace there. He also knows he can do his rehab anywhere, and this assignment is over for him.

No, Jake's on a crusade to save someone he began to fall in love with a long time ago. I think it all started with that first meeting. Then, there is that photo he's been carrying around everywhere inside his shirt. There is you, Mr. Alexander, and he's become extremely fond of you. He's spoken to all of these people who know and love your daughter enormously. In his mind, there is a fixation about her. I'm with Regina on this. He loves her, but he doesn't quite realize it consciously."

Charles spoke up, "So, Tony, since you know him longest and best, do you believe this is a good idea? I mean, throwing them together out there like this?"

Tony said, "Yes, I do. If they find they can both work this out together, then that's as good as it gets. I'll tell all of you, no more interference, because they will both resent it. From everything I've heard about your daughter, she's nobody's fool. So, if she believes this is a fix-up deal, we'll end up with two rabbits running off in different directions."

Charles replied, "I agree wholeheartedly with you, Tony. You're a bright young man, and I mirror your thoughts totally. We'll just let nature take its own course."

Duke interjected, "I took the liberty of writing him off for the next three months. Tony, you and I are going to have to hit the ground running. Brett told me this morning. We had two difficult cases that need to be looked at tomorrow. I'm so screwed up on time. We can stay in Santa Cruz overnight or wherever and head back on the first-morning flight to Sarasota."

Charles jumped in, "Nonsense. You will stay the night where I have already made arrangements. Let these two young people spend some time together. You know, Major, we have faxes and computers with e-mail. Besides, this boy has a father to see, and this plane will take him there. You're going to escort him for moral support. Levi and I are going on a trip to Alaska. It's something we've always wanted to do and never got around to before. We're going to go up there by boat. First, a train ride, and then a cruise, and I'm really looking forward to that train ride. I haven't been on one since I was a kid. We'll have a private stateroom, and of course, Levi is officially retired.

"We will continue to share quarters now as friends and family. I didn't quite realize it, but I've made him a wealthy man. I told him we would split the expenses, but we will see some things before considering the president's offer. I know unless he really screws something up, he's going to win reelection. As much as I hate those people in DC. I believe you have to be prepared to make changes from within or surrender your rights to complain.

That also reminds me, Major. Jake must spend all his time on this Foundation, and you can contribute as well. Human trafficking is a huge problem, and someone with the intelligence and resources has to tackle the problem. I've decided with your firm's expertise and my connections and resources. We can make a severe dent in this problem. That's the other reason I'm going to Washington. I can cultivate the right resources and get the government to take this problem more seriously. Hell, we go running around pissing off more than half the world with our foreign policy, and we wonder why we have to worry about terrorism. People worldwide are stealing upwards of one million of our children and using and debasing them in the most horrendous ways. I'll tell you, if I can't help change this, then everything I've worked for my entire life means nothing. I'll let you know something else; Levi feels precisely the same way. I'm sorry to get on a soapbox, and I know I'm preaching to the choir on this fact."

Duke said. "No, sir, this is a great lesson for these young people. Our country works this way. When people like you see a problem and are willing to devote your resources to it, capital you've performed a lifetime to acquire and attack this problem head-on, well, I've never heard it put any better except maybe by Jake himself.

"You know when we first met, I rented him an apartment of mine. We both had the Marine Corps in common, but not much else at first. Anyway, we started having lunch every couple of days, and then dinner and a like-mindedness developed between us.

One day, the topic of his previous work with the police department came up. I was curious as to why he left, and he began to tell me all about the Missing Persons Department. Adult people are missing and don't want to be found, but most are trafficked for the sex industry or kidnapped for ransom. Most of them are children and young women. I admit, I'd never even heard the phrase *human trafficking* before, but as he started to explain it to me. These young children and women were being abducted. I was spellbound not only by the topic but the personal way in which he related to all of it. He associated with all those people who had lost their children.

"It took time, but not long after that, I talked him into this as a business. I realized why the whole thing was so personal for him. I don't know if you know this, but Jake is a highly spiritual man. Not always a popular thing to say these days, but he believes in acts of contrition, as he was taught many years ago in our church.

His entire life, in that sense, is a single act of contrition for his days as a Marine. I think with this latest situation, and from what Tony has told me, he's finally made peace between those two beliefs. I heard Levi said a battle prayer before they stormed that house, and they all prayed together.

I believe we can end this chapter, and I agree with whoever said it. It's time to allow Jake and Julia to have peace in their lives. Because if there have ever been two people who have earned it by their acts of compassion more than these two, I sure as hell never met them."

Regina looked at everyone. "Since I'm the only woman present, I get to have the last word. Let's get you guys something to eat, but allow him to continue to sleep. We still have a long way to go, and I'll fix his dinner when he wakes up."

Chapter Twenty
Carmel-by-the-Sea

I'd never taken the ride around the seventeen-mile drive, and I mentioned it to Charles in passing. So, of course, we had to make the detour to do this scenic drive. I have to admit, it really was as beautiful as I've been told. Things like this road usually fail to live up to our expectations, but a strange thing happened as we drove on this beautiful winding path. We came to what they call the Lone Cypress. This tree sits by itself on an outcropping of rock overlooking the sea below. For some reason, it made me think about my father, but not in a negative way. No, it was as if something or someone was telling me everything's all right, and I was where I should be. Near the sea, we both loved so much.

Charles interceded in my reverie, "Are you okay, Jake? You look especially distant?"

I said, "Yes, My dad popped into my head, and for the first time in a long time, I realized his memory gave me peace and not the sorrow I usually feel."

He said, "That's as it should be, Jake. I'm very sure he'd want you to feel this way. He must have been one a hell of a man, your dad."

I asked, "What makes you say that?

Charles said, "Because we are all in our own way the sum total of all our fathers' and mothers' dreams and aspirations. That's how we all live on through our children, and I know he would be as proud of you as I am and, and of course, Julia. We love all our children, but there is always the one who comes closest to what we thought we might be ourselves."

I said, "You know; he died before I finished college, and that's always bothered me."

He said, "Jake, he knows you finished. Because he knew you always achieve whatever you begin. It's one of your most admirable character traits."

I said, "Well, Charles, I have to admit, my stubbornness

has been described to me in many ways, but as an admirable character trait? That's a totally new one for me."

He replied, "You show me a man who's worth his salt, and I'll show you a stable temperament, and believe me, Jake; you're looking at a man who has blisters on his ass from the kisses of others. Some people would have played me like a piano had I have given them a chance.

On another subject, while you were sleeping, I talked to my office and Levi. As we sit here, we are getting season's box seats at Yankee Stadium. I know Levi and I are two old farts, but we'd love to see some of those games with you."

I said, "Charles, nothing would make me happier."

He went on, "You were asleep when I told everyone. Levi and I are leaving to go on to Alaska by train and then a cruise. I'm going to impose on you a bit more and ask you to look in on Julia while you're out here in California. Would it be asking too much for you to keep an eye on her?"

I said, "No, not at all. I remember Julia likes to run, doesn't she?"

He replied, "Yes, and from what Levi told me, she has already begun. He said he couldn't keep up with her. That would be excellent if you could run with her a few times a week, but I don't want this to interfere with your rehabilitation."

I said, "Well, I don't want to interfere with her rehabilitation."

Charles said, "That's funny. She said the exact same thing about you. I think she feels guilty about your being wounded in the process of facilitating her rescue."

I responded, "Well, that's nonsense, and I'll make that clear to her. I made a blunder, and like all stupid mistakes in a combat situation, you pay the price. I'm only glad my error in judgment didn't result in her being injured. Besides, it was she who saved my butt."

He said, "I can see you both have different recollections of those events, but I'm sure you'll resolve it between yourselves."

We'd gotten off the seventeen-mile drive and were quiet for the duration of our ride. Carmel Valley is a strange place in that it's only a short drive from the Monterey Peninsula, but the temperature change is dramatic. You go from dense, cold fog to a pleasant, warm, and sun-filled valley with little humidity in a matter of miles. It's gorgeous, and I could see why Bart decided to abandon Los Angeles and move up here. We made a right turn by a grove of trees onto a dirt road and drove another three hundred yards to a series of newly constructed buildings surrounded by a large central structure. It looked to be about ten thousand square feet in size.

As we pulled under the portico, I saw Bart standing there with a massive smile on his face. I got out of the car, and his hug came brutal and inescapable. We danced around for a few moments. Then, he said, "It's so good to see you, buddy. How do you like my new setup? Isn't it terrific? We have the main house here and twelve cottages for the guests who are staying with us. Mr. Alexander, you really are becoming an international jet-setter. I guess you want to see Mr. Chapman and your daughter. They're down by the stream next to her cottage, drinking ice tea, I believe."

Charles returned with, "That's great, but I need to ask you something first. I have some of Julia's friends over at the Delmonte Lodge. I want you to tell me if you think she's up to join us for dinner. Everyone there had had something to do with her rescue. Maybe you think the emotion of all that might be too much of a strain?"

Bart asked, "What's the second thing you wanted to ask?"

Charles said, " Mr. Chapman and I have made tentative plans for a trip, which will take us away for two or three weeks."

Brad said, "The trip, I heartily endorse, sir. Both of you, although well-intentioned, are smothering her. It was great initially, but it's now Julia's time to be alone in small doses. She must concentrate on her own inner healing. When you two are here, frankly, her mind is focused on trying to please everyone else. You're showing fear, and sir, there should be nothing in this place to frighten her. She's going to be unhappy going through this process. That's to be expected, as Jake can tell you. She has a personal journey to make, and all we can do is create the proper setting and the right ear to allow her to make that passage in her own time.

As to what I think you really fear. Julia's already walked up to that door and turned away. So, you needn't concern yourself about suicide attempts. About the first question, if I've been able to make myself understood, then you already know the answer as to what would be best for her."

Charles said, "Yes, I understand, Doctor, but in my absence, if you have any arrangements, you would usually talk over with me, refer them to Jake. He has my full authority for Julia in my absence. Please humor an old man on this matter. Doctor, no one's going to interfere with what you do here. In fact, Jake instructed me to bring my daughter to you. His confidence in you stopped me from seeking help closer to home.

Make no mistake, you have been checked out by the best. I could tell you things about yourself you had forgotten. Don't be offended, please. It's my way, as Jake can attest to. I'm a comprehensive man when it comes to whom I entrust with my family's welfare."

Bart said, "I can assure you, sir; I'm not offended. Let me get Jake settled into his cottage and give him the tour. I will see both you and Mr. Chapman before you leave this afternoon. As to that second question, if I made myself clear, you already know that answer."

With that, Bart picked up one of my bags, and we started

walking down a path that ran parallel to a beautiful stream moving eastwards towards the mountains. We stopped at a lovely cottage with only the number 11 to differentiate it from the rest we'd passed. They were all built of logs and had porches with and without screens on each side.

Bart stuck a key in the door, and we entered a deceptively oversized living room done in the same log cabin style with a grand stone fireplace and a large bedroom with a bath in the rear. There was a small kitchen to the left and a table with four chairs placed in an alcove next to a beautiful bay window. Then a view of this lazy stream. Two French doors off to the right led out to the screened side porch with a hot tub placed at the rear, overlooking a more full part of the stream.

We walked back into the living room, with its cathedral ceilings all done in exposed beams and a blue-and-tan color scheme on all the furniture. It had a genuine homey feeling to it. I put one of my two bags on the floor and sat in one of the two large oversized couches.

I said to Bart, "This is a big step up from LA. Where in the world did you get all the capital to build all these dwellings?"

Bart said, "Well, the short story is, I have a very wealthy benefactor whose kid I helped through a bad drug problem. He arranged a donation to help me make this a first-class operation with the stipulation that we would still treat the indigent. It's the old Robin Hood theory: those who can pay, pay up the ass, and those who can't pay, pay nothing.

I said, "Well, hell, I can probably pay, but I could also go to the YMCA, and Charles Alexander isn't going to pick up my tab. Do we understand each other, Bart?"

He said, "Yes, I do, and you're correct. He wanted to pay the standard rate for you, but I informed him, and I told him I consider you a colleague. I know what you do for other people. You were one of the models for how I wanted this clinic prepared. So, as my friend, you might say founding father, you stay, and you and I will jaw out some of what happened. In repayment, you're going to lead some talks in-group for me. You know this process better than anyone I have on staff. Anyway, we're not going to argue about this because you and I are the only two people who have made this journey together."

I said, "Okay, Bart, I'll give it a try. If I'm not up to it, I'm going home to my boat. Now, I would like to get a shower and some sleep. I don't even know what time zone I'm in."

Bart said, "Listen up, chow here comes three ways. There's a restaurant in the main building with a pretty good evening chef. Otherwise, it's a short-order menu. There are things in your refrigerator if you want to cook yourself, and you can call a number here and get cabin-room service. You have access to any of the five jeeps, so you can go off property anytime you want when you can drive with that arm. We would appreciate knowing when and for how long you'll be gone. If you have a physical therapy appointment or an appointment with me, we expect you to keep your commitments. You are not under any restrictions, so there are some excellent California wines and imported beers in your refrigerator. We ask that you confine your drinking to the cottage as we have patients here dealing with these types of issues. Anything else you need, call me, and please lock up when you leave your house.

"Julia's cottage is number twelve, which is the next cottage upriver facing east. She doesn't know where you are, and as you can see, these cabins are somewhat far away from one another. Jake, there's a question I need to ask. Are you here to safeguard her? Is my facility in any danger from outside forces?"

I said, "First of all, my responsibilities to Julia Alexander ended with her repatriation from that hell-hole. I am not here to watch over her because that's your job, Bart. Secondly, no one is left to harm or pursue her in any way from that nightmare she experienced. There's no one left alive. That's what I'm here to deal with. However, if having both of us here at the same time complicates things for her or you in any way, then I'll go home tomorrow."

Bart said, "Jake, you're strung as tight as a banjo, and for now, it's not a problem. Down the road, you may need help coming to terms with some of this crap. I caution you on one thing only.

When you see her, she'll want to discuss each part of her rescue. Maybe there is a time and place for that, but not at present. If she asks, say it's a subject, and she must concentrate on herself for another time.

"Like you, she is by nature, a remarkably selfless person, and again like you, the hardest part of helping her is going to be getting her to concentrate on her own experiences and feelings. The impact of this on her emotions has been devastating. I would say, at this time, she's a fully functioning victim. You and I know where she has to travel to from that point. Look, get some sleep, and if you need anything, use the phone. Tess will pick up and find me immediately."

I said, "Thanks, Bart. I apologize for jumping down your throat like that."

He said. "It's no problem, my friend. It's really great to see you again."

As soon as he left, I looked around and decided I could be very content staying here, especially when I opened the refrigerator and found three cold bottles of Graves. Levi must have left me a gift. I removed the cork with some difficulty and poured a generous glass. Then I went to rest on the screened-in porch.

I no sooner sat down when I heard a faint knock on the front door. I opened it, and there was Levi's standing tall and straight as an oak. I asked him in and thanked him profusely for his gift of the wine. I asked if he could stay a moment and what could get him to drink. He replied yes, and that he wanted a beer.

He queried me when I returned with the beer. "How are you feeling, Jake? Do you have a lot of pain from that shoulder?"

I said, "It hurts a little, but it's nothing I can't live with."

I told him I was glad he stopped by before leaving, and for a moment, we sat there together quietly.

Then he spoke. "You understand that I'm not always good at expressing the things I need to say. I want you to know how much you have come to mean to me personally. I'm sorry I ever doubted you for a moment back when this whole thing began."

I stopped him. "Levi, serving with you on this mission has been one of the greatest honors in my life. I will always be there by your side whenever you need me."

He returned, "I feel exactly the same way about you, son. I, too, will be there for you no matter what. Whatever comes tomorrow. One last thing, Jake, I want you to give some considerable thought to Charles's Foundation. Don't answer, but promise me you'll give it your deepest thought. You must realize you're now a part of this family. We won't allow you to disappear into anonymity."

I replied, "I promise; I'll give it a great amount of consideration for him and for you."

He said, "That's all I or anyone can ever ask of you, Jake."

Then the door opened, and Charles strolled in. "Levi, we have to be on our way. Can you join us for dinner, Jake?"

I answered, "I'm sorry, Charles, but I think I'm kind of wrung out from all that travel today."

We all said our goodbyes with hugs all around. They both left, and as I watched them walk down the path, I thought of how I had come to care so much about each one of them.

I sat down and fell asleep after drinking that one glass of wine. When I awoke, it was three in the morning. I was cramped as hell from sleeping on that couch. My shoulder was throbbing, and I opened my bag and located some pain pills and a sleeping pill. I recognized that I'd roam around half the night if I didn't take the sleeping pill. After a half-ass shower because of the dressing on my arm, I went in to lie down on that queen bed and fell asleep dreaming about dogs. Great water dogs—I so love dogs. I want a male golden retriever, a red one, not the blonde color that's so in fashion today, a huge fellow who can sail with me.

Chapter Twenty-One

Julia

I faltered momentarily on the first step. I'd spied Julia sitting at a small table in the morning sun on the deck of the main building. She caught me looking at her from the steps below. I was up early for my appointment with Bart, hoping to grab a little breakfast first.

The first thing I noticed was her golden skin color had returned. I began climbing the stairs when she said, "You've been here two days without even stopping by to say hello. For a girl whose life you've saved, I guess, I'm only one maiden in distress in a long line of needy women. All you superheroes are the same. It's a real pain in the ass. I had to get kidnapped even to get your attention. I guess you still have no interest in seeing me. I find it hard to believe all those nice things my father said to me about you."

I stammered, "Wait a minute; any reluctance on my part should not be misconstrued as anything other than someone trying not to interfere with a woman who is attempting her recuperation. You're not really going to hold those non-returned phone calls over me forever?"

She came back at me with. "Are you always this serious in the morning?" That was said with her old, familiar, luminous smile. That was what I saw in her photo and in my mind over such an extended time.

I had no recourse but to laugh. "All right, let's begin over again. How are you this beautiful day? You do look lovely under this California sun."

She said, "I'm excellent, Jake Reynard, and if you'd only accepted some of my dad's money, then Ms. Alexander would be fine. However, since you didn't, I guess it will have to be Julia."

I said, "You think you're pretty clever, don't you?"

She said, "I'm sharp enough to handle some old torn-up Marine. As you know, I was brought up by one of your larger brethren."

I replied, "You weren't raised by any Marine. You were carried to safety by a legend in our Corps."

Julia said, "Yes, someone told me all about that. Levi would never allow us to question those exploits of his life. So, am I to believe that you hold Gunnery Sergeant Levi Chapman in some form of high esteem?"

I said, "I hold him in the very highest esteem imaginable."

She went on, "Will you please sit down? I'm getting a creak in my neck from looking up at you. You're a big fellow, you know?"

I replied, "My mother used to say that. She'd say, 'Jake, come down here with us mortals. I wish to speak with you about your current behavior.'"

That brought out a small laugh, and I said. "I actually came up here early for some breakfast."

She said, "You're in luck as here comes mine. You can order or share mine if you don't mind eating off the same plate."

Sure enough, a young woman came through the door with a tray, and after Julia made introductions. I ordered a steak and three eggs with toast and coffee. When she left, Julia caught me looking at her again, and I felt my face growing red.

She asked, "Why are you blushing like that?"

I decided, for the truth, "I keep looking at you because I've been carrying a picture of you around in my shirt for over two months. You're even more beautiful than you were in that photo. I thought that particular image of you was inordinate."

She replied, "I thought I knew your face, but all I remember was an off-duty cop that came to spend a day with me at my shelter. He never returned any of my calls. Not a Marine lieutenant, or was the other guy your brother? He was cute and possessed a great sense of humor and really knew how to kiss a girl."

I said, "Okay, you got me, but I never thought you'd remember me in a thousand years. Your father reminded you, didn't he?"

She said, "No, actually, I waited for you to show up at my house or the shelter for quite a while. I figured, in the end, you were just a flirt with no real substance or character. Jake, I have to ask you something seriously, and it's important to me. Are you here to watch over me? Did my father get you to come here for that purpose? I don't mean for money, but out of some loyalty you've developed for him. Levi told me you; two have become quite close. My god, he even had you stay in both our houses, and nobody has ever had that license before. I understand he sat up with you for three nights after your surgeries in Germany."

I said. "If you're done, I'll tell you what you want to know point by point. First, I am not here to look after you. Any plans for pumping me about what happened over there are to be postponed until a later time. Next, I was the one who told your father to bring you here. I once had to battle with post-traumatic stress myself. I'd developed a drinking problem after an action I was involved in, and I needed help badly. Bart guided me on that journey; I had to make to regain self-respect.

"As to the rest of your question, I'd be lying if I were to say I don't bear a great affection for your father. He's an exceptional man. All men of purpose are drawn to one another. Finally, I do not flirt with all the ladies of my acquaintance. However, as you and I know, we are from entirely different worlds. Women from your position in life, don't engage with third-grade detectives. I knew with you; it would have to be serious, and I was panic-stricken by the feelings I had at the time.

"Now, your dad, Levi, and I have an upcoming mutual interest in some activities with the New York Yankees. In fact, the three of us intend to see a few games together, and I am going to take them both sailing with me."

No sooner had I have gotten these words out of my mouth when she began laughing so hard she almost fell off her chair.

I asked, "What did I say that's so funny? I don't get it."

As the young lady named Lynn put my food down, Julia began to regain a sense of normalcy.

"Oh, I'm sorry, Jake. It's only that father loathes baseball. Jeanette and I used to beg him as kids to go with us when Levi would take us up to the Bronx for a Yankee game."

I stared at her and began to calculate for myself. Why in the hell would he do all this for me?

She went on. "Don't you get it? I do; It's all so clear to me now. You're the son he never had, and you're the total package. You're a Marine Corps hero and someone who can turn down millions of dollars without batting an eye. I bet you get to disagree with him. No, don't tell me. I already know you put my sister in her place. I understand he took your side in that as well. Levi told me it was you who inspired him to create this Foundation for trafficked and missing people. All these girls and young boys who have been stolen and sold as if they were pieces of garbage to the highest bidder, they'll get a second chance at freedom. That's because men like you and my father are willing to challenge these monsters. Neither of you will allow those evil bastards to win this battle for our lives.

"I knew something had changed in my father. I was aware it had something to do with losing me and giving up hope. However, now I truly understand it. You've given him hope in something higher than what he has already accomplished. You've given him hope in changing this entire evil practice.

"You have to understand that in the world he lives in, there are so many con artists. He began to despise the very people he serves each day. It took my mother's death for him to appreciate Levi's love for our family. Levi is the only true friend he has aside from Jeanette and me. That's because he has such a difficult time displaying his emotions. He thinks it belittles him to show his feelings, and I guess what happened to me must have hurt him most of all. I'm so glad you talked him into giving me this time out here. I need to repair what was taken from me. I can't have them huddling around me while I attempt this journey. As far as you and I, being from different worlds, you are way off base. Of course, now it's changed because I've been used. I'll never be good enough to be sought after by any man ever again."

I barked at her, "Julia, never say that to me again. I can understand how you feel at the moment. It took me a long time to find Bart and learn how to deal with my problems. I had a father like yours. Who supported and believed in me my entire life? You are not a used person because you still possess all that exceptional substance that is you inside. I never want to hear you say that crap about not being good enough for anyone ever again. I'm glad you told me all this, but never think that way about yourself because it reeks of self-pity. That's not who you are, Julia."

She asked, "Where's your dad now, Jake?"

I replied, "I lost him four years ago to cancer, and I still feel remorse over that loss every day."

She said, "You know that Patty, my girlfriend, and I ran that shelter with each other for three years. I found from that experience that God has a way of putting the right people together at the proper time."

I said, "Yes, I know about your shelter and a whole lot more about you. Your shelter is how we met that first time. That's why this is so comfortable for me to sit and talk with you. It seems, at times, I've known you all my life, and the greatest regret in my life was not keeping that family dinner date. I've lived with that act of stupidity for a long time as well."

She replied, "That's the other thing about this entire affair. I know some things about you, but not nearly as much as you discern about me. That makes me feel sort of unclothed in front of you."

I said, with a smile, "Well, I've never seen you naked because I'm sure I'd remember that, but I did sleep on your bed in New York. As to the rest, I'll share it with you as long as we stay off the operation's side of what happened in Qatar. That's a discussion for you and Bart, which reminds me, I have an appointment, but I understand you run, is that so? I mean, your jogging here on the compound?"

She asked, "Yes, but are you up for running with that damaged shoulder?"

I answered, "I might hold you back a little in the beginning, but in the end, I think I can keep up with a long-legged gal."

She said, "Why don't we meet up at seven tomorrow at my cottage? That is number twelve, and give it a try."

I stood up and walked inside, thinking about how remarkable she still is. She possessed that same breathtaking beauty. She glowed, and for the life of me, I couldn't believe from her manner; she'd been through this terrible ordeal. She was from all outward appearances healthy, funny, and vibrant, at least until that self-piteous comment that I called her out on.

I pounded on Bart's office door. Someone yelled for me to walk in and take a seat.

Bart said, "Well, partner, are you all settled in?"

I shook my head in the affirmative, and he handed me a sheet of paper.

I asked, "What's this all about?"

He said, "It's a schedule for your stay with us. Starting tomorrow, you're to begin physical therapy, and as you can see, I've blocked out some time for us."

I said, "This sounds good. The quicker you can get me up and running, the faster I can get home to my boat."

He replied, "Planning a trip, are we?"

I said, "All the way here on the plane, all I could think of was the Dry Tortugas and anchoring in the Switchel for some bonefishing."

He asked, "Are you alone on this trip, or is there a lady currently in your life?"

I answered, "I'm alone, and it's been that way for a while. I can't seem to make these connections people all tell me about. However, don't lecture me because you're no better than me."

He said, "That is not quite accurate, Jake. I've been engaged to Tess, whom you have yet to meet for over a year. As a matter of fact, we're getting spliced in two months."

I said, "Well, that's it. Everyone I know is getting married. This has become an epidemic."

He asked, "Is there someone else you know that's getting married?"

I said, "Tony, my buddy, and Regina, a girlfriend of Julia's, are getting married. Julia and I are supposed to stand up for them. They've only known each other since the mission began, and in no time at all, it's love and marriage. I don't understand it."

He said, "There's that famous line from the movie *When Harry Met Sally*. It starts something like, 'When you finally meet the person you want to spend the rest of your life with, you want the rest of your life to start right away.' I don't suppose it's the amount of time you know someone that matters—it's those other things. Look, we have a lot of work ahead, so why don't you start by you telling me what happened from the beginning. Don't leave out any of the feelings that go along with this entire experience. I also want to know all about your emotional state towards the other people involved, and I mean all of them. Jake, take me on the journey like we did it before."

I began with the phone call on that first day and went on from there. It was easy at first, and by the time we had to stop, for the day, I'd put us in Canada. I could see his feelings changing from a disinterested observer to someone beginning a journey with me. I could tell by his expression that he was sensing the experience, if not living through it, with me.

At the end of our first hour, he asked if I had seen Julia since I'd been here. I told him about our encounter this morning. When I mentioned how I had made her laugh and then called her on the self-pitying remark, he thought, for a moment.

I said, "Was that unwise to call her out? Did I do something stupid?"

He said, "No, I think it was a reasonable response. You've both experienced a shock together. You barely know each other, but you can laugh together. Just don't start crying, or you may never be able to stop. Besides, Julia sees you as a pillar of strength, and you and I know that's not true. However, for now, it's all right. She needs to believe that not all men are beasts. She's been through something, you, and I can never completely understand. Right now, it's a nightmare, and that part of it; you do understand."

I said. "Maybe it's not all right with me. Did you ever think of that? I don't want her to view me as some courageous force in her life."

He replied, "Listen, Jake. I know all about your vows never to kill again. I imagine that has something to do with you being here. We're going to come to terms with all of that in due time. If you're interested in her long-term welfare, then continue being her confidant for a while."

I said, "Yes, but—"

He said sternly, "No buts. This girl has been through something far worse than you or I could ever imagine. She's had her real sense of herself destroyed. The woman has returned, but she's here and not at this side of things. Surely you can understand that."

I said, "Of course I can."

He went on, "Most of all, she believes she's unclean, and no man will ever desire her again. So I don't care if she thinks of you as her hero or her brother now. It's phenomenal she's even talking to anyone who is a man except her father and this Levi, the giant man."

I said, "That Levi guy not only raised her and her sister, but he is an exceptional man in his own right. It would pay you to remember that in any dealings or conversations with Julia about him."

Bart sat and thought about this for a moment. "Jake, I've never known you to be so familiar and defensive about anybody as you seem to be about all these people. Is there something more here that I should know more about in treating her?"

I said, "No, I've just come to care and respect these people like family. As for Julia, I arranged to run with her tomorrow. Do you think that's a good idea?"

He said, "Yes, go ahead and have lunch or dinner together. Do what you feel like doing. Only stay away from the abduction for now."

I said, "I was thinking about taking a day and going to Tassajara while I'm out here."

He said, "That's a wonderful idea, and you know it's very close. Now they have cabins you can rent for a night or a few days. Besides, the mineral waters would be excellent for your shoulder. Tess and I have both spent some time with the monks there."

I said, "I didn't plan to go soon, but before I leave."

He said, "Listen, Jake, I think we've made a decent start today. I'll see you tomorrow at the same time."

I expressed my thanks and left his office. I saw a thin red-haired guy with an odd facial tick waiting outside to go to his office.

I said, "Good morning," but got no reply.

I walked back to my cabin and found Julia sitting on my front porch in the rocking chair. "Hi," I said. "To what do I owe this honor twice in one day?"

She said, "I thought you might enjoy a walk around the property to familiarize yourself with the surroundings. I'm volunteering to be your guide. Is that acceptable to you?"

I replied. "Sure is, but I'm going to have a beer first, then we can take a walk."

She said, "Make that two beers."

I said, "Really? A Park Ave. The girl who drinks beer. What will they think of next?"

In a firm tone, she said, "All right, Jake, we can do away with the rich-girl crap right now. I've never made money in my entire life. It's my father's money. None of it's mine. I couldn't care less about it, except it helped me do some things for people who've suffered from true hardship."

I unlocked the door, and she followed me inside.

I said, "I know all about your work among the poor, and I'm sorry for the wisecrack. I didn't mean it quite the way it sounded. It was meant to be funny."

She rejoined, "Apology accepted. Now, what have you got for beer?"

I said, "Let's see, ah, two very cold Labatt's."

She asked, "What exactly is a Labatt?"

I said, "It's a Canadian beer, and it's rather good."

We both grabbed a beer, took sips, and she nodded her approval as we walked out the front door. I followed her, and I had to admit that the view from behind was significantly absorbing in her hiking shorts.

I found myself having errant thoughts. I knew that was wrong, but very difficult to restrain myself. I walked alongside her and began to look at the surrounding woods. We turned a corner and came upon a smaller path, about a mile up, the trail from my cabin. We walked for about thirty minutes and were a mile or so from the cottages when the river expanded into a pool about sixty to seventy feet across and eighty feet long. Beavers built a dam at the far end of the stream. We both took a seat on a large rock and finished drinking our beers.

I asked. "How did you ever find this place?"

She answered. "I was racing Levi, and I made a wrong turn and stumbled upon this place."

I said, "It's certainly peaceful and calm."

She asked, "Do you want to take a swim? The water's cold at first, but it's great after you get in if you can handle it with that arm."

I said, "I don't have a swimsuit with me."

She said, "You have underwear on, don't you?"

I said, "My, but you're a brazen lassie."

She said, "If you're too uptight to swim with a friend, then the hell with you." There she was with that fearless attitude and defiant look again. That's when I recognized she'd be okay.

I said, "Is that what we are? Friends? You hardly know me at all."

She said, "Listen, I know you as well as you know me. From all the mutual friends we share, yes, we're friends, and given what we've experienced together, we'll be friends for the rest of our lives. Jake, forget everything else you did for me. You believed in me and my ability to survive when everyone else gave up, even the people who loved me the most, and that alone makes us bonded in a way few people will ever understand. Now, if I've embarrassed you, I'm sorry."

I said, "No, I'm just not used to this kind of candor. Do you always say exactly what you feel and think? I ask because that's so difficult for me, but I agree with everything you said."

She asked, "Now, do you want to swim with a semi-naked girl or what?"

With that, I chucked my pants, shoes, and shirt and stepped in, turning to look if she had been putting me on. She stood there in a pair of very sheer panties with no bra and dove into the water like a professional. I won't attempt to explain what she looked like that first day. It was fortunate that the water was cold, especially for this Florida boy. We paddled around for a few minutes and settled down next to a large boulder on the other side of the pond.

She said, "Now, aren't you glad you came in?"

I said, "Yes, but I have a nagging feeling when I get out; I'm going to be chilled to the bone."

She asked, "Are you always this serious and gloomy? I mean, is that your true nature?"

I said, "Not always, but I admit that being a cop and a Marine has had its impact on how I perceive the world. I think it's made me a stronger person, and that's a good thing in its idiosyncratic way. However, I have a few problems of my own to settle while I'm out here."

She asked, "Do you have anyone special in your life? I don't mean to be nosey."

I said, "I love it when people say that. 'I don't want to be nosey,'' but then they ask you very intrusive questions. The answer is no. The way I live doesn't lend itself to a home with kids, and in the end, that's what most women want, isn't it?"

She replied, "Your damn right they do, a life-long relationship.

It completes a woman in a way no occupation or political cause ever can. I love girls who try to deny that. You know, my friend Patty?"

I said. "Yes, I sure do, and Tom also. They're both very decent people."

She said. "Good case in point. While we were working at the shelter, Patty told me that I could never marry on more than one occasion. This feeling of being helpful to all these people is all I'll ever require.' The truth was that we were two girls who had such high expectations of someone else; we needed a person to be spectacular. Well, it didn't happen for me because the guy I liked wouldn't even come to dinner, but it did for her when she met Tom. She flipped out over him. She told me after her second date, she was going to marry him. I asked her if he knew that, and she just laughed and said, 'Believe me, he doesn't stand a chance in hell of escaping.'"

I rejoined. "Will I ever be forgiven for that stupid mistake on my part?

She said, "Perhaps. You've come a long way to me, conceding with the gratitude you deserve."

I asked, "Is falling in love and getting married right away how it really happens?"

She said, "Come on, Jake. At your age, you've been in love before."

I said, "No, I never have. I've been in lust, and I've liked a few women whom I've known pretty well, but I can't say I've ever been in love like Tony and Regina. What about you and that Peter fellow from Vermont? Was that real love?"

She said, "No, that was always only friendship, and it could have never been anything else."

I replied, "You'll have a lot of time for that search. I know you're right about one thing: we're going to be friends for a long, long time. In fact, we'll be the very best of friends always. Speaking of that, did you make dinner plans tonight?"

She answered, "No. Are we planning a prison break?"

I couldn't help myself, and again, I began to laugh and explained that with my injured arm, I couldn't drive. However, if she can, I know of a great restaurant in Carmel with the most exceptional seafood. That has been missing from my diet for some time. She jumped up in the water, kissed me on the cheek, and said, "You really are my own Parsifal. He was a knight in shining armor."

I was providing a small escape from all her terrible self-reflections. I knew too well how that could feel. We swam to the other side and took turns averting eyes while the other one got dressed. As we started to walk back, I said we should meet at six at my cottage if she could get a car.

She suggested meeting at her cottage as she wanted me to see it. I agreed, and when we got to the front of her cabin, she turned and said, "Thanks for this afternoon, Jake it was, well . . . I knew from the very beginning, you were an awesome man."

I looked at her and couldn't help myself. "I think you're pretty great yourself, Julia. I've carried that feeling with me since we spent that day together so long ago."

Having said that, I turned and ambled away. I was tempted to turn and glimpse back, but I didn't dare.

Chapter Twenty-Two
Carmel-by-the-Sea

Her cottage was much larger than mine, with a full-sized kitchen and two bedrooms, the master of which contained a king-size bed. She told me it was the largest cottage, and her dad had insisted on having the extra room here if he or Levi wanted to stay over. We shared a glass of vintage wine and afterward went off to find my restaurant.

The drive to Carmel was pleasant, and we listened to a beautiful jazz station coming out of Pacific Grove. The top was down on the jeep. The music was great, and Julia was in a blue summer dress with open white high-heeled sandals. She epitomized the essence of summer itself.

Finally, she asked where we were going. I told her, "Although I don't usually eat in hotels, a good friend told me about a place called the Pacific Edge at the Park Hyatt Hotel in Carmel."

She said, "So let me get this straight, you're luring me to a hotel, and then the idea is to eat fish, and what else?"

I replied, "You know, I'll need some time to get used to your humor and sense of wit."

She said, "Yes, you will. You keep expecting me to have the screaming Mimi's, and I can assure you that I do, but not here, and certainly not with you. You make me feel safe."

I said, "If you get them bad, I want you to know I'm close by. I've been through all this before, so I'll be there for you."

For a moment, she looked at me very seriously and said, "Will you be there for me, Jake, with no more running away this time?"

I said, "You bet your ass, I will, especially if you begin looking at the road."

"Wow," was all she had to say to my admonishment.

We handed the Jeep over to a nice-looking young fellow who directed us to a hostess at the rear of the hotel. I gave her our names, and she said she had our reservation. I'd made the reservation this afternoon for a table at the window that overlooks the Pacific.

The waiter said, "Ah, yes. Please, Mr. and Mrs. Reynard, please follow me. I have your table ready."

We looked at each other at the same time and snickered.

We were escorted by the waiter to a table for two. The table itself faced west, overlooking the entire Pacific. It was given its phenomenal vista by a large glass wall that fully displayed the sea below. There wasn't a wrong table in this whole room. I usually avoid tourist spots, but I had to admit the view here was unrivaled.

Julia said, "Oh, Jake, It's fabulous. Look, you can see sea otters down there. I think I saw a seal go underwater."

She was like a child again. To see her smile like this was more than satisfactory for me. I promised myself even if the food was lousy, I wouldn't express a negative word.

The waiter came to take our drink order, and Julia said, "Since I'm driving, dear, I think we should only have wine, but not just any wine." As she said this, I began to laugh. Then she started, and the poor waiter had to wait while we composed ourselves. I began to apologize, and he interrupted me while smiling and said. "Sir, we get many honeymooners here, and we are used to all the laughing and giggling, and for myself, I say God bless you. I only hope for the rest of your lives; you remember these precious moments, especially when things are not as carefree as they are now."

All that he said only brought on a fresh round of lighthearted gaiety.

Julia began again, "Sir, we are in desperate need of a bottle of Dom Pérignon, and we will remember what you said. We both thank you for your thoughtful insight. We will be counting on your advice when it comes to the menu here. We have not eaten at this hotel before, but we are in the mood for some outstanding seafood."

The waiter enjoined her, "Madame, how would you describe your palates?"

Julia said, "Very sophisticated, and we are well-off. However, we haven't gotten out too much lately. My husband can't keep his hands off me, so you know it's been most days spent in our room. Please tell the chef to make us something exceptional, and would you also bring us a tumbler of cassis on the side to mix with our wine?"

He told us he would procure it with the wine and hurried off to speak to the chef.

I said, "You know, you're incorrigible. You have ruined my chances with every female in a twenty-mile radius."

She began to look serious. I knew then; my stupid attempt at humor fell flat. I recovered with, "On the other hand, being viewed with someone as beautiful as you can only serve to enhance my overall reputation for good taste."

Then her tears began to fall, and I asked, "Oh God, whatever did I say to upset you? I'm so damn thoughtless sometimes."

She said, "No, Jake, it's not you. I'm just so soiled that no one will ever truly desire me again. You might not believe me, but I was a virgin before this happened."

Then I couldn't help myself. I stood up and walked around the table, grabbed her by the shoulders, lifted her with my one right arm, and spoke firmly as hell. "Don't you ever say that to me, as it's not true, and anyone lucky enough to be with you will know how unparalleled you are?

What happened to you is now a part of who you are. This makes you a fighter. You've proven you have real character. I know, from what Levi and your dad have told me, you've always had that in you. Now you've shown real courage to go through a terrible experience that all of us can only guess at, and you proved you can survive on your own terms.

"You're here, and you can smile, laugh, and add something special to everything you share with people. You'll have some more pain ahead, but I know you'll get through this entire ordeal. The Julia that comes out the other side of all this will be stronger and more special if that's even possible."

She asked, "Do you really believe that, Jake?"

I said, "Your damn right. I do, and you had better too."

She said, "Jake, we're making a scene in front of all these people."

Then as she said that, I held her even tighter and said,

"Who cares. Let them look. Even in tears, you look completely magnificent."

We sat and sipped Kir royals and observed the setting sun. I felt no need to speak any further for the moment.

On the way home later, Julia spoke. "Jake, I don't want to take advantage of you, but while you're here, could we do this again occasionally?"

I said, "I have a better idea. One night, we'll eat at your cottage, and one night we'll eat at mine. Mind you, we will do the shopping together, and cook in cooperation, but whoever's cottage we eat in is the chef of the day. Then two days a week, we'll go out to eat—one day; I think Wednesday; we'll dress casually, and on Saturday night, we'll dress up and find some snobby place with music. How's that sound to you?"

She rejoined, "Jake, it all sounds wonderful, and on those other days, I can let out the screaming Mimi's. It will give me something to look forward to."

I kissed her on the cheek at the door like a brother and sealed our contract. I got to my cottage, and I sat up for a while, speculating on the idea that if I'd only met her in different circumstances. If she was a secretary instead of an heiress, what would it be like? I decided that we would be sailing on the Gulf of Mexico aboard the *Switchel* bound to the outer islands. In my heart, I knew this girl was for another man. Marines and ex-cops don't travel in the same circles as she does, no matter what she says or believes now.

This will be our particular time, and somehow it seemed enough. I mean, you couldn't look at Julia and not become aroused. It helped to know what she had been through at the hands of these bastards. Tonight's upset at the table drove home how she truly felt about herself. That would never do. She has to be brought back by someone who was not only gentile and understanding but was willing to call her on the self-pity crap; otherwise, it could devour her.

Yes, if only she was who she purported to be in private and not the daughter of Charles Alexander, the next Secretary of Treasury of the United States, then I'd take her in my life with no reluctance.

My mother was constantly ill, and I could never understand

how my dad could be so resolute in his love for her. Now, I think I realized that to a whole new extent.

I spent enough time thinking about all this. It was a full day, and the feeling that somehow I might be a part of Julia's return to normalcy didn't concern me one little bit.

Chapter Twenty-Three
The New Routine

We began our schedule of running each morning the following day. Our sessions with Bart midmorning taught a workshop speaking about those transformative aspects of self-esteem, two days a week. It was during the second week when Bart queried me about my current situation with Julia.

I said indignantly, "There is no situation with Julia. We spend a lot of time with each other."

He said, "Jake, people in love do many things together. Are you smitten with her?"

I said, "No, but she needs to feel like a human being again. She requires acceptance, and besides, we laugh as if we were children when we're together. It's really a new experience for me as she does the most outrageous things you could ever conceive."

He said gently, "I'm not saying it's a bad thing, Jake. In fact, since you two have begun cooking together and eating out in town at night, I've seen a marked improvement in both of you. It's only that her self-worth has been completely trampled. She doesn't feel she's good enough for anyone yet."

I said, "I know about that aspect of her situation. I try every day to dissuade her from these types of thoughts."

He said, "Am I to understand she's spoken to you about all she's experienced?"

I told him about our first night at that restaurant in Carmel and whatever I expressed to her about the dangers of self-pity.

He asked, "You roared and then said all that to her?"

I said, "Yes, I did. Was I wrong to be so forth-right about it?"

He told me, "No, you did exactly the correct thing. That next day, she began opening up to me in our sessions together."

I said, "Since then, we haven't spoken about her incarceration.

I try to keep things healthy, and it's not really that difficult. Yesterday, when we went shopping, we got this idea to buy some music. We went through the record place and went kind of wacky. It was surprising because we like most of the same music for all of our ten-year age difference. So, we decided to share some of our favorite music with each other.

"Last night, when we cooked dinner at her cottage, we listened to Pavarotti, her choice, and when you listen to this gentleman sing, and you understand the music, it's magnificent, and I especially loved the piece called 'Nessun Dorma' or something like that. It was so powerful. I was making pasta sauce as I listened to him sing, and I was conveyed to another era in time."

He asked, "How do you feel about what we were talking about yesterday? Have you been giving any further thought to the idea?"

I said, "Yes, and I feel there are things we do, and they are very black. Like the way I killed those people. I know no matter how badly I feel, it's not enough. I have to ask for God's forgiveness and understanding. Maybe, I'll be at peace again after I do an act of contrition. I broke the covenant that I'd made with him."

He said, "I agree with you because of your powerful beliefs. When do you plan to go to church and get this handled?"

I said, "I thought since tomorrow is Sunday, I'd go to church. I know Julia and I are going to someplace in Pacific Grove tonight where they have dancing. I'm only fearful we might be out too late for mass the next morning."

He responded, "Maybe you should go before dinner tonight. There's a church in Carmel-by-the-Sea that has a six o'clock Mass on Saturday. I know because Tess and I have gone to that Mass many times."

I responded, "It's an idea. I'll ask Julia first. I don't know how she is with her faith, given what she's experienced."

He said, "She remains strong in her faith. She's a Catholic also, and in the beginning, she wavered. However, I reminded her that she wouldn't be with us now if God had truly deserted her. I think it will do you both good, Jake. There will come a time when you'll have to leave here and here. You're aware of that, right?"

I responded, "Bart, I know there's a part of this passage she has to accomplish on her own. Will you let me know when it's time for me to leave?"

He said, "Yes, I'll tell you, and how are your physical injuries coming along?"

I said, "The leg is almost a hundred percent. I can keep up with Julia on our runs, which I couldn't do before. The shoulder is another matter. It's going to take some more time before these ligament damages heal. I can move it, and it bears weight, so I think it will eventually come all the way back. By the way, have you heard any news from our senior travelers as of late?"

He said, "Yes, they are flying in on Monday, and of course, they call me at least every two days. They drive me a little crazy. If these were the old days and you and Julia were my only patients, it would be easy, but listen to their latest brainstorm. They asked if the property next to us was for sale. I told them, 'Not to my knowledge.' Anyway, that was last week, and yesterday they told me their foundation had bought the fifty acres' adjunct to our property. He said I should begin to think broader and start looking for more therapists. I mean, what in the hell is it with these two guys?"

I replied, "Bart, you've been caught up in the Alexander maelstrom. I'm going to give you some good advice. Speak up to him if he tries to intimidate you. Remember, he's one of the greatest people you will ever have the pleasure of knowing. He just put one billion, that's with the big B, into this Foundation to find and help to miss and trafficked people. That's only the beginning, as he has three billion more to donate without asking for any outside contributions. He's also going to be the Secretary of the Treasury for the United States. He likes you, and when he likes someone, he tries to get him or her to think about their dreams. I believe over this holiday, they've been doing some brainstorming. He had his lawyers buy that land next to yours as an adjunct for this new Foundation."

Bart said, "Jake, I already have a partner, and he's not that rich, but he's a humanitarian too."

I said, "Bart, he knows that, and Charles has probably already spoken to your benefactor. I'll bet you dinner in town on that for the four of us."

He said, "You're on, but you know this is way out of our protocol."

I said, "Protocol, my ass. It's only two old soldiers and a couple of girls having dinner together."

He said, "You know, he's gotten hold of six of the girls who were with Julia. They're flying in on Tuesday. He's paying for their treatment."

I asked, "What do you think about that? I mean, will it have positive or negative implications for Julia?"

He answered, "You know Julia. She has that instinctive benevolent nature. I think it will do her good. She'll have her own baby ducks to watch over. She thrives in that type of nurturing environment. I think this is an excellent time for her to get back to fostering others with her problems."

Later, I remembered it was our dress-up night. I went to retrieve her, and she was standing on the porch attired in a tiny black backless cocktail dress that took me right down the river. "Julia, you look . . . ah . . . ah . . ."

She said, "You better spit out something, Marine, or I'll have Levi pick you up and drop you on your head. I just paid a small fortune for this dress."

I quickly added, "I was trying to say you look extraordinary!"

She said, "That's better. I haven't dressed up for a while, and I wanted our formal night out to be flawless. I didn't want to disgrace you. So, I went into town and bought this dress."

I asked, "Do you have a shawl you can wear over that dress until we get to the restaurant?"

She replied, "Yes, but why do I need to cover up my new dress?"

I said, "I thought if it's all right with you, we could attend mass in Carmel."

She said, "Jake, are you inviting me to go to church with you?"

I said, "Yes, I guess that's a general idea if it's satisfactory with you?"

She answered, "No one besides my sister, Jeanette, has ever

asked me to church. Yes, I think that's wonderful, and I'd be proud to accompany you to celebrate mass."

We went to a lovely old stone church done in an original Spanish style at the center of Carmel-by-the-Sea. The Priest said. "Turn to your neighbor and say, 'Peace be with you.' We fell into each other's arms, whispered the words, and were unable to separate from each other. Finally, we turned and shook hands with everyone in the congregation standing nearby. The sermon was on bravery in the face of adversity. It seemed tailor-made for her and me. He spoke of God being our copilot, and we looked at each other and didn't stop holding each other's hands throughout the entire Mass.

The rest of the evening in Pacific Grove was filled with an atmosphere of great food and wine, with a jazz quartet playing in the background. Later, we heard the best young African American chanteuse; I've ever heard in my life. We danced to all her favorite songs, and for a guy who doesn't waltz, I did damn fine—some of those lessons my mother sent me to in eighth grade finally paid off. Julia felt beautiful in my arms, and it was challenging to keep my mind focused on the music.

I decided, when the band took a break, to introduce something new to our conversation.

I asked, "Are you aware that there are some ladies who were with you in Oman, and they are arriving on Tuesday?"

She replied, "Yes, I do, and at first I thought, no way; it was going to bring that entire nightmare back. However, now I know I can help support one another. We understand one another better than anyone else."

I said, "Julia, you absolutely amaze me. I don't want our schedule of dinners to interfere with these additional responsibilities you're going to assume with these women."

She said, "Jake, if you are trying to back out of our deal, I'll murder you. This is what keeps me in balance. I need you and me to continue swimming, shopping, and cooking together."

I said, "You're right. If it wasn't for the things we share together, I'd have gone home a long time ago."

She said, "Oh my God, I never even thought of that. I'm keeping you here with all of my demands."

I said, "Nobody is keeping anyone anywhere. Are you doing exactly what you desire doing?"

She said, "Oh, yes, Jake. I'm happy being here with you?"

I replied, "I'm having the time of my life. My mother is looking down on us, and she's saying, 'You see, I told you those dancing lessons would come in handy one day.' Listen, I have an idea about tomorrow. Would you like to hear it?"

She replied, "I'd love to hear about tomorrow."

I said, "I found a place in Monterey where we can rent a pretty decent-sized sailboat. I thought if you want, I will take you sailing tomorrow."

She said, "Oh, Jake, I would love that more than anything else."

I said, "Then it's settled. Tomorrow, I'll show you where I get my life sorted out. No matter whatever's happened to me, even my mother's and dad's deaths, which was the worst, I've always found total peace on the sea."

She said, "Jake, I need to speak to you about something. I

get a little confused at times as I've observed these two sides of your nature. In Oman, I saw a fearless warrior who went on and on even with a knife sticking out of his shoulder. When I first saw you, I knew it was that same you from before. It was so hard to believe, but there you were. You were so clear in your purpose, and that filled me with great confidence. Then I saw you severely wounded, and Regina knew there was something terribly wrong and transfused you with my blood. I thought I was going to lose you all over again. You are gentle and sensitive, and I wonder, which is real, or is this only a figment of my imagination? I mean, you have come to mean so much to me, and I couldn't stand losing you again. What I am trying to say is, I can accept that you are noble, compassionate, and fierce."

I said, "Julia, I don't know how to explain it, but I feel the same way about you. If there is any part of me that is gentle, then it's because of you in my life. This time we've shared together has altered me forever."

As she stood, we caressed, and all our words stopped. We shared a very silent journey back to the center.

We called it an early night because of our sailing trip in the morning.

When we said "Good night" at her front door, she reached up and kissed me with an embrace filled with passion and promise. It was definitely not a brotherly kiss. I would have taken her up in my arms there and then, but common sense prevailed. I walked away with her kiss, still burning on my lips.

I sat with a glass of wine, trying to sort through all the complicated feelings I experienced. I knew what was best for Julia from the very beginning. I had always put not hurting her above everything else, but it seemed these last four weeks together changed us in new and unexpected ways.

This was no longer a phase. I had rescued Julia, and in her mind, I was her knight. I didn't count on that it might be myself who would have the problem of letting go of her. From the shopping to sitting on the porch playing scrabble, everything we did had become precious to me. I felt a change in myself in her presence. There was little doubt as to the influence she was having on me.

I'd known women before, and it usually moved into the

bedroom rather rapidly. When that first heat slacked off, nothing left to bind me but this habit of being together. Lately, I'd been putting more of an effort into these liaisons, but to no avail. With Julia, I was beginning to learn the value of true friendship from a woman.

When I bought the *Switchel*, its refitting had consumed most of my time. I didn't even care when Ann decided to try it again with her husband, Bradley. I actually felt relief if the truth were to be told. I had never experienced what Tony described to me about his feelings for Regina. I knew what he felt now. He'd found his other half.

I kept this thought in front of me because of what Julia had experienced in her abduction. That had followed the physical feelings I held in check, but it became more challenging to be around her without displaying the affection I felt within.

I knew when the other girls showed up, it would all move back in on her. That might be the right time for me to leave. I made up my mind on my return. I was going to take the *Switchel* for a few weeks and get my head straightened out. I needed to get out of this whirlwind of emotions because this wasn't my method of reasoning.

Chapter Twenty-Four
Sailing

The morning came another beautiful day, and I heard a knock at the front door while still in the shower. I yelled for whomever to come in, and two minutes later, Julia was standing there in my bathroom.

I yelled, "Hey, I'm not decent, little girl!"

She said. "I was only thinking of that first day we met, sailor."

I said, "You're in a curious mood. I only hope you don't get seasick out there. Could you please toss me a towel?"

She replied, "No, but I'll hand you one."

With that, she strolled over to the shower towel in hand, as brazen as can be, while I was standing there stark naked.

I said, "Are you satisfied, you reckless hussy, now that you've thoroughly shamed me?"

She replied, "Jake, from where I'm standing, you have nothing to be ashamed about."

I grabbed the towel, shooed her out of my bathroom, dried myself, and threw on a pair of old faded jeans.

I walked outside, and she'd already made coffee.

She said, "See the service you receive when you inspire a girl so early in the morning."

We drank our coffee and headed off for the Monterey Pier, where I'd rented a 1967 twenty-five-foot O'Day sloop. I took over ten minutes explaining the various lines and procedures for coming about through the wind. We had a perfect day for sailing, fifteen-knot winds blowing steady from the east, and this boat was beautifully maintained. We went out of the dock slowly under power, watching the seals and otters as we motored out to the opening, to the sea.

You had to avoid this massive amount of kelp that filled the bay. Observing these animals close up is a great experience. We'd gone out on the run, and I had to decide whether to turn north or south at the mouth of the bay. In speaking to the dockmaster at the marina, he suggested a southerly course and gave me some excellent compass bearings. He said it was very scenic sailing south toward Big Sur and gave me some landmarks to begin my sail home.

Julia was curious about everything I was doing. She made me drill her on the names of all the sails, sheets, and lines. I don't know if Julia was kind-hearted because she knew how much I loved to sail or if she was truly fascinated. She seemed to enjoy it immensely, and when I made the turn south, I let her handle the wheel. I put out a one-ten genoa that I reduced to 70 percent, then set both sails for a broad starboard reach.

We were moving along with the wind at full speed. My heart quickened with the increasing wind on the outside. We were both lost in our own thoughts. There is not much need to speak at sea, and she seemed to appreciate that fact. Bless her, as people who prattled while I sailed drove me crazy."

An hour of this, and suddenly there was a big whoosh twenty-five yards off the starboard side, near the bow as a colossal humpback whale sounded alongside us. We both happened to be looking in the exact same place at the right time. All that came out of Julia's mouth was, "Oh, Jake! Look!"

I observed her. She looked back, and we both smiled as if we'd discovered the secret of life together. I had only seen one other whale in my real-life sailing, and it was nowhere near this close to the boat. I was actually frightened as she could have come up under us and flung us into an icy cold sea.

The Alaskan current runs up the coastline, and we wouldn't last ten minutes in this water. I decided there, and then I would never tell Julia and ruin this beautiful moment we were sharing.

"Oh, Jake," she said, "when we're together, we experience some of the most wonderful things."

I thought to myself, *Yes, we do, and some of the most horrifying as well*, but I said nothing and only gave her my biggest smile.

Our whale kept pace with us for almost a half-hour, and then she sounded and didn't reappear.

Julia had been lugging around an ice chest all morning, and I thought it was time to find out why she brought it along.

I asked, "Julia, do you, perchance, have any food in that thing, and if so, where did you get it at five this morning?"

She replied, "If you hadn't suggested this sailing trip, I was going to propose a picnic. So, I arranged yesterday afternoon with the chef. I bribed him. The chef was a little put off when I called him at eleven last night to make new arrangements for an earlier pickup, but they all think you and I are a bit screwy anyway."

I said, "Let's head up into that cove over there and anchor in. That's a two-man job, so I'll set the anchor forward after we drop sails, and you'll have to operate the motor. All you have to do when I signal is to put it in reverse here and apply a little throttle, and that will set in the anchor."

She replied with a great smile, "Aye, aye, Captain! I stand fast in my duties."

I said thoughtfully, "No fooling around because this deck is wet, and if you jerk the boat into reverse, I will go into the drink, and that's freezing cold water. Understand?"

She said with a sly look, "Jake, would I do something like that to you?"

I said, "Yes, you'd do it in a heartbeat. It's my experience that girls who sneak into men's bathrooms to take a peek at them showering are capable of anything."

She said, "Ha-ha, you're right, I would, but we don't have dry clothes. I'll save that trick for Florida after you've forgotten you told me."

We anchored in without a hitch, and the cove offered us decent shelter from the east-blowing winds. She opened the cooler and started exposing amazing things like foie gras and a grand Château Margaux with cold chicken in a green tarragon sauce, and the baguette, fruit, and a marvelous cheese rounded out our lunch. We were soon stuffed, and I decided to take a little nap on the lazaretto cushions. The wine, the sun, and the gentle rocking of the boat received their toll, and I was asleep in a matter of minutes.

I'd slept for about an hour, and when I awoke, the first thing I saw was Julia looking at me. Tears were streaming down her cheeks. I jumped up and said, "What's the matter? Did I say or do something stupid in my sleep?"

She said, "No, you, silly ass. Don't you know girls sometimes cry when they're delighted?"

I said, "No, I didn't, but what I know about women, you could put on the head of a pin."

She said, "I don't believe that, Jake. I think you know how to make lots of people happy. You have this wonderful gift for motivating people—my dad, for instance. And by the way, they're flying in tomorrow and want us to join them for dinner. I told them they were interfering with our dinner schedule, and they both laughed. They asked if we could join them if that's all right with you."

Suddenly, her face grew grave, and she said, "Jake, do you mind if I go below for a minute?"

I said, "Of course not. You can do anything you want, but if you're going to use that bathroom, there are directions on the wall you have to follow regarding the pumping device."

She said no and took another bag she'd brought aboard and went below, stepping nimbly.

I was sitting on the lacerate, thinking about how confusing women can be when she called below for me to come down. As I descended the three steps down to the cabin floor, I saw her standing there naked. I said nothing for a moment as I drank in all her exquisiteness. When I began to speak, she took the three steps necessary to move closer and put her hand softly on my lips.

She said softly, "Jake, I need you to let me speak. No matter what you do or don't feel for me, I have to know what it's like to be with a man without abuse and debasement. I'm asking you, no; I'm begging you to help me feel like a woman again. I know you look at me when you don't think I see you. I also know about your honor, but you will do this if you really want to be noble to me. Make love to me because you're the only man who could, the only one I can trust."

I looked down at her beautiful face and knew if I didn't do this, it would be a greater sin than if I did. Saying nothing, I put my hands on the sides of her face and kissed her deeply and gently. Then I picked her up in my arms and kissed her repeatedly on her opened mouth. I laid her on the double bunk and quickly removed my clothes. I laid down next to her, and she moved into the crook of my right arm. Then we began that dance as old as time, but in a way, I'd never experienced before.

No thinking or speaking, only tender and loving caresses of our two bodies. Julia's hair, and lips, and breasts were all mine. I lingered at each step, never even thinking of completion. Her beautiful behind was caressed by my left hand until after a period of exchanging kisses, I moved slowly down her body and took her into my mouth. She was already wet, and that drove me into a frenzy as I began to softly lick the edges of her mons. In a matter of moments, she began to quiver, and I breathed her in as her first orgasm began its release.

A short respite and she took me in her hands and said, "Jake, I need you inside me now."

I asked, "Is that acceptable to you?"

She answered, "Yes, yes, please, Jake, join your life to mine."

I allowed her to guide me into her. I lay a moment inside her, and something in me began to drive me. It was somewhere

where needs, wishes, and physical desires became all muddled together. These emotions I felt were so strong they threatened to overwhelm me. We climbed together, reaching out for each other's mouths with our tongues, and we came within seconds of each other while looking deeply into the other's eyes. The kiss had been overwhelming as it took me over human boundaries. When we were spent and lay there looking at each other, a smile glistened on her face, and she said, "Oh, Jake, you are my ultimate love." I was her most faithful secret.

Her hands had been firmly locked around my back, and I remembered her pulling me in even more profound when we came. I'd never experienced that before. Speechless, I looked at her. She very slowly began to roll her hips, almost imperceptibly at first. Her mouth sought mine out again, and I felt myself becoming hard once more. Her small thrusts moved me to a heightened state of magnified sensitivity.

This was a new first for me, becoming excited so swiftly after having just climaxed. This time as I grew to full strength, Julia slowly rolled over the top of me. That wasn't new, but the way she did it was. She lifted herself up straight in the air and then came down on me even slower. I can't explain the impact of this, but it didn't take long for us to arrive at that amazing place that had become ours alone. Everything was so simple yet so loving and intimate.

I've read books about people concluding this act together, but in my experience, you gave a woman an orgasm, so you didn't leave her high and dry. Unbelievably, my father gave me that advice before I left for boot camp. It stood me rather well until this moment. There was no contrivance or forethought here. We were only two people who cared deeply for each other, seeking new means of expressing the ultimately inexpressible.

This was all beyond words and without pretense. Julia removed herself slowly, and I felt a physical loss at extraction. She grabbed my hand, and we went topside naked, where she pushed me into the cushions and laid down in my arms.

She uttered, "Jake, I'm not going to become mushy with you. Nevertheless, you can't imagine what you've done for me today. No matter what you may believe, you will always be in the very deepest part of my heart."

I said, "You as well, Julia. I can't express what I feel now. I think we said it all, so I'm going to lie here and experience the moment."

She said, "Yes, that's true. Sometimes words only get in the way."

We laid here until the afternoon sun began to burn deep into us, then we weighed anchor and started the two-hour sail back to Monterey. We arrived just when the sun was setting, and the dockmaster said he'd become concerned. I explained we had done some sunbathing, and he said, "You sure did. You're both as red as beets. You two better lay down in a tub full of tea."

"Tea?" I asked. "What will that do for us?"

Julia said, "Yes, Levi told me about that a long time ago. It has something to do with the tannin in tea. It takes away the sting of sunburn."

On the drive back, we were quiet. It wasn't an awkward silence, but a relaxed kind of what could be a sense of inner peace. It was exactly like the way I felt after Mass last night. We arrived in camp and decided on this rare occasion. We would go to the restaurant in the main building of the clinic for dinner.

We no sooner walked into the dining room when we saw Bart and Tess sitting, at a table, waving us over. I turned to Julia and said. "You realize they're going asking us to join them, and I think we both look like two cats who just ate a canary."

She says, "Well, I don't know about you, but I didn't eat any canary. I just had this great-looking guy screw the living hell out of me. I've never experienced that in my entire life."

That was it. When these outlandish things came out of Julia's sweet, angelic face, it totally cracked me up as she knew it would. Here we were, walking over to them. She had this straight face, and I was almost crying from laughing so hard.

Bart said, "What's so funny?"

I said, "It's this female patient of yours. She knows exactly how to strike my funny bone, and she takes great delight in it. I believe underneath, she's a true sadist."

He said, "Well, why don't you join us? That is unless you're headed for the infirmary. How in the hell did you both get so burned?"

I answered, "We went sailing, and I guess we fell asleep at anchor."

Bart asked, "Didn't you wear some kind of protection?"

Now it was Julia's turn to laugh. She started to say, "Not really," but set about laughing in the middle of her own reply.

Tess turned to Bart and said, "You know; for a psychologist, you don't grasp people worth squat. They were obviously having fun. You remember the fun. That's what we used to do before you decided to work twenty-four hours a day, and I was crazy and stupid enough in love to join you in all this insanity."

I stepped in, "Hey, we don't want to start a family squabble."

Bart said. "No, no, please sit down. It would be great to have a meal with friends for a change. Tess is right. We hardly get to do anything together anymore."

Julia said, "Bart if you're nice to Jake and me before we

leave, I'll let you in on a secret that will solve some of those problems for you both."

Bart said, "Oh, first you tease him, now you're going to begin on me. What is this secret?"

She returned, "Sorry, not until we leave. It's our secret for the moment. I promise before we leave to share it with you. Is that a deal?"

He replied, "I guess I don't have much choice. Don't you guys hurt from that sunburn?"

Julia said, "Yes, we have a date with a bathtub full of tea after dinner."

Tess asked, "Tea, like the kind you drink with lemon?"

Julia said, "Yes, an old sailor told us all about it. I think I'm going to try it. I don't know about Mr. Macho here, but I'm up for whatever takes away the sting."

We ordered dinner, and Julia told Bart she wanted to help with the new girls coming in on Tuesday. He explained that he wouldn't need her on Tuesday because he had set up indoctrinations with all his staff with that many people coming in at once. He said. "What I'd really like, if you can spare the time, is for you to organize a group and lead it twice a week. You're the kind of person they can relate to in sharing the same experience. They'll know they can come to you with their problems." He told her that by participating in the recovery of the others, her own healing would speed up dramatically.

She looked at me, and I said, "He's right. Whenever you talk out these emotions with someone who's suffered the same experiences as you, you begin to recall effects. There are things you haven't thought of that start to click in your mind, and the suppressed experiences begin to complete themselves. Once that cycle is complete, you'll have taken back your life.

"Besides, I am going to have to get back to Duke and my former occupation. There is Tony and Regina's wedding coming up. You and I are supposed to stand up for them. I can't stay here and let you keep babysitting me."

She said, "I knew this was coming, and I'm going to be a good scout. When I return to Florida, you're taking me sailing again, and that's a pact?"

I said, "Yes, Julia, I wouldn't dream of giving your bunk to anyone else. It's yours when you feel up to it. Maybe, I'll even show you the Leeward Islands."

Bart and Tess were looking at us as if we were speaking in tongues.

I said, "Julia took to sailing like a duck to water. I think she likes it, or she's shining me on to spare my ego."

She said, "Save your ego! First of all, I truly loved it, and the experience with the whale was unbelievable. You guys understand a *berth* means 'a bed on a ship' and the job that goes with it. I didn't do too badly for the first time out, did I, Jake?"

I said, "No, as a matter of fact, I've never sailed with anyone who, on their first sail, could remember the names of all the lines and sheets."

Bart began laughing like hell, and except for Julia, we all looked at him, wondering what was so funny.

Bart said, "Jake, my friend, you've been had in the loveliest way possible. You have been had even so. Our Ms. Julia Anne

Alexander, summa cum laude graduate of . . . what was it? Brown?"

Julia said, "Yes, Mr. Smarty-Pants, and if you don't stop right now, I'll never tell you about that secret place."

Bart replied, "Sorry, but this is a guy thing. She came to me two weeks ago and borrowed *Sailing: The Basics*. The author is David Franzel or some world-renowned sailing character."

I looked straight at her, and she just gave me that smile of hers, saying, "I thought if ever you asked, I could benefit from a little knowledge beforehand. Alexander's are like that, and right now, Daddy is probably walking around with books on baseball and driving Levi crazy, asking him questions about batting stats and the infield fly rule. If we care about someone, we try to share his or her interests. That doesn't nullify the fact that today was still one day in a million on so many different levels."

Tess jumped in and asked, "What was all that about a whale?"

I began to explain, "We were sailing down the coast when a

humpback sounded not twenty yards from the boat."

Bart said, "You must have been frightened out of your minds?"

"No, actually, it was quite the opposite. It was all very soothing and a little otherworldly," I shared.

Julia jumped in, "When you're cruising, you get this feeling of how tiny we all are and how immense God's universe truly is, so it follows that our problems, no matter how large on land, seem to diminish when you're on the sea. It's all a matter of proportion. The whale only added another dimension, and it overwhelmed us. It's as if God was telling us, 'My world is great and immeasurable. I made it all for you. All living things, large and small, are for you and are a part of you.' I don't know if I'm saying this correctly."

I looked at her and said, "I've been sailing since I was a kid. I've always felt precisely like what you just said, but I've never been quite able to express it as perfectly as you did right now."

When we said "Good night" later, I felt I should kiss her. The surroundings made me feel somewhat guilt-ridden. Had

I done the right thing today, or was I playing with emotions that could backfire on me? This was someone whom I cared for more than anyone else was in the world. I caressed her and walked away.

I was lying in bed, and in no more than five minutes, I heard a noise. Then a couple of moments later, Julia was standing next to my bed, disrobing. She paused in the moonlight, and it played against her beautiful breasts and long legs. She turned back the covers, slid in next to me, and said, "Knowing you; I can already imagine the conversation you're having with yourself. Even if not, one thing you're thinking is true unless you're thinking that it was the most amazing experience of making love you've ever had. Jake, I want you to hold me now and let that all go. I don't want to sleep in that big bed alone, and I intend to take full advantage of your body in the morning. You had better get some sleep because you're going to need it. Please don't second-guess today. It's been one of the best days of my life, and I need it and you to stay exactly where you are in my heart."

When she said that, I rotated her into my arms, kissed her

long and deep, and we spooned like children for a good night's sleep. I slept like a child. She'd expressed it all for me.

We spent all the next day making love in every nook and cranny of my cottage. We did it in the bed, the kitchen table, the couch, the hot tub, and the big comfortable chair in front of the fireplace. We ate and talked about a thousand things except what we were doing or thinking.

I asked her where she obtained her love of baseball. She admitted it started with a crush on Gary Jetter, but she began to love the game in the process. We played a game of statistics on all the Yankee World Series players for the last fifty years on my chest.

Yes, she knew all about Murderers' Row, which completely stunned me. She also learned about Don Larson's no-hitter in the World Series of 1956. He pitched the only perfect game in postseason play up until then.

We spoke of fantasies unfulfilled; dreams lived worth repeating and about doing all these things with someone's special. The right someone would be genuinely exceptional. Mostly, we agreed that simple everyday things were best when shared.

We skirted all other issues in light of the last two days that could possibly diminish this feeling. We wanted nothing to ruin these precious moments together.

At one point or another, the world tried to invade us with telephone calls and missed appointments. We claimed we were not feeling well while turning down offers of assistance. Sunburn was the culprit, and we blamed it for everything that was keeping us in my cottage.

We slept in my cottage that night in case her father and Levi showed up ahead of schedule. There was no going back from the course we'd set upon.

At seven the following day, we went to her cottage, and the phone began ringing. It was Charles explaining they would be here in time for dinner. With a temporary stay of execution at hand, we decided to spend the day at our pool in the woods.

Making love in cold water is challenging. What is life without some small challenges? I'd discovered in being with her that I had everything figured out incorrectly. I must look her through the eyes of pure emotion and love her with all my preconceptions absent. It had never been like this with anyone. I failed to understand how I missed all this in the past. I lost count of how many times we made love in the last three days. In the afternoon, we were sitting on our boulders, being silent, when she turned to me and said, "I have secrets I want to share with you. However, I need your pledge; they will stay between us."

I said, "Okay, you have my scout's honor."

She went on, "Before the Marine Corps birthday party in November, it's going to be announced that General Wingate will take over as the new Commandant and receive his fourth star. He's called to check up on our progress. He's really a very nice man and unusually sensitive, which I didn't expect. Anyway, at or before the party, he will ask Levi to stay onboard and become the new Sergeant Major of the Marine Corps. He polled all the senior NCOs, and they all agree that Levi would add to what your Corps desperately needs today. He said Levi's old-fashioned values and sense of loyalty are what is missing in your Corps. Is this job essential, Jake, or is it only a ceremonial position?"

I said, "It's the top soldier of our entire Corps. It can be as important as the guy who takes it on makes it. Our legends are dying off, and with their deaths, a bit of the true values that make the Marine Corps so special are dying as well. I can see the general's point. Levi is a symbol of both his prior actions and demeanor. He epitomizes what the Marine Corps is all about, and the great thing is, he wouldn't be afraid to make those necessary changes. Yes, he should take it, for himself and for the Corps, we both love so dearly."

She said, "That leaves another difficult situation as Daddy will be moving to Washington. He must put all his holdings in a blind trust and give up his directorship of this new Foundation to take up the President's offer to be Secretary of the Treasury. The same trust agreement goes for Levi as well. Daddy says it wouldn't look right to have the sergeant major of the Marine Corps heading a billion-dollar foundation. I know Daddy named you as the third man. In fact, you're already on the papers and all the Foundation bank accounts."

I said, "Yes, I know, and I told him he had no right to do

any of that. I don't know a thing about handling this type of finance. I planned on settling this with them when they make an appearance today."

She said, "Jake, sometimes you're a little impenetrable. This is not Daddy's way of a backdoor to reward you for finding me. If he wanted to do that, he'd just buy a ton of stock and put it in your name without you even knowing it."

I asked, "Well, then, what is it? I mean, I think it's a wonderful thing he wants to accomplish. However, there are many famous people out there who would gladly do this for only the honor involved."

She said, "You're right, but don't you see? Daddy has had a lot of dealings with famous people. He doesn't trust any of them. He trusts you, and he's going to get you all the help; you'll need to do this job. You're going to be able to name all the directors; you want to work with you. You would have to be in New York two or three times a month for a few days or more. If you're on a case, then one of your co-directors could stand in for you. You'll have our apartment all to yourself. His one request is that he doesn't want to let anyone on staff get laid off. Besides, on occasion, you'd have a friend to take to dinner, and you might even get a little decent sex out of this deal."

I said, "That's the only thing. You've said so far that tempts me in the least."

She went on. "Daddy said if you turned him down, he would have to let this Foundation lie fallow for the next four years. He's that determined. Jake, and I want you to follow your destiny. I think you should think long and hard about this offer. I can tell; he's come to love you, and he wants to see you fulfill your true purpose in life. There's another matter. I'd like you to do this for all the other missing women and me still out there awaiting rescue."

I said, "Well, you might as well give me all your requests at one time. What are the rest?"

She said, I want to see Levi receive his honor, and I want you to escort me to the Marine Corps ball. I promise I won't embarrass you. I'll make you proud to be with me."

I looked at her sitting there shining like the sun, totally

naked and beautiful beyond description. I was hooked. I was in love for the first time in my life. This would be agonizing, excruciating because we lived in different worlds and had such dissimilar existences. I could do this for Charles. I'd get Duke to help me, but could I, in a few months, stop loving her and allow her to get on with her own destiny? Let her find that one person she's supposed to be with forever?

I made a vow sitting on that rock that I would because I cherished her so much, and there's nothing selfish about loving someone like this. You're compelled to honor that love above all else.

I said, "Okay, I'll do it, Julia."

She asked, "Okay, to which of my requests, Jake?"

I said, "I'm willing to do all these things that you want of me. I mean everything you asked for, I will try with all of my heart to achieve them."

Someday I will tell you what it can do to you inside, and not everyone has someone like you to make them feel worthy again."

I said, "Julia, nobody could ever destroy who you are—nothing. You were hurt badly, but you have that heroic stuff within you in vast abundance. That comes along rarely and in very few people."

She said, "Jake, you don't know what it feels like to hear you say that to me. From you, it means the entire world, and what about the birthday ball? Can we go together?"

I said, "Ms. Alexander, I would be proud to escort you to the ball on one condition."

She asked, "What's the one condition?"

I replied, "You must wear more clothing than you have on now. Even the most battle-hardened Marines are susceptible to heart attacks when confronted by such naked loveliness."

We both cracked up, and I looked at the time. I realized Charles and Levi were probably waiting for us at the cottage by now.

I remarked, "I hope; I didn't leave anything in your cottage, like underwear or any other clothes."

Julia said, "Jake, we're adults, and I don't want to place our personal life on parade, but it's our private business. I'm enormously happy about what we share. Are we clear on that part of this?"

I said, "You know; you're beginning to sound more like my mother every day."

She replied, "Good because boys always seek out girls who act like their mothers."

Chapter Twenty-Five
Dinner Out

As we came across the clearing near Julia's cottage, Charles and Levi were sitting on the front porch.

Charles spoke first, "We thought you two had gotten lost out in the woods."

Julia said, "Daddy, Jake has something to tell you that will make you very happy. I'm going inside to make some lemonade. I'm going to make it fresh, so you have about twenty minutes to gossip about me until I reappear. Then we will bathe, and Jake and I are taking you to a small restaurant we found in Pacific Grove. You're going to see otters, seals and have a great meal while this fabulous chanteuse sings her heart out for both of you."

With that, she turned, not requiring any reply, and went into her cabin.

Charles said. "What did you think of that, Levi?"

Levi spoke up, "I think she's starting to sound like our old Julia. She's taking over, and I think it's wonderful."

Charles added, "Yes, I agree wholeheartedly."

I said, "You mean, she always bosses you two around like that?"

Charles said, "Yes, and she's very good at it. It's never about anything for herself. Do you mean she doesn't boss you around?"

I answered, "Well, not directly; I don't think. I get to make most decisions on where to eat, what we're going to eat. Anyway, it's not important. You're correct. Julia's usually right about everything."

Charles asked, "You mean you've been eating together all this time?"

I said, "It's complicated. We got into this thing where we ran in the mornings, and then we cooked together one night, and that became two and three nights, and there's a casual night out, and on Saturday, we do a dress-up night. We've become close throughout the time we've spent here.

"We went sailing yesterday in the Pacific. We had a whale sound right next to the boat. We both got sunburned. Well, that's another whole thing that is a long story."

They were looking at each other as if I was speaking like a crazy person. Charles said. "It sounds great, Jake, that you've become such great friends. I assume that accounts for the change in her voice over the phone these last several weeks."

I said, "Listen, I'm not stupid. I know Julia likes me. You know, the guy who rescued her and all that crap. She needed to have someone nearby to depend on, but now I think she's ready to go on alone."

Charles responded, "She told you that?"

I answered, "In her own way. I told her she should become more involved with these other girls who shared that horrible experience with her. Actually, by serving them, she will help herself with some of those lingering feelings."

Levi finally spoke, "What you're saying makes perfect sense. If you leave now, do you think she could regress?"

I said, "Hell, no. This girl is powerful and courageous."

That little reveal made them stop and glance towards me. I said, "Look, it's not what you're thinking, so ease off on any judgments you may make."

Charles asked, "What is this happy news you have for us?"

I said, "I don't know what good I'll do, but I'll take on this Foundation job on certain conditions."

He asked, "What are those conditions exactly?"

I said, "First, I need Duke McGarrety to work with me. He will keep your Wall Street sharks honest. He knows how to organize things, so we can get the money to where it's needed most. He won't be conned in the process. I'll handle the tactical, meaning I'll put together small teams of investigators and instruct them and meet with your fellows regularly. We will select the projects or individual cases to see if we can affect the outcome positively.

"We'll need a name, something that people will recognize when they've lost a loved one or a child. I thought, why not name it (The Missing Child Foundation).

"I learned something significant during our situation. These new Special Forces guys have the training and equipment to make these types of extractions. We're dinosaurs when it comes to what they know today and the types of equipment they have."

At this point, Julia came out with a tray, and we all took a glass of lemonade from her plate.

Charles began, "Jake, it's my turn. Levi and I agree with all your conditions. Like you, we see this as an agency outside the manacles of government. At some point in the process, you will have to bring them into the loop. Julia, is this conversation going to upset you?"

She replied, "Upset me? Didn't he tell you who browbeats him into accepting this job? Do you know he's an extremely stubborn man?"

Charles said, "Yes, we're familiar with that aspect of his

personality. However, it's shown itself to be extremely effective. Now, to get back to where I was, you must know this, son. I have spoken in person with the president, and the Treasury Department is in a mess, so with that advantage in hand, I told him my agenda for acceptance was for him to put the subject of Human Trafficking on his platform for reelection. He agreed, and his speechwriters are working on it as we sit here. Actually, he thought it was a brilliant idea. It will be introduced at a major press conference next week. Now, for the choicest part, I'll let you tell him, Levi."

Levi spoke up, "Jake, you know the Corps had always gotten the short end of the stick when it came to training and equipment. These people in DC have woken up to the idea that future engagements will call for more specialized soldiers. More Delta Forces, Seals, Air Forces PJs, and more Force Recon are about to be united under a single banner and become the Special Operations Regiment. Everyone will be brought up to speed in the next one to two years, and all those units will be expanded no matter who is elected. Army and Navy and Air Force, and Marine Corps Special Operations units will work with each other under that single command. They will live and train at Mac Dill Air Base in Florida and Coronado in California. They all will get the latest gear and still handle all their individual mission assignments.

He went on. "You of all people know these people have a high degree of unit pride. So that will be their cornerstones for excellence. The way it works is, no matter how enlightened our military becomes, it's still military-style rational. When it's your needs from these Special Operations guys, you can't always come to us for influence. That's best used for bigger problems. So it was General Wingate's idea, and we agreed to make you a permanent captain in USMC Reserve with the understanding. You would complete the war college course next summer. It's only four weeks, including time at Fort Meade, to bring you up to speed on new weapons and tactics. Before you go crazy, you will still be able to draw your salary at the foundation. That is two hundred and fifty thousand dollars a year plus living expenses because we knew if we gave you what anyone else would require, you'd turn us down flat. You have to accept that. If you want to donate it or burn it, that's your choice."

All this time, I said nothing. Julia was looking at me with extreme intensity. It was as if she was feeding me her brain waves telepathically.

I sighed, trying to take it all in, and realized Julia wanted me to do this for her. For some reason, it was important to me that she remained proud of me no matter what would happen between us. However, I wasn't going to roll over all that easy.

I said, "Pardon me, Julia, but you know you; guys do a lot of meddling in other people's lives. What's frightening is no matter; whether you're right or wrong, you seem to believe that it's okay to do this to people."

Charles began to speak, "Now, Jake, please. "

I said firmly, "You wait, Charles; I'm not done. First, you get me entangled in this Foundation without speaking to me. I mean, you went and filled out all those papers. Now, suddenly I'm back in the Marine Corps. Since I accepted the initial commission, they have me locked in. There's something called to service at the convenience of the government. You two have put me in a position that if they say tomorrow, 'Jake, go to Iraq,' which, by the way, I think we have no business being involved in; I would have to go. Go into harm's way for something I don't believe in. What's more, no matter what you say, I'd go because it would be an order, and I'd be a Marine officer."

Charles spoke. "Well, Jake, I don't think Levi or I thought of it that way. Does this mean you're going to turn us down?"

Julia looked at me and shook her head, no. She was standing behind them where they couldn't see her.

I asked, "What about my business in Florida? I just hired Tony, and now I'll need him to render his service to this foundation. I'll have to resign from my own company. You can't do anything like this half-ass because it wouldn't work."

Charles spoke again, "We thought of all that. Actually, Regina was about to give up her apartment when I stopped her. Mike, George, and Regina now work on the plane, transferred on paper to the Foundation yesterday. Again, we're only suggesting, but we think you should hire Tony full-time, and Brett and Duke will serve with you as your inside people, on extremely first-class salaries."